THE ROMANY PRINCESS

by

Margaret Brazear

Copyright © Margaret Brazear 2013

http://www.historical-romance.com
http://historical-fiction-on-kindle.blogspot.co.uk

CHAPTER ONE

"Funny really, getting this," the old lady commented reflectively. "I never had much time for royalty. Always thought they were a waste of money."

Clutched between her twisted fingers she held the royal telegram, crushed into a ball like so much waste paper. It didn't seem to mean much to her, living long enough to claim her prize.

Stella watched her uncomfortably, wondering how coherent she could expect her to be. She was Stella's Great Aunt Bess, the sister to whom her grandmother had not spoken since the First World War.

Although they had never met before, she knew the story well. Their quarrel had been talked about frequently and with bitterness by Stella's grandmother, who had been engaged, at the age of sixteen, to a handsome sailor. She had loved him dearly, but her own sister had set out to destroy the romance. Bess had met him first, had been jealous when he transferred his affections to Edith, and her jealousy had festered as their wedding plans took form. So she had lied, had told him Edith had been unfaithful, and he had accepted her story. Since then, the two sisters had had no contact with each other.

"So you're Mary's girl, are you?" Bess said now.

Stella nodded.

"That's right," she replied. "I'm Stella MacKenzie."

"Edie's granddaughter," she murmured thoughtfully.

Seeing her now, it was hard to believe that she had ever been young, had ever been susceptible to the yearnings and schemes of a teenage girl. She had become a grim parody of a human being, shrunken and withered by the common enemy of good and bad alike.

Stella's uneasiness on first accepting her invitation faded a little when she heard her cracked voice, saw the way arthritis twisted her limbs. There are few of us who do not feel the desire to protect and cosset the very old, to absolve them of past sins as though they had been committed in another lifetime.

Stella had prepared for this visit with a blend of apprehension and curiosity; she wanted to meet the woman she had heard so much about, the woman of whom her own mother had recently remarked: 'even Jesus doesn't want her; that's why she's still alive.'

She wanted to hear her side of the story, for she had no doubt that it was that which the old woman intended to tell her. If someone so very ancient felt the need, in her twilight days, to ease her conscience, Stella felt it would be wrong to refuse her.

She still lived alone, tending to her own needs with the aid of a home help two mornings a week, which aroused Stella's grudging admiration. She had not expected everything to be so modern and functional. She was expecting her environment to be as archaic as the lady herself, but that assumption was to do her an injustice, for she had made the place easy to manage. There was a deep red fitted carpet with a small pattern of black woven into it; the three piece suite had removable covers which went into the washing machine and the fire was one of the modern, coal effect gas models.

Her only visible concession to the past was a massive walnut sideboard which stood against one wall, laden with greetings cards of various shapes and sizes which obscured the few photographs in their silver frames.

She sat in a high backed armchair beside the fire and looked at Stella expectantly, her dark eyes wandering over her as though searching for some hint of familiarity, while Stella tried to think of something to say to her, something that would not reveal her pre-conceived notions about her. But she could not seem to project her thoughts beyond the fact that this woman was born into this world one hundred years ago today.

Inevitably, she could do nothing but wait for Bess to speak. There was no delicate way to prompt the regrets Stella was sure she wished to voice, and she felt like a benevolent arbitrator, awaiting a confession. She believed that her aunt was suffering an angry conscience as death drew near for her, and she had come prepared to accept a belated apology on her grandmother's behalf. Her complacent beliefs were shattered when Bess said:

"I want to tell you about Rose."

Stella looked as startled as she felt, and she could feel the anger mounting within her. She realised the old woman had no intention of trying to atone for the past. That had never been her purpose in bringing Stella to her home, and she had never pretended that it was. Stella felt embarrassed by her own folly and assumptions. And she had absolutely no idea who Rose might be.

The old woman raised an eyebrow sceptically, as though she had read Stella's thoughts, and a slow smile crept over her mouth, revealing a subtle ghost of the beauty that had once been hers. She had small, even features and large, almost black eyes, even now only slightly faded. Her hair was almost entirely white, but there were streaks of black still visible beneath. She bore no resemblance whatsoever to Stella's grandmother.

Bess shifted in her armchair, seeming to settle herself more comfortably, and Stella was afraid she was getting ready for a long story. She glanced at the clock on the mantelpiece, hoping she wouldn't take too long about it. But, restless though she was, she couldn't quite believe she was meeting her at last.

Her reference to someone Stella had never heard of made her doubt that she really knew who her great niece was, and she seemed to read that doubt in her face.

"You needn't look at me like that, Miss," she snapped. "I suppose you thought I was too senile to understand, did you?" She sighed softly. "That's what most people think when you get to my age. They treat you like some sort of backward child. You'll find out one day."

Stella's grandmother had always said that her sister had a tongue that could cut glass. It was clear that time had failed to mellow Great Aunt Bess.

"Edie's granddaughter," she repeated. "You don't look like her. Not a bit."

"I've been told I resemble my father."

She shrugged.

"Never met him," she said. "Never met your mother, either."

Stella felt resentment gathering once more. She was prepared to be forgiving, but if her aunt wanted to be belligerent about the quarrel, she saw no reason why she shouldn't have her say.

"I know about the feud between you and my grandmother," she replied. "From what I've heard, you played no small part in it."

She smiled, but it was a menacing smile that made Stella wish she hadn't spoken.

"Is that what you heard?" Bess said, then swung away from the subject with: "Mary must have been knocking on a bit when she had you."

"She was in her forties," she replied stiffly.

"I'm glad you don't look like Edith. I wouldn't have liked that. I've kept my secret for seventy-five years. I don't think I could tell it to anyone who reminded me of Edie."

"I can't believe you still hate my grandmother," Stella protested.

"I'm not surprised you don't know about Rose," Bess went on, ignoring her. "That stuck-up bigot Edie married thought he was too good for the likes of us. He wouldn't have let her mention Rose." She leaned forward suddenly and peered into Stella's face. "Is he dead?" She demanded sharply. "Reg, I mean."

"Yes, he is. He died about twenty years ago, actually."

"Good."

Stella could feel the shock taking shape on her face. She had never met anyone who would say such a thing about the dead, no matter how much they had disliked them.

"I know you didn't get on with him," she said defensively. "But he was my grandfather."

"That's your misfortune, dear." She relaxed back in her seat. "I could tell you a thing or two about Mr. High-and-Mighty Parrish!"

Stella bit down on her animosity. She told herself firmly that her aunt was an old lady, that she must try to be tolerant.

"Don't take it personally, love," Bess said. "I've got things to say, a story to tell, and I've already had thirty years more than the Bible allows."

She leaned forward once more, wincing with the arthritic pain in her spine, and her eyes glowed with an intensity that convinced Stella to hear her out. "It's only fair, you see," she went on. "I've done what Rose wanted. I've kept my promise, all my life I've kept it. But I won't take the truth to the grave with me."

Stella was growing impatient with her cryptic references to someone she knew nothing about.

"But who is Rose?" She demanded.

"Rose was my sister," Bess answered quietly. "The eldest of the lot of us; well, all of us that survived, that is. There were many before her, and a few after her, but they never lived long enough to notice."

"Your sister?" Stella repeated stupidly. "There was another sister? I always thought you were the eldest."

She shook her head slowly, her eyes misting with fleeting sorrow.

"I often wondered whether you and your mother were ever told anything about her. That's why I asked you here, to tell you all about it."

Stella nodded her agreement, somewhat reluctantly. There didn't seem to be anything else she could do. The old woman had aroused her curiosity and she didn't want to risk offending her and have to go away without ever knowing what she had to say.

"Fifteen children my mother brought into the world," she began, "and there were just the five of us left. Rose, me, Edith, Billy and Nina."

Stella nodded eagerly, relieved to hear familiar names.

"Billy was the one who died of pneumonia," Stella said.

"That's right. And it was his death that started it all."

CHAPTER TWO

She said nothing else for some minutes, while Stella waited with mounting impatience. At last she sighed wearily.

"We lived each day as it came in those days," she went on. "There was no welfare, no social security, and if you didn't work, you didn't eat. Either that or you ended up in the workhouse, and that was worse than starving.

"As we grew up, we all got work to help out, to keep us fed, and that's how we went on. We were happy in our own way, we had our good times, until Billy died. Mother just never could accept that he was really gone."

She shifted her tiny frame once more, seeking a more comfortable position.

"There were three of us at home that afternoon," she began. "Me, Rose and Nina. You know who Nina was, I suppose? I can't recall her doing anything to make Reg decide she didn't exist."

Stella refused to rise to the bait.

"Yes, of course," she replied.

"Nina wasn't quite twelve years old when Billy died," Bess went on. "She was standing at the table, her little arms immersed up to the elbows in greasy, grey water, and tears streaming down her face. She'd been at it all day, crying like her little heart would break, and I remember how she tried to wipe at her face and eyes with the dry part of her sleeve, sniffing all the time. She dried the cups, then her hands, on the bit of rag she was using as a drying-up cloth. Then she lifted her skirt right above her knees and dabbed at her face with it.

"We'd put up with her weeping all day, me and Rose, and Rose kept putting her arms round her, trying to comfort her.

"I was sewing. I was always sewing, every spare minute I got. I used to embroider, and I had a lot of customers for my embroidery among the well-to-do ladies. You needed a bob or two to afford my embroidery, I don't mind telling you. People would pay a lot to have me put some flowers on a plain blouse or maybe decorate a nightgown for a wedding night."

She paused and held up her hands to inspect them, a little grimace crossing her face.

"You wouldn't think it now, to look at these mangled paws, would you?" She laughed, her laughter emerging as a broken cackle, then dropped her hands back into her lap. "It comes to us all in the end.

"That day I was mending a blouse, and I was taking all my anger out on that blouse, stabbing at it with my needle as though it was somehow to blame for Billy's death and the awful noise of Nina's sniffling. It was getting dark too, and I wanted to finish it while I still had a little light from the window above the bed. There was no escape, either, because that room was all we had. We all lived in one room over a pub in Shoreditch, and it didn't seem to matter how the numbers went up and down over the years, we were always able to squeeze them in somewhere."

"My grandmother didn't come from Shoreditch," Stella interrupted before she could stop to think about it. "She didn't come from London at all."

Bess watched her for a long moment, until Stella could no longer hold her gaze. Then she laughed heartily, but she made no reply, merely carried on as though Stella hadn't spoken. Perhaps she doesn't understand, Stella thought. She is, after all, a centenarian.

She didn't protest again. It would have been useless, as had already been proved.

"All we had," she said, "was a single, straight backed chair, the old fashioned sort with carving on the wood at the back and its upholstery shredded with age, the horsehair stuffing spilling out all over. The table had been scrubbed so many times that the surface was a pale cream colour, while the sides and legs remained the deep brown of the wood. The bed I was lying on was piled with three feather mattresses, two of which we'd spread on the floor at night, one on top of the other, and that's how we'd sleep – some of us on the bed and some on the floor. The only other furniture we had was an ancient cooking range in the fireplace, a few shelves holding cooking pots and other utensils, and an old clock which stood on the mantelpiece.

"Everything in the room had been donated by a friend of mother's, a Jewish dealer in second hand furniture, who kept a shop in Ridley Road. He tended to pass on what he knew he would never sell, but we were grateful just the same.

"The window above the bed looked out onto the street and across the other rooftops, all much the same as ours. At night, we could look down at the men as they left the pub, usually the worse for wear.

"On the other side of the room was another small window that overlooked the yard at the back, which was the way we used to come and go.

"I remember how windy it was that night. I was sitting with my back to the front window and every now and then a gust of wind would shake the window frame and send a cold draft down my neck.

"We never seemed to notice things like that at the time. We'd never known anything else you see. I don't suppose we noticed the peeling paint on the walls or the patch of damp high up dear the ceiling, either. They were just things we lived with, things we accepted because we had no means to change them."

She was quiet for so long, Stella thought she had fallen asleep. She had assumed that all old people fell asleep half way through a conversation. But that was still early in the day, and she didn't know Great Aunt Bess.

"I'm still awake, if that's what you're worrying about," she said suddenly, making Stella start. She sighed heavily before going on.

"Nina had put away the clean cups and was trying to lift the bowl full of dirty water down from the table.

"'Leave that, Nin," Rose took the bowl from her. It was one of those heavy, galvanised metal bowls, oval shaped with a handle at each end. 'You can't carry that all the way downstairs,' she said.

"'Give it here,' I said, jumping up.

"I opened the window, then took the bowl from Nina.

"'What are you going to do, Bess?" Rose asked me suspiciously.

"'Chuck it out the window.'

"'You can't do that," she argued. "Someone might be walking by.'

"That made me chuckle.

"'Good," I said. 'We could do with a laugh.

"All the tension of that day must have got me down more than I realised. I didn't even look to see if anyone was down there. I just held the bowl out of the window and tipped it over, emptying the water into the street. There was an almighty yell from below.

"'Oi! What the bloody hell d'ya think you're doing!'

"I slammed the window shut and we all shook with laughter, covering our mouths with our hands so as not to be heard by the soaked man in the street.

"The laughter felt good. We all needed the release after the hours of waiting.

"Rose shook her head at me as I went back to my sewing, giving me that indulgent maternal look she liked to use sometimes.

"Nina sat herself down beside the cooking range to warm her hands. It was one of those iron ranges with the fire in the middle and an oven either side. Her face quickly sobered and I knew what she was thinking, what she'd been thinking all day. Her and Billy were always close; she'd miss him more than any of us. He was her big brother, used to tease her and play with her. She'd been writing to him every week since he went to that place.

"We all thought of it as 'that place', the home where they sent young offenders. Billy wasn't a criminal. He's just got himself mixed up with the wrong crowd, got caught throwing stones at a shop window. He wouldn't have stolen anything, not Billy. He wasn't a thief, but the court hadn't seen it that way. The other boys had run away when the coppers arrived and they'd got off scot free.

"Rose put her arms round Nina, held her close against her shoulder.

"'He was only fifteen, Rose,' Nina sobbed. 'He can't be dead.'

"'Pneumonia, love. It's very cold up north. Thick snow.'

"We'd had the letter two days before, telling us about Billy's death, but I had little grief to spare for a brother who got himself in trouble with the law for the sake of a few laughs.

"Mother had been gone all day, gone up to Cumberland to bring back his body for burial. The neighbours had all had a whip round to pay for her fare. It seemed daft to me, but that's the way they were in the East End then. Still are for all I know. It didn't matter how hard up you were, you had to have a grand funeral. I've got a drawer full of memorial cards to prove it, all printed with fancy black edging, even if we didn't have two ha'pennies to rub together.

"The light had almost gone by then, so I put down the mending and got up to go down and get some water.

"'Mother'll be home soon,' I remarked as I got to my feet. 'She'll want a cup of tea and a warm up.'

"Nina sat up suddenly, her little eyes swollen from crying, but full of alarm.

"'She's not bringing the body here, is she?' she asked. 'Where will we put it?'

"I had to laugh. There she'd been, breaking her heart all day over Billy, but she didn't much fancy sharing our little bit of space with his corpse.

"But I had another reason for going downstairs. I wanted to see if there was any sign of Edie."

The old woman looked at Stella pointedly, a challenge in her eyes.

"I know she was your grandmother," she said. "And I know you think I shouldn't be saying a word against her, but she was a self-centred, flighty little piece in those days and that's a fact, whether you like it or not.

"She was supposed to be home. We'd all agreed, it would be nice for mother if we were all there when she got back. But where was Edie? Out flirting with all and sundry again, I shouldn't wonder.

"I scooped up the old wooden bucket from beside the door and made my way down the narrow stairs. Those stairs always creaked; I knew every step by its own special noise.

"The wind lashed my skirts about my ankles and tore through the worn, wool dress. I wish I'd taken the time to put on a coat, but I wasn't about to go back upstairs for it. I didn't even have a shawl to protect me from the cold.

"The sound of the water as it hit the bucket made a dull, rhythmic thud that grated on my nerves as I waited. The water trickled out of the tap, while I stood and shivered, my teeth chattering.

"The yard was a mess. There was an old tin bath leaning upright against the wall; an equally old mangle, painted green and peeling, stood beneath a lean-to shelter beside me. Mother used that mangle, for the family's wash and for anyone else who cared to pay. That was in between scrubbing doorsteps for a couple of coppers a time.

"The trapdoor to the beer cellar rattled in the wind, its wooden slats rotted with age and damp and an old penny-farthing cycle was balanced on the cover to keep it down. The landlord would have to start charging a reasonable rent for our room if he was ever to afford a new door for his cellar. But Tom was a good sort. He undercharged us outrageously and in return, we cooked his meals and cleaned the bar and his small living rooms. And while he had Rose to sing a few songs for his customers on Saturday nights, he was happy.

"She had a lovely voice, Rose did. She'd been singing to herself over the washing up one day in the summer and her voice had drifted down through the open window. Tom had heard her, and he'd asked her to sing in the pub. Mother wasn't keen at first. A lone woman in a public house in those days always got a bad reputation, but we needed the money and Rose made quite a tidy bit in tips down there. The men loved to listen to her, but what she really wanted was to sing in the music hall. I knew she could do it, it was just a question of getting the right people to take notice.

"At the far end of the yard, leaning against the back fence, was the wooden outhouse which we shared with the landlord and all his customers. The wind hadn't kept the rats at home that night, either. I could see them scuttling about in the shadows, and I could hear the swaying of the 'Angel' pub sign out the front as the wind caught it, making it creak on its hinges.

"It seemed to take forever for the bucket to fill up. I reached across to turn off the tap and lifted it with both hands, balancing it carefully in front of me. I climbed the stairs slowly, each step splashing a little more water over my dress. I knew I'd be soaked through by the time I reached the top.

"Rose was just stoking up the fire when I opened the door and Nina ran forward to help with the water, but there was still no sign of Edie and I couldn't bite my tongue any longer.

"'Little trollop's out giving herself airs again, I expect,' I grumbled to no one in particular.

"'Oh, Bess, don't say that about your own sister.'

"That was Rose, always ready with a good word for anybody, whether they deserved it or not.

"'Someone's got to say it, Rose,' I said. 'You don't see the harm in her, I know, but she's been too full of herself lately. Ever since she got that parlour maid's job, she thinks she's Lady Muck.' I couldn't wait to put down the water and squat in front of the fire to get warm. 'Did you see her yesterday?' I said. 'She crossed the road when she saw us coming. Didn't want to be seen with factory girls.'

"'She didn't see us,' Rose insisted, sticking up for her as usual.

"'Rubbish! She saw us, all right. She couldn't get away fast enough.'

"That's when we heard mother's tread on the stairs and that shut me up, or I would have said more. In fact, I had a great deal more to say about sister Edith.

"The door opened and mother shuffled into the room, dragging her feet as though they were too heavy to pick up off the floor. She looked exhausted, and she seemed to have acquired more lines on her face than she'd had when she left home that morning. She was Romany, you know, my mother, and very dark like the rest of us. All except Edie, that is. She had the ol' man's colouring."

Stella looked up sharply at her great aunt, but she didn't seem to notice. It was the first she had heard about having Romany blood; it was the first she'd heard about her grandmother coming from London, or working as a maid. She wasn't sure she believed Bess; how could she, when she had been raised on anecdotes of wealthy ancestors in Hertfordshire? Perhaps the old lady was a little senile after all, she thought. Perhaps she was imagining all this.

"I've often wondered," Bess went on, "just what my father had that made her run off with him. That's what she did, you know, eloped with my father. My grandfather disowned her; they all disowned her, put a curse on her, they did. The only one of them she saw after that was her sister, Ann.

"Mother's face was drawn and weary, but she managed a smile when Rose jumped up to take her coat.

"'How did it go, Mother?' She asked quickly. 'Come and get warm. The kettle's on and one of us'll go out for some eels when we're all here.'

"Mother shrugged out of her black coat, letting it drop into Rose's arms. She always wore black. I don't know whether she was in permanent mourning for all those babies she'd lost, or whether she hoped to make everyone think she was a widow. It played on her mind, that she had no husband and all those kids. She had moral standards to match Queen Victoria's and it worried her, what people might be saying.

"I made room for her at the fire, but I was concerned about her and I suppose she must have seen it.

"'There's no need to look like that, Elizabeth,' she snapped. Her head came up proudly. 'I've got some news for all of you. Billy is alive.'

"I wasn't a bit relieved by that. Her statement got me even more worried and I was the only one close enough to see the strange look in her eyes.

"'It weren't him,' she said quietly. 'All that way to bring my boy home, I went. But it weren't him.'

"We were all watching her as she sat there, warming her hands, all saw the secret little smile that softened her mouth. I glanced up at the others, trying to read their thoughts. Rose looked a bit wary, but Nina just looked relieved. I couldn't let it go on. I knew, you see. I knew Billy was dead the moment it happened, long before we got the letter from that place. I always have known when someone close dies. It's just a feeling I get, a feeling of something missing. Romany blood, you see.

"'Did you see him then, mother?' I asked her. 'Did you speak to him?'

"She shook her head.

"'They've got him hid somewhere,' she answered.

"Rose opened her mouth, but I put up my hand to silence her. I felt that we had to tread very carefully around this one. That little light of unreality still shone in mother's eyes as she stared at the flames, her gaze fixed as though she was seeing things that we could not. Something was very wrong.

"'Why don't you lie down and have a rest?' I suggested, keeping my voice low. 'The tea won't be ready for a while.'

"Mother just kept looking at the flames for a few more minutes, then her head snapped around suddenly and she jumped to her feet.

"'Nothing wrong with me,' she declared. 'Lie down? At this time of day? What d'ya think I am, one of them fancy ladies you do your sewing for?' She looked about the room, as if she had only just realised where she was. 'Where's Edith?' She demanded.

"That's what we'd all like to know, I thought, but I held my tongue.

"'Not home yet, mother,' Rose answered quickly. 'I don't suppose she'll be long.'

"Mother nodded knowingly.

"'They work her too hard at that house,' she said. 'I daresay they've kept her late again.'

"I had to bite my tongue at that, I can tell you. Now, your grandmother was mother's favourite. She had a sly way of creeping round her, and it annoyed me no end. I couldn't see why the silly woman never saw what Edie really was. Working late, my Aunt Fanny! The worthless girl never worked late in her life.

"I knew I wouldn't be able to keep quiet if I had to listen to any more, so I grabbed my coat down from the hook behind the door and threw it over one arm. I got an enamel basin down from the shelf and started toward the stairs.

"'I'll go and get the eels,' I said when I reached the door. 'I'm not waiting any longer for her.'

"I hurried downstairs before anyone could stop me, pausing at the bottom to slip into my coat. I pulled it tight and buttoned it as I walked through the yard, round the side of the pub and out into the street. It was a dirty part of London then and it's still dirty today, but it was more than usually depressing that night. The wind had caught up all the rubbish that perpetually lay about the streets, and blown it into heaps. There was debris floating about in the air above my head, bits of paper and straw, mostly. The wind seemed to be getting worse if anything and I had to walk with my head down to keep it from getting in my face and taking my breath away.

"My eyes were fixed on the pavement when I spotted a pair of brand new boots coming toward me, their heels tapering then spreading wide again at the bottom, what we used to call Louis heels. They had buttons all the way up the side which disappeared beneath a red skirt at the ankles. They were the sort of boots I saw every day, the sort that Rose and me had our respective parts in putting together at the factory – the sort of boots that cost a lot of money. It wasn't often you saw a pair like that in our part of London.

"I had to raise my head, had to have a look at whoever it was who was wearing those boots. You can imagine my surprise to find myself face to face with Edie's smirking countenance.

"She was the only one of us who bore any resemblance at all to our father. Her eyes were hazel, and her hair was a sort of light brown, more the colour of a field mouse than anything else."

The contempt the old lady still felt for Edith, Stella's grandmother, cried out in her every word, and Stella began to consider that there might be more to the story than her grandma had told them all. Great Aunt Bess would scarcely feel such rancour if she were the guilty party, would she?

"She was always smartly dressed, though nothing too expensive," Bess was saying. "New boots that week; the previous week it had been a new hat – or was that the week before? Edie didn't earn enough for all these extravagances and what she did earn went towards feeding the family, just like everybody else. But I knew where the money came from and the knowledge infuriated me.

"Edie had a boyfriend, a sailor whose ring, with its three tiny diamonds, glittered on the third finger of her left hand. But the engagement meant as little to Edie as Sam himself, for while he was away at sea, she made sure she was never lonely."

Stella's heart began to beat rapidly. The old lady couldn't know that she had heard all about Grandma and her sailor, and she was unsure whether to contradict what she said, or keep quiet until she had heard her side of the story. She decided on the latter course, mainly because she didn't want to start an argument.

"I couldn't help looking down at my own boots, bought from a second hand stall in Petticoat Lane and ten years out of date, like everything else I stood up in. I had never had anything new in my life and neither had Rose, or Nina. Don't get me wrong. I wouldn't have begrudged Edie any of her finery, if it hadn't been Sam's money she was spending.

"Edie stopped in front of me, while I let my glance rest once more on the new boots, then moved my eyes slowly up to look into hers.

"'Sam sent you some more money, did he?' I asked her accusingly.

"'As a matter of fact, yes, he did,' she replied. 'What's that got to do with you?'

"I ignored her question.

"'And, of course, you've put it away with the rest he sent you.' My voice was heavy with sarcasm. 'You must have quite a tidy bit saved up by now. For when you get married, isn't it?

That is what he sends it for, isn't it, Edie? For you to save?'

"'That's right,' she answered, pulling her kid gloves tightly over her wrists. 'Not that it's any of your business.'

"'I think it's time I made it my business,' I said. 'I think someone ought to write to Sam and tell him just what you've been doing with his money.'

"Edie's mouth opened in a gasp that was lost in the wind.

"'You wouldn't dare!' She cried.

"'Wouldn't I?'

"She tried to push past me, her lips pressed together in a grim line, but I clutched her arm tightly.

"'Mother's home,' I told her abruptly. 'She says Billy's not dead.'

"'Well, that's good news,' she replied with a little smile, pleased to have the subject changed, I expect.

"'No, it's not,' I said. 'Do you think the people at that place would have got mother all the way up there for a mistake? She didn't see him, just keeps saying the body wasn't Billy.'

"'What are you talking about, Bess?' She demanded.

"'I'm talking about delusions. I think the old girl's cracked.' Edie stared at me as though she thought I was the one who had cracked. 'Fifteen children,' I said to her. 'Fifteen children in as many years, and only five of them made it past a few months. She had a husband who went off and left her to get on with it; God alone knows where he is! And she's worn herself out trying to keep us out of the workhouse. I think this business with Billy is the final straw.'

"I suddenly remembered who I was talking to and I wondered why I'd bothered. As far as Edie was concerned, the whole world could fall apart so long as she had pretty things and plenty of boys to flirt with.

"'I'm going to get the eels,' I said and dropped her arm so abruptly she was pushed off balance. Then I strode off across the road toward the evening market.

CHAPTER THREE

"I felt in both pockets for my gloves and cursed, only then remembering that I'd lent my only pair to Nina that morning. I'd made her wear them when she went out on her regular Saturday morning chore of selling the lace mother made in what little time she could spare.

"Now my hands were turning blue and I had lost all feeling in my fingers. I walked as quickly as I could, across roads and down gloomy little side streets toward the light of the evening market. Many voices called my name as I went, people I had known all my life, all with the same question on their lips: 'How's Rebecca taking things?'

"They all knew about Billy. They had all contributed from their meagre wages to bring my brother home to rest.

"I could only shrug and murmur a non-committal 'not so bad'. I had neither the time nor the patience to explain the situation now. How could I make them understand that mother was denying Billy's death, or that I didn't believe her.

"'Walk with you, Bess?' Somebody said.

"I turned toward the voice which had drifted out of a shop doorway, and saw a thin, dirty woman in her early thirties with dyed red hair. Pulled close about her shoulders, she wore a tattered crochet shawl which might once have been white.

"May was a well-known local prostitute and the only time I'd agreed to walk along with her, I'd found myself the unwilling object of a very persistent customer.

"'Sorry, May,' I answered her as kindly as I could. 'You know what happened last time.'

"The woman laughed and stepped out of the doorway to walk away, throwing a friendly wave behind her as she went.

"I watched her retreating figure, wondering as I often did what it was like to earn a living as May did. I found the subject fascinating, even while it repelled me. My mother would have had a fit if she knew I spoke to people like May. She would have had a fit if she'd realised I even knew what it was that May actually did. We weren't supposed to know about things like that in those days, but it was difficult to remain ignorant when you had been brought up in one room.

"I only mention May because it was the last time I saw her. She was found dead the next day, murdered by one of her customers. It quite shook me up at the time and everyone started recalling the twenty year old crimes of Jack the Ripper, not too far away in Whitechapel. But May wasn't mutilated, that God. She was a good sort, really; just didn't have any other way to survive. And there were many more like her where we lived. There was nothing unusual about going out in the evening and coming across these poor, dirty wretches, huddled into doorways with various men. But while mother crossed the street to avoid them, Rose and me would exchange a greeting. We felt sorry for them and they never did us any harm.

"I could smell the market long before I saw it. You couldn't help it with the wind blowing the scents of candle grease and hot chestnuts right up your nose. Most of the stalls had gas lamps by then, but some still used oil or candles to light their stalls.

"The market was teeming with people, some with baskets over their arms, intent on the best bargains for their Sunday dinners, many simply wandering, inspecting each stall with no intention of parting with so much as a penny.

"I hurried to the eel stand, hoping not to meet too many people who would ask about mother; and about Billy. I wasn't concerned with meat for Sunday – it would be cheaper to buy in the morning.

"The smell of hot eels made my stomach contract with hunger and I realised I hadn't eaten at all that day. I handed over my basin and waited, watching the fresh eels, still alive and squirming about in their tank.

"Death was very much on my mind that night and I found the snake-like creatures with their grey, shiny skins fascinating, as though I had never seen them before. I thought about them for the first time, that they were alive and in a few short hours, their lives would be severed. Just like Billy's had been.

"I worried about mother too, because I knew at the precise moment when Billy departed this life. I always knew. I had lost count of the times I had woken in the night, knowing beyond any doubt that one of the babies had died. I would rise from my bed and tiptoe across the bare, wooden floor, to peer at a lifeless bundle in the old crib. Sometimes the knowledge had come to me as I sat at my desk at school, and later amid the noise of the factory, and I would have to wait all day to confirm what I already knew.

"I can't explain it, and few people knew about my peculiar 'gift', but just as I knew for certain that my brother was no more, so I also knew that my mother had started on the downhill trek toward mental instability. She would not recover from this, of that I was certain. She would only get worse and she would need to be cared for, perhaps for the rest of her life.

"But I lived in a world where death was commonplace, a world where, if children lived beyond infancy, their parents counted themselves blessed. Billy's death at such a young age was nothing unusual, my mother's hardship was likewise."

She stopped speaking so abruptly, it was a few minutes before Stella realised the old woman was just watching the fire, as though she could see her memories come to life among the flames.

Stella had to stop herself from urging her on, although she was still a little sceptical. She could not quite see her sedate, middle-class grandmother as the painted floozy that Aunt Bess had described. As for Sam, Stella was not yet prepared to accept that the great love of Grandma's life had really been no more to her than a meal ticket, someone whose money she spent as though he fished it out of the sea.

It was a long time before Auntie Bess looked up from the fire and sighed deeply.

"Just thinking," she said.

There was a catch in her voice, as though the memories had caused her pain, and Stella couldn't help mellowing a little toward her. She was already finding it difficult to keep her resolution to dislike her. Whatever the truth might be, she had done Stella no harm and she seemed so very fragile.

"I can come back if you're tired," Stella offered, hoping she'd refuse. She didn't think she'd be able to sleep that night if she had to go home still wondering.

The old lady shook her head.

"I'm all right. Just got a funny feeling, that's all. Here I am, talking about things that happened more than eighty years ago, and they seem like recent memories to me."

She pushed on the chair arms, moving herself up in the seat.

"Can I get you anything? A cup of tea or something?"

"No thanks. I want to tell you what happened the next day. As I recall, it was thick frost on the Sunday and freezing in our room. We'd put blankets along the bottom of the windows and against the door, to keep out the draught, but we none of us wanted to move far from the fire.

"Rose had been down the market and got us a scrag end of lamb and that was bubbling away in a stewpot on the range, filling the confined space with steam along with an aroma which was as overpowering as it was savoury.

"Nothing had been said about Billy. No one wanted to stir things up, to remind mother about him, but the effort of not mentioning him had resulted in an overall reluctance to say anything at all, for fear of saying the wrong thing. And mother had been unusually quiet since she woke up, as though she were deep in thought – too deep in thought to even notice her surroundings.

"By the time the church bells had begun to ring the end of morning service, I was sitting in my usual spot, on the bed beside the window, the only place I had enough light for my embroidery. I wore thin, white cotton gloves to sew, because my hands were rough and stained with the polish and dye we used for making boots. No amount of scrubbing could get that off.

"Mother sat beside the other window with her cushion in her lap, making her lace, the bobbins flying about as though they had a life of their own.

"From my window I could see all the way down the road and I was watching particularly that day. Auntie Ann always stopped in on her way home from church on Sundays, and I was worried about what she might say to my mother to set her off. She always meant well, but she had a talent for saying the wrong thing.

"Then I saw them, two women with small, leather-bound prayer books clasped in their hands. Ann was dark with a keen resemblance to my mother except that while mother was thin, Ann was what Rose liked to call stout. I wasn't so polite. To me, the only word for Auntie Ann was fat, and as she marched along, throwing her sturdy legs out before her, swinging her arms back and forth in time with them, her ample flesh swayed and wobbled. Auntie Ann would have been mortified to know she presented a comic figure; she always liked to think herself dignified, but I could never resist a tiny chuckle when I saw her.

"Beside her, as always, was a thin little woman, no bigger than a child of perhaps eleven or twelve, with sharp features and grey hair, her short legs almost running to keep up. This was Auntie Ann's friend, Maud, who shared both her house and her fervent religious commitment.

"'Here comes the God Squad,' I commented with a little laugh.

"'Don't be so wicked!' Mother protested, knowing at once who I was referring to.

"I only grinned at her. Mother's objection to the mockery of religion was based on her fear of all things supernatural. As far as she was concerned, religion fell firmly under the heading of the supernatural, and she was constantly afraid of offending gods who may or may not exist. But me, I always believed that if God gave us a sense of humour, then He must have one Himself, since we were all made in His image.

"The two visitors settled themselves as best they could, Maud perched on the edge of the bed, whilst Ann's surplus flesh overflowed the rickety chair. She sipped her tea with great care, as the chair rocked and creaked beneath her weight with every movement, threatening to launch her onto the floor.

"Ann always brought Maud with her when she came and, as far as any of us knew, they went everywhere together. The curious thing was that Maud never spoke. Whether this was from shyness, or a simple lack of any coherent thought to be voiced, nobody was quite sure.

"The little woman sat sipping her tea, her eyes darting about, never resting on anything for longer than a second. It was a habit we had grown accustomed to, just as we had long ago given up any hope of engaging her in conversation.

"Ann was never comfortable in our little home, but I always believed her discomfort only added to her sense of nobility in the duty of visiting.

"'Really, Rebecca,' she said, and not for the first time. 'I can't understand why you don't all come and live with us. Here you are, huddled into one room, and Maud and I have that big house all to ourselves.'

"She had persisted, since my father was last seen, in trying to share her house with us, and her own conscience was the motive. My grandfather had been a wealthy man by his standards, having a careful eye for a bargain and a bit of profit wherever he travelled, and he had left everything he owned to Ann. Mother no longer existed as far as he was concerned and his only son had died young. Ann always felt that the inheritance ought to be shared, whether old Sampson had wanted it or not.

"'Of course you do,' mother muttered, half under her breath.

"'Sorry, dear. What did you say?'

"'She said,' I couldn't resist putting in, 'that you have that big house all to yourselves. That's because you got all grandfather's money.'

"Words died on everyone's lips. The subject of grandfather's wealth had always been carefully stepped over, tiptoed around, never spoken of except by veiled hints. I thought it was time someone brought the subject out into the open.

"Ann turned a stony glare on me, but it quickly faded when her eyes met mine. I wasn't afraid of her; I wouldn't let her intimidate me. And I've always said what I thought. That's probably why I've never been too popular. Most people don't want to hear the truth.

"'Come on, Maud,' Ann said haughtily, half rising. 'We're obviously not welcome here.'

"'Don't go off in a huff,' said mother, pushing her back into her seat. 'We've been through all this before. We won't take charity.'

"'Hardly charity, dear,' Ann muttered, only slightly mollified. She drained her cup.

"She did not, in fact, want us any more than we wanted to go, but she was a great one for what she called her Christian duty.

"'Besides, Ann,' mother went on. 'You know you're not going to have room in the house. My Billy's not a child any more, you know. He's a young man now and he'll want somewhere to live when he comes home.'

"She had taken Ann's cup as she spoke and was refilling it. She didn't see the startled look on her sister's face and would not have noticed if she had.

"Auntie Ann looked at each of us in turn, even to little Nina who she didn't normally bother with, seeking an explanation for her sister's statement. She hadn't mentioned Billy since she arrived, perhaps feeling the subject was best left alone until someone closer to the boy chose to speak of it. She looked across the room at Maud, whose grey eyes ceased their endless movement to meet hers.

"'What......?' She began.

"'Shut up, Auntie,' I cut her off quickly, and rudely, my eyes fixed on my mother.

"Ann's glance followed mine, while Maud's began once more to shift nervously from one person to the other, the cup in her small hand beginning to clatter. She swallowed the last of her tea quickly, almost choking with the effort.

"Rose leaned over Auntie's shoulder and provided her with a whispered explanation.

"An uncomfortable atmosphere had gathered in the room, a tension felt by all save mother. Ann decided that the best course would be a change of subject.

"'I was hoping to hear, Rosina,' she said, 'that you had found yourself a nice young man at last.'

"'No one special, Auntie,' she replied, giving me a significant glance.

"It was a question Rose had come to expect from Auntie Ann, who was determined that none of her nieces should suffer her own fate of remaining a spinster.

"'I don't understand it,' she said. 'A lovely young girl like you, you should have men lining up for your favours.'

"'I have my moments,' Rose replied.

"She certainly wasn't short of admirers, you can take my word for that. We both collected our share of wolf-whistles and saucy remarks on our way to work and back, but it was all a bit of a giggle to us. And Rose was a romantic by nature. She read a lot of love stories, and she'd never have been content with anyone she couldn't adore. As for me, I'd long since made up my mind to stay single. I'd learned very early in life to distrust the opposite sex. It wasn't only the women afraid of being left on the shelf; behind all the admiring glances and chat up lines, there was usually a bloke in search of a skivvy.

"'You ought to be thinking about a husband and a home of your own, Rosina,' Auntie Ann was saying.

"'There's always Alfred,' I suggested with a chuckle.

"'Rose's eyes rolled heavenward.

"'Oh, yes,' she agreed. 'There's always Alfred.'

"'So you do have someone then, dear,' Ann said happily. 'Now, I want to hear all about him.'

"Rose and I collapsed into fits of giggles, while Auntie just looked bewildered. She couldn't know that Alfred was a standing joke between us two. He worked in the factory, going round with a box full of leather, making sure we workers never ran out of materials and didn't have to waste time getting them ourselves. That was when he wasn't skiving off in some corner or cupboard somewhere.

"He was a tall, skinny fella with brown hair and small hazel eyes which sat too close together. His eyebrows met in the middle of his brow, which my mother always said was a sign that a man was born to be hanged. That proved to be somewhat ironic, as it turned out.

"He had been sniffing round Rose ever since he started work there. I say sniffing, because that's what he reminded me of – a randy dog. I couldn't stand him, but she used to say it wasn't his fault he was so obnoxious and it was unkind to be openly hostile.

"When we had recovered our composure, we saw that Auntie Ann was looking affronted. There's nothing worse than somebody enjoying a joke that you don't share. Stiffly, she turned her attention to Edie.

"'Your young man will be home again soon, won't he?' She asked deliberately. 'I expect you miss him.'

"Remembering our little talk of the night before, Edie looked quickly at me and I made no attempt to keep the mockery out of my eyes. Her cheeks flushed, but she managed a non-committal reply.

"'And have you set a date for the wedding yet?'

"'No. Not yet.'

"'Best get it settled, dear,' Ann persisted. 'Handsome young fella like that, away at sea. Some other pretty girl'll snap him up, you mark my words.'

"Ann was very certain of her ground with this piece of advice. After my mother had run off with George Shaw, old Sampson had learned not to trust young men who came calling and when Ann had wanted to marry, the old man had stubbornly refused to allow her to rush into anything. He had practically kept her locked up to keep her from seeing Will, despite her protestations that she adored him. And he had got tired of waiting and found someone else.

"'Edith's only young yet, Ann,' mother said sharply. 'No need for her to rush off and marry the first one who asks. Sixteen's no age to be tying herself down.' She can't have forgotten that she had herself been only sixteen when she eloped with my father. She turned her attention on me then, her mouth clamping down into a grim line. 'As for you, Elizabeth,' she said sternly, 'you're older. It's high time you and Daniel tied the knot.'

"Perhaps I was a bit dim in those days, but I'd never realised until then how my friendship with Daniel might appear to everyone else. And that's all he was to me, just a friend. We had a lot of laughs and we got on together, but no more than Rose and me did.

"If I'd had any hopes for my future at all, it was as a much sought-after seamstress, running a little business perhaps. One thing was certain, there was never a man in my dreams of the future, and I had never considered Daniel at all among those dreams.

"I stopped sewing and stared at mother, my needle frozen over my work. I was frankly astonished to realise that she was expecting me to marry, but that wasn't the only idea that made me pause. If mother expected marriage, what did Daniel expect?

CHAPTER FOUR

"'Me and Daniel?' I answered at last. 'Who said anything about me and Daniel getting married?'

"Mother scoffed quietly.

"'Everyone knows you've been courting for months. Stands to reason you'll get married sooner or later. Better make it sooner, my girl. That'll be one less mouth to feed.'

"How dare she say that, when I put more money in the kitty than any of us? I forgot my promise to myself to be tolerant with her; she didn't deserve it.

"'I'd like to see how long you last without my money coming in,' I retorted angrily. 'For your information, I've got no intention of marrying Daniel – or anybody else for that matter!'

"'What d'ya mean "anybody else"?' She asked archly. 'No one else'd have you, not with that tongue of yours. Sharp as a woodman's chopper, that tongue! Men like a woman to be soft and gentle, not sharp and hard like a pickaxe!'

"I should have known better than to expect her support. She was born of an age when a woman would suffer anything, however harsh, rather than have it supposed that no one had wanted her. Surely she would have been happier had she never laid eyes on George Shaw. Auntie Ann was certainly better off with her church and Maud than her sister had ever been.

"I gathered my sewing into the little box where I kept all my embroidery things and quickly got up. Then I put my coat on and had reached the door before I turned back to face mother. I could feel my tongue running away from me.

"'Being soft for a man certainly did you a lot of good, didn't it?' I demanded, and I slammed the door as I left.

"I've never been given to storming out when things got heated, but I couldn't stay and listen to such nonsense any longer. I had to see Daniel, had to find out what his feelings were.

"I hated to think that I might be leading him on, and if I was, if I found that he saw it that way, then things had to be put right at once.

"I have to admit too, that I've always had an obstinate nature. If someone tells me what to do, then I will do the opposite. It could be that my stubborn streak played a part in my actions that day.

"I had known Daniel for just under a year. We had met in the park, of all places, one Sunday afternoon in the spring. I'd gone there to finish the embroidery on a baby's christening gown, because the light was good and the sun was shining and I needed a little peace and quiet. I had not been pleased when he came over to my bench and started to speak to me. It wasn't the accepted thing to talk to strange men in parks, and I really wanted nothing more than to be left alone. But I wouldn't be a woman if I hadn't noticed how good looking he was, with his blonde hair and blue eyes and his gentle, teasing smile.

"He worked as a barber, in his father's shop near Cheapside, and that made him socially superior to an unskilled worker in a boot factory. He was the only person I knew whose parents owned their own home, and his mother considered her son to be far too good for the gypsies who lived above the Angel. She was probably right.

"Daniel didn't seem bothered by any such social niceties. He had come round to our meagre little room, introduced himself to my mother and sisters, played with Nina and managed to resist the advances made by Edie. She of the fancy boots and hats, had first met Sam when I introduced them and she always imagined she'd lured him with her charms. After several attempts at flirting with Daniel, she had been left to pout for three days because he refused to transfer his interest from me to her. I can't deny feeling a little smug about that.

"I was very fond of Daniel, but I couldn't consider a future for myself with any man. One reason, if I'm honest, was because I was scared. It was all different in those days. Once married, a woman had very few rights. I couldn't imagine having someone expecting me to cook and clean for him and have children for him, and I could hardly bring myself to think about how the children were made. I had my memories, and they weren't very pleasant.

"As a little girl, living and sleeping in the same room with my parents, I knew very well what else married women were expected to put up with. I had nightmares even then about the strange, gasping sounds and jerky movements coming from my father. We might not see him for months on end, while he gallivanted off Lord knew where, and then one night, I would wake up to the noises and see my mother lying still and rigid with a grim line of distaste across her mouth. The memory made me feel physically sick and I'd never harboured a single doubt that I wanted to remain unmarried and untouched.

"I expect you think that's peculiar, don't you? Growing up with different values, being young today, when people talk about things."

Stella had to smile. It had been a long time since she'd been called 'young', but she supposed when one has lived for a hundred years, everyone else must seem juvenile.

"Not at all," she replied. "I might feel the same if I'd had to witness such goings on. And she didn't love him by then, did she?"

Auntie Bess chuckled, but the grim set of her mouth remained.

"I don't know if that would have made much difference," she said wryly. "Mother used to say that if a man really loved you, he wouldn't expect you to do that."

Stella had never heard that curious point of view before and it seemed a somewhat tragic one to her.

Bess went back to her tale, her voice still as firm as when she'd started.

"I hadn't seen my father for seven years then. None of us had heard from him since his last, brief visit, a visit which led to yet another mouth to feed. But the last little girl was badly deformed, her little spine sort of scrunched up and her fists permanently closed. She only lived for a week. I tried not to let myself get fond of her, but I must have failed because I still knew, the very moment her young life left her.

"After that, mother had finally gone to the Metropolitan Police Court and applied for a separation order. The court awarded her six shillings a week maintenance from my father; six shillings a week to feed herself and three children still at school. It didn't matter. She never got a penny, anyway.

"I waited outside the barber's shop for Daniel that day, beneath the red, white and blue pole. I knew I wouldn't have long to wait. The shop was only open for a few hours on Sundays, just long enough to catch the trade of men coming out of church and heading toward the pub. I'd spent a few precious coppers on the tram fare, an extravagance I could ill afford, but had I walked I wouldn't have been in time to catch him before he left.

"He emerged to find me standing with my shoulders hunched and my arms folded against the cold. I had once again forgotten to retrieve my gloves from Nina.

"'Liza!' He cried when he saw me.

"He was the only person who ever called me that. It was his own special name for me and it wasn't until then that I stopped to wonder why should need one.

"He walked to my side and bent to give me a swift peck on the cheek, the most intimate gesture he had ever made.

"'What a lovely surprise!' He said. 'Are you all right? Nothing's happened, has it? I mean, I heard about your brother.'

"I frowned crossly, annoyed to think our private business was being talked about so freely.

"'How did you get to hear about it so soon?'

"'Is it true? Is he still alive?'

"'No. Mother insists he is, though, and I suppose it's best to humour her.'

"I was still not sure of the best way to approach the subject. I, who was always ready to speak my mind, found myself curiously tongue-tied when it came to Daniel.

"'I need to ask you something,' I finally blurted out.

"'Yes?'

"I looked up at him, at the sunlight shining on his hair, making it glow with little golden lights, and wondered for the first time if I was doing the right thing. He was a powerfully built man. The top of my head came no higher than the middle of his chest, and his size made me feel overwhelmed and insignificant, but he was always ready with a mischievous smile. He never could take very much seriously.

"Of course, if I hadn't cared about him, it wouldn't have mattered what I said. I realised that. But it was because I cared that I had to do this. He deserved better.

"He had waited patiently for me to speak, and when at last I did, I still hadn't thought of any tactful way round it.

"'Are you expecting us to get married?' I asked him, the words tumbling out brusquely.

"It was considered very unseemly to ask a man about marriage. You were supposed to wait until he asked you, but I didn't want it to go that far. If he had any hopes in that direction, I wanted to squash them before he got too involved.

"He looked surprised for only a moment, before a little smile of amusement played about his mouth.

"'Is that a proposal?' He asked.

"'No.'

"'Shame. You sure? It certainly sounded like a proposal to me.'

"'Well, it wasn't. I just wanted to know, that's all.'

"It was his turn for thoughtful silence. His eyes searched mine, as though considering his next words with great care. After a moment, he answered evenly.

"'I can't say the thought hasn't crossed my mind.'

"It wasn't what I wanted to hear, yet, perversely, I couldn't help feeling flattered. I looked at my feet, wondering what to do next, but there was nothing I could do but tell him he was wasting his time.

"'What's this all about, Liza?' He finally prompted.

"'Something my mother said. She wanted to know when we were getting married. It never occurred to me that anyone expected that, least of all you.'

"'Well, since the subject has come up, how do you feel about it?'

"'I can't marry you, Daniel,' I replied, still studying my feet. 'I've never wanted to get married. I'd only make you miserable.'

"He drew a quick breath and stuffed his hands into his pockets. His shoulders hunched against the cold and a little grimace crossed his face.

"'Let's walk,' he said, taking my arm. 'I don't want everyone to hear our private business.' After a moment, he went on. 'I'm not like your father, you know. I would never treat you like that. I'm even on the side of these wretched suffragettes, though I think they're going about things all wrong.'

"I could scarcely believe it. He really wanted to marry me, he was trying to persuade me. I had seen the way girls looked at him, giving him the eye, and it crossed my mind that I must have a screw loose to be refusing him.

"But, no matter what he said, I couldn't help wondering if my father had once said the same things. I couldn't afford to trust him with my whole life and if I allowed myself to be sentimental, I might end up like my mother and I knew I would rather be dead. Besides, I could not forget the other thing.

"I couldn't find the right words, and I thought I'd die of embarrassment. But it had to be said.

"'There are other things that men expect,' I muttered, forcing the words and casting my eyes across the road so they wouldn't have to look at him.

"'Oh?'

"'You know what I mean.'

"'Yes. I know what you mean. I suppose this has something to do with being brought up in one room, does it?'

"I stopped and looked up at him. He always understood, straight away, what was in my mind. His eyes met mine and I felt my cheeks begin to burn.

"'Elizabeth! I'm ashamed of you!' He said, suddenly laughing. 'I never thought I'd live to see the day when you would blush!'

"'I'm not blushing!' I insisted. 'It's the cold, that's all.'

"'Yes. Of course it is,' he agreed, but I could see he wasn't convinced. 'Well, at least my mother will be pleased. She always said you weren't good enough for me.'

"I burst out laughing at that, all my embarrassment forgotten. His mother was such an old snob, I'd have enjoyed marrying her son, just to annoy her.

"'You see, Liza,' he said, suddenly serious. 'Any other girl would be insulted at what I just said, but not you. You think it's funny. No wonder I think you're special.'

"We had come to Shoreditch Park by then, the place where we'd first met, and we made our way to a little bench. It was quiet in the park that day. The ground all around us was white with frost and the bitter cold had kept weaker souls at home in the warm.

"'Did I ever tell you about the day I met a very special girl?' He began as we settled ourselves. 'I was walking here, in this very spot, like I always did on Sunday afternoons, when suddenly I saw this vision, sitting there sewing. She had gleaming black hair, shining in the sunlight, and the prettiest nose I ever saw.'

"'Dan, stop it!'

"He went on, ignoring me as if I hadn't spoken.

"'I thought she must be a great lady, the way she sat, with her back dead straight. I had to talk to her; it was out of my control. I thought, when she speaks, she'll sound like the Queen and I'll know she's not for me. That's all I needed, really. To know she wasn't for me.

"'But then I noticed her clothes. Clean they were, well starched, but old and mended and she had white cotton gloves on her hands while she sewed. Now why, I wondered, would someone wear gloves to sew? Downright inconvenient, I'd have thought.'

"'Daniel...'

"'Don't interrupt. I'm telling this story.' He paused and gave me a half smile, then he went on. 'Well, being a reasonably intelligent sort of chap, I guessed that she'd wear gloves for sewing if her hands were rough from hard work. She wouldn't want to snag the material, or the embroidery. Such pretty embroidery it was, too. Of course, I didn't know about the stains from the boot factory as well, not then. But I wasn't far wrong, was I?

"'So I went up and spoke to her. That was my mistake, I suppose. I was caught, from that moment on, like a haddock in a fishing net.'

"'You'll find someone else, Daniel,' I said quickly, wanting to silence him. I didn't want to hear anymore.

"'You think so? I expect you're right. There must be someone in this world, if I look long enough and far enough, who's maybe half as special as you.'

"'Daniel, please don't say that.'

"'Why shouldn't I? You're the one who's always saying a few home truths never hurt anyone.'

"I didn't answer him. What could I say, when I knew he was right? I wanted to be able to walk away, to feel no remorse, and he was making that impossible. But what else did I expect? Why should he make things easy for me? I was ashamed to feel tears forcing their way into my eyes.

"Daniel was looking at me and that little smile appeared again.

"'This is indeed a day for revelations,' he said. 'You crying? For me? I suppose I should feel flattered.' He got to his feet and took my hand to help me up. 'Best be going. There's no point in prolonging the agony, is there?'

"But he kept hold of my hand when I had gained my feet and, before I had a chance to protest, he pulled me into his arms and kissed me. It was the last thing I expected to happen, but I clung to him instinctively, feeling suddenly warm and thrilled. And I realised all at once that I had been existing in an emotional void, my sensations barren and stagnant.

"We were unconcerned about the curious stares of the few people brave enough to be out. When he released me, his hands cupped my face for a few seconds before he finally stepped away.

"'What...what was that for?' I asked quickly, my cheeks beginning to burn again. 'You've never done that before.'

"'Something to remember me by,' he answered quietly. 'Something I would always have wondered about.'

"He walked away from me then, leaving crisp white footprints across the frozen grass, while I watched him go, ready to give a little wave when he turned around. But he never did.

CHAPTER FIVE

"That was the day I discovered more about my sister Edith, than I really wanted to know. You won't like what I'm going to tell you, I don't suppose, but it's all part of the story. And I want you to know the truth."

"I already know," Stella said accusingly. "You fell out with my grandmother over her fiancé. She told my mother and I all about it."

Bess eyed her steadily, her face impassive. Stella knew a moment of shame for having spoken harshly to such a very old person; she felt that she was bullying her and she wasn't happy with that image of herself. She should have realised, even on such short acquaintance, that no one could have bullied Great Aunt Bess.

"Did she now?" Bess finally replied. "I wonder what Edie told you? She was always good at blaming everyone else for her own misdoings."

Stella opened her mouth to argue, but she silenced her with a raised hand.

"No, don't tell me. I can imagine the tale she told, how she twisted the facts to suit herself. Told you I was jealous, did she? That the row was all my fault? I can't make you believe me, but what I'm telling you now is what happened, untwisted and ungarnished. I've got no reason to lie, have I? I can't afford to when I'll be meeting my maker so soon.

"I walked home from the park that day. The cold was seeping into my coat and I had my hands deep in my pockets to keep the blood circulating, but I begrudged paying for another tram ride. It wasn't a long walk, but long enough to ponder over the afternoon's events, and to ask myself honestly if I had done the right thing. Maybe I should have taken more time to think about it, instead of rushing off like that because of what my mother had said. Good men were hard to find, as mother was very fond of saying, and I was sure that I'd thrown away the only good man I was ever likely to meet. But I didn't want a man, good or otherwise. That's why I did it and I'd expected to feel relieved to have the matter settled. But after it was done, all I could feel was regret. And I'd never been kissed before, not like that. We didn't in those days. I think if someone had kissed my mother like that, she'd have been insulted, but I must admit I was pleased. If marriage entailed only a few kisses, I thought, I could have been happy with Daniel.

"As I drew nearer to home, I looked about at the grim houses that made up my neighbourhood. There are a lot of those houses still standing in London, with their grey bricks and their tiny yards backing onto more tiny yards. There were alleyways every now and then to give access to the back gates, alleyways just wide enough for one person's width, with high walls on either side. All we could see from our window on Mondays were rows and rows of fully laden washing lines.

"I was born there, had never known anything else, except the occasional visit to Hyde Park and a quick look at the ladies in their fine carriages. I had never been happy, but I'd never been unhappy either, not until that day. That day I was very unhappy with the thought that I might never see Daniel again. But what else could I do? I just couldn't bear the idea of being married and I was afraid it wouldn't last. I was scared he'd change once the ring was on my finger and I'd end up hating him. We'd end up hating each other.

"I was nearly home when I saw Edie. She was huddled in one of those narrow alleyways with a man. I recognised her straight away, even though she had her back to me, and I'd have known that silly giggle of hers anywhere.

"I'd never seen the man before, but Edie was certainly behaving as though she knew him well enough.

"I had no wish to hear any of the silliness my sister might be engaged in, but I made up my mind to tell Sam about her as soon as he came home. He worked hard, Sam did and he deserved better.

"I have very clear memories of Sam, with his bright red hair and his sailor's tattoos. He was tall as well, taller even than Daniel, and I had met him at a church social which Auntie Ann had dragged Rose and me to. We had gone out a couple of times, but I knew what I was doing when I introduced him to Edith. He was starting to get serious and I wanted to let him down gently. Edie had been the ideal solution, or so it seemed at the time, but I never imagined he would stick with her.

"Now my scheme had come home to roost, as they say, and I felt sort of responsible. I would have to interfere; there was no other choice.

"They still hadn't noticed me, so I took advantage of the opportunity to study what I could see of the man. And I really don't know what she saw in him. He wasn't much taller than she was, and we bred very small women in our family. He was skinny too, and I never could abide a skinny man. He wore a little bowler hat perched on his head and I wondered how he kept it there with all the groping that was going on.

"Seeing her so friendly with this chap made me ashamed of her and I couldn't wait to get away. I didn't let on that I'd seen her, but just as I passed by, I glanced back and I couldn't believe my eyes.

"There she stood, her arms locked round his neck so tight it's a wonder he could breathe, while his hand was busy crawling up her leg, beneath her skirt!

"I knew Edie was flighty, and I knew she liked to flirt, but I didn't really believe she'd have taken things any farther than that. I don't suppose it sounds like much to you, but we had different ideas then. We didn't wear long skirts to keep our legs warm or because it was fashionable. No respectable woman showed her legs.

"I was boiling over with rage and disgust. We might not have had much, but we always maintained a strong sense of decency. She was shaming the whole family by carrying on like that.

"'You trollop!' I shouted at her. 'You dirty little whore!'

"They broke apart quick enough then and Edie at least had the good grace to blush.

"'Bess! What are you doing, spying on me?'

"'I've got better things to do with my time than watch your disgusting behaviour! It's bad enough you're after anything in trousers, but to do it in public! It's obscene!'

"'And I suppose you'll tell mother?'

"'Tell mother? The state she's in, thinking Billy's still alive to come back one day? You might not care about anyone but yourself, young lady, but some of us do!'

"The man spoke then for the first time. He had a little patronising grin on his lips which stoked up my fire a bit more.

"'Now then, ladies,' he said. 'Let's not argue in public.'

"I snapped my eyes on him, giving him the full benefit of my sharpest glare. I've always been told I could radiate looks as good as Medusa's, and right then I hoped it was true. I would have enjoyed seeing the pair of them turn to stone. I noticed, when he spoke, an attempt to improve his accent, to give himself the air of a better class than he actually was. He was always like that, pretentious, but I didn't know that then.

"'You don't seem all that bothered about what else you do in public!' I spat. 'Who the hell are you, anyway?'

"He cleared his throat and drew himself up to his full height.

"'I am Reginald Parrish, Miss. And you are?'

"'She's my sister, Reg,' Edie answered for me. 'My sister, Bess, that is.' She turned to me and added with a self-important air: 'Reginald's in banking. A head clerk.'

"'I don't care if he's the Lord Mayor of London!' I replied, giving her a withering glare.

"He cleared his throat again and I turned back to him.

"'I'm very pleased to meet you,' he said.

"He extended his hand but I wasn't about to shake it. I merely let my eyes rest on it for a long moment, then turned back to Edie.

"'Haven't you got to be at work or something?' I demanded.

"'I'm just going. By the way, I wouldn't be in a hurry to get home if I were you. Mother's still ranting on about what you said to her before you left. She says Billy will have to write to you,' she went on, and a little smirk appeared on her mouth. 'Him being the only man of the house, that is.'

"Her amused contempt was the final push that I needed. Before either of them could move, I flung back my arm and slapped Edie across the face.

"She screamed and her hand shot up to nurse her injury. Her cheek was rapidly turning crimson and was the definite imprint of a hand across her face. I got some satisfaction out of that, I don't mind telling you.

"'Now then, Bess,' Reg stepped forward. 'There's no need for that.'

"'It's Miss Shaw to you,' I corrected him. 'And I'd thank you to keep your long nose out of my family's business. I don't know how long you've known this fast little piece, or how long you think you'll last before she gets fed up and finds someone else, but I'll tell you this much. You're not the first man to do what he liked with her and you won't be the last!'

"I turned away and marched off angrily toward home. I was still trembling, furious with my sister and with the man for his lack of respect for her, though just why any man should have respected her, I'm sure I don't know. I couldn't help thinking of Daniel and how he had always behaved like a gentleman. He would never dream of even attempting to take such liberties as I'd just seen my sister consent to.

"My heart was still thumping with indignation when I reached the Angel and hurried toward our entrance at the rear of the building. Rose was waiting for me, standing in the yard, her hands tucked under her arms to keep them warm.

"'Bess! Thank goodness.' She grabbed my arms as she rushed forward, a little worried frown creasing her forehead. 'Mother's in a terrible state.'

"'I know. I've just seen Edie. Something about what I said to her, isn't it?'

"Rose nodded.

"'Among other things,' she replied. 'You did go a bit far, you know.' She sighed deeply. 'But that's not all. Auntie Ann left in a mood because mother wouldn't pray with her for Billy's soul. Kept saying he wasn't dead, that the body was some other kid. Bess, what if she keeps on saying it? You know he's dead, don't you?'

"I nodded.

"'Yes, I do. But if the old girl won't accept it, there's not much we can do but go along with her. All this arguing won't help.'

"'But if she won't admit he's gone, then that place'll bury him themselves.' Her mouth drew itself down into a grim line. 'It's terrible for him to have to lie in a pauper's grave.'

"I just stared at her. I never could understand why it was so important to have a decent grave. After all, you're in no state to care once you're dead, are you?

"Medical science can have me. Perhaps they can figure out why none of my innards have gone off in a hundred years.

"'Rose!' I said at last. "How can you talk like that? I thought you had more sense. What difference does it make where he's buried? He's dead and that's an end to it. Pauper's grave, indeed!'

"She nodded doubtfully.

"'I know you're right,' she said. 'Billy's gone to a world far better than this one, but still it seems all wrong to me that he won't have a decent funeral.'

"'I'm more concerned about the insurance money, to tell you the truth,' I went on. I seemed to be the only one who had thought of it. 'Mother'll keep paying it in, so she's got enough to pay for his funeral when he does die. It's such a waste.'

"Rose sighed and shook her head again.

"'I hadn't thought of that,' she replied. 'Perhaps when the death certificate comes, you and me can do something about it.' She paused briefly, then asked: 'How did it go with Daniel?'

"'You knew where I'd gone then?'

"She nodded.

"'Did you tell him what mother said? What did he say?'

"I shook my head, not wanting to recall the meeting.

"'It doesn't matter now, Rose. It's over, whatever it was. It should never have started in the first place.' I squeezed her hand, then turned away. 'I'd better go up, see how she is.'

"'Bess.' She caught my arm. 'Are you sure you've done the right thing?'

"I frowned at her. My head was full of the recent scene with Edith, and it took me a minute to realise what Rose was talking about.

"'To be quite honest with you,' I answered, 'I don't know.'"

***

Bess asked for a cup of tea then and her request jolted Stella back to the present with a start.

After the modern conveniences of the living room, her kitchen came as no great surprise. It was fitted with modern wipe-down cupboards and she had an electric oven, a microwave, and even a small dishwasher.

As she waited for the water to boil, her grandmother's image crept into her mind and lingered, her expression concerned, as though warning me away from the knowledge her sister was about to impart. Stella felt disloyal for even listening, but the temptation was too great to call a halt now, even had she known how to.

The clock on the mantelpiece struck midday as she gave Bess her tea and sat down, and she wondered if she would reach the end of her tale that day. She need not have worried; her aunt was determined to speak her piece, even if it took all night.

"It wasn't long before I started to miss Daniel," she went on between sips of tea. "Thursday was his day off, a luxury limited in those days to people who worked for their own fathers and, in the past, he would always be found waiting at the factory gates when Rose and me came out. I looked for him that Thursday. I was even puzzled to find him missing from his usual place, leaning against the wall just inside the gates. It was a moment or two before I realised he wouldn't be coming.

"Rose noticed his empty place as well. Either that or she saw what was in my mind.

"'It's odd, not having Daniel here to meet us,' she said.

"'We'll get used to it,' I replied, trying to sound as though it wasn't important.

"'I wonder what he's doing instead?' She persisted.

"'Who cares?'

"'You do, I think. Of course, if I'm wrong, and you really don't want him, I might seek him out and flirt with him myself. A girl could do a lot worse.'

"Her words produced an image in my mind that made me furiously jealous. I halted my steps and looked at her angrily, only to see the teasing smile she wore, and I knew that jealousy was precisely what she had intended me to feel.

"'You stick to Alfred,' I replied with a short laugh.

"'Oh, yes! I mustn't think of being unfaithful to Alfred.'

"We went off down the road, arm in arm, giggling like two silly schoolgirls. We did a lot of laughing together back then, and the other workers who poured out of the gates around us took no notice. All except one.

"'Share the joke?' Alfred's voice sounded in my ear, making me jump.

"'Nothing you'd find funny,' Rose answered pleasantly.

"'No boyfriend tonight, Bess?' He asked me.

"I glared at him crossly, putting an end to the humour for that day. I had no intention of discussing Daniel with him."

Her smile faded with her last words, and Stella recalled Grandma's stories and how she'd told us that her sister was a spinster because nobody had wanted her. More lies, more deviations from the truth? They had to be, for it didn't seem likely that Auntie Bess had invented Daniel.

"So you stayed unmarried through choice, Auntie?" Stella asked.

She was beginning to feel quite fond of the old lady by then, and the 'Auntie' slipped out naturally. Bess gazed at her for a moment and smiled.

"You could say that," was her cryptic reply.

CHAPTER SIX

"Edie had worked for Lady Metcalf for about a year then and she had always had Sunday as her day off. She would arrive home late on Saturday night, stay over until Sunday evening, then return to Hanover Square. A few weeks after I'd seen her with Reg Parrish, she began to spend her weeknights at home as well. It seemed an odd thing to do, considering the distance between our room and the place where she worked, and it also seemed that she was taking an unnecessary risk. She could lose her job if Lady Metcalf discovered her missing and it was a good job, too. Girls of our class didn't often get to be parlour maids, I can tell you.

"Mother didn't seem to think her behaviour was in any way unusual, but both Rose and I were suspicious of her excuse that she could sleep better at home.

"'There's something going on,' I said to Rose one morning as we walked to work. 'You can't tell me she's more comfortable coming all the way home, late at night, and going back at some unearthly hour, than staying put. It's been good enough for her all this time, so why now?'

"'Well, I can't think of any reason. Perhaps she's fallen out with one of the other servants. That could be it, couldn't it?'

"'It's possible. Still, I can't see Edie letting anyone chase her out of the house. There's more to it, you mark my words.'

"'But what?'

"'I don't know. But I intend to find out.'

"Edie had to be up even before me to make it back in time to prepare the house for Lady Metcalf. It was too early for any transport, so she used the old penny farthing cycle from the yard.

"She presented quite a picture, did Edie, wobbling about as she rode down the street on that thing, her skirt hoisted up to keep it from getting caught and the wheels creaking so loud you could hear them long after she was out of sight. But mother was more concerned about her showing her ankles than she was about her falling off and breaking her silly neck.

"There had to be a better reason for all this than insomnia, you can be sure of that.

"I always woke early – Rose and me had to be at the factory by six – and the next morning I lay there listening in the dark as Edie made getting-up noises, tiptoeing round the room to gather her clothes, slipping into her shoes and coat. Mother snored with rhythmic vibrations and I could hear the distant cries of the street pedlars as they made their across London. It was always a very lonely hour, listening to the sounds of London coming to life. You almost felt as if you were the only person left alive in your part of the city and everyone else had forgotten all about you.

"Edie neither ate nor drank anything. The moment she was dressed, she slipped through the door and closed it quietly behind her. I was straight out of bed, pushing my arms into my coat sleeves and shoving my feet into mother's slippers. My mother was the only member of the family who owned a pair of slippers, and they were men's, left behind by my father on one of his fleeting visits.

"I crossed to the door and peered out. Edie had reached the bottom of the stairs and was running across the yard. I was just in time to see her, with her hand covering her mouth, throw open the door to the outhouse and hurry inside. I crept up and stood close by, listening to the retching noises from within, and Edie's reason for staying at home became very clear indeed.

"The scene was repeated the next morning, and the next, confirming my suspicions. My sister was determined to suffer her morning sickness far away from the prying eyes of the other servants in Hanover Square.

"'She's pregnant,' I told Rose.

"'She can't be, Bess,' she argued, her eyes wide with shock. 'Sam hasn't been home for six months.'

"I had little sympathy with her naivety. She'd never think of two timing a man herself, so it wouldn't occur to her that her sister could.

"'Well it's not the Immaculate Conception, Rose!' I cried impatiently. 'That girl's pregnant, I tell you, and if you think she's kept herself to herself while Sam's been away, you want to wake your ideas up. I know she's been seeing someone else; I saw her with him.'

"'You never said anything.'

"'Well, I didn't think it was any of my business, not enough to talk about anyway. Besides, I hoped it might all blow over. Too late for that now, though.'

"'I'm sure you're wrong. Maybe she's not feeling too good. There's nowhere like your own home when you don't feel well.'

"'We'll see,' I replied, but I was certain in my own mind that I was not mistaken.

"I decided to give Edie the benefit of the doubt, and for a long time I waited to see how things would develop. I thought it just possible that an announcement might be made, that she might tell us about an engagement to Reg. I was sure Reg was the one responsible, though I didn't much relish the idea of having him as my brother-in-law.

"But when Sam's letter arrived telling Edie he would be home at the end of February, I was forced to abandon any hope of my sister doing the right thing for once in her life.

"'Sam's coming home!' Edie declared, clutching the letter to her as if it was Sam himself. 'I'm going to persuade him to name a day. He's not going to fob me off with excuses about me being too young, not this time. I'll talk him into marrying me before he goes back.'

"'And before he finds out,' I couldn't resist retorting sharply.

"Edie's smile faded and she looked at me with a touch of panic in her eyes.

"'Finds out what?' She asked, but she was having trouble keeping her voice steady, you could see that.

"I didn't answer for a moment. I just watched her, wanting her to worry. I had reached the point of disgust with her the day I'd seen her wrestling with Reg. Now I'd gone beyond that point; I felt nothing for her but contempt and I just couldn't believe I'd been gullible enough to hope for anything better from her. There wasn't an ounce of decency in that girl. I thought I must be getting as bad as Rose; she was always trying to find honesty where there wasn't any to find.

"'Finds out what?' She repeated, and her voice was rising toward hysteria.

"I raised an eyebrow suggestively.

"'About the money, of course,' I answered. 'Unless there's something else he doesn't know about.'

"Edie's relief was apparent as she put the letter away in her little wooden box where she kept all Sam's letters. As soon as she had gone out, I opened the box and read the letter. It told me what I needed to know – which train he would arrive on. Edie wouldn't waste her day off just to go and meet him. She'd re-arrange it so she could see him the day after he arrived in London, the same as she always did. I intended to get to him first.

"I daresay you've heard this tale before, or at least some version of it. But what else could I do? What would you have done? Sam trusted Edie, trusted her with his money as well as his affection. She'd betrayed him on both counts, and I couldn't stand by and do nothing.

"I saw him at once. Amid all the other sailor suits rushing along the platform, their kit bags hoisted onto their shoulders, I spotted his red hair easily. He stopped dead when he saw me and gave me a worried frown.

"'Bess? What are you doing here?' He said. 'What's happened?'

"The concern in his eyes only made me angry. What right did Edie have to provoke so much consideration from a man like that? He was a good deal older than my sister, perhaps ten years or more, but he had loved her for two years. All that time, she had deceived him, spending the money he sent for her to save for their wedding, wearing his ring as bold as brass and pawning it frequently to pay for her fripperies.

"'It's all right, Sam,' I said, trying to make my voice sound gentle. Somehow it never did sound gentle, even to my own ears, not once I no longer had Daniel to talk to. I still missed him; I looked for him everywhere I went. Firmly I pushed the treacherous thoughts away – this was no time to get sentimental.

"'Come and have a cup of tea with me, Sam,' I said. 'I've got something to tell you.'

"He followed me to the station buffet, asking questions that I refused to answer. He paid for our teas, knowing full well that I couldn't afford to.

"'Well?' He asked as soon as we were seated. 'What's it all about?'

"'You won't thank me for telling you this, Sam. At least, not now you won't. But someone has to.'

"'What are you talking about, Bess? Out with it. It's not like you to hold back.'

"'You're right,' I said at last. 'What I've got to say has to be said, and it won't wait either. That's why I skived off work to come and meet you. It's about Edie.'

"His eyes met mine sharply, his frown one of anxiety tinged with anger.

"'You told me she was all right.'

"'She is. At least, she's not ill or anything.' I drew a deep breath to give me courage. 'The fact is, Sam, Edie's pregnant and I think she plans to rush you to the altar before you find out.'

"He shook his head slowly, disbelievingly.

"'She wouldn't do a thing like that.'

"'Oh, yes, she would.' I sipped my tea slowly before I spoke again. I didn't want to have to be the one to tell him, and I was trying to find some words of comfort so he wouldn't be hurt so much. 'You don't know her, Sam. You're away so much, you've never had a chance to see what she's really like.'

"'Did she tell you? That she's in the club?'

"I shook my head.

"'We all live together, remember? You can't hide something like that, not when it's right under your nose. And I know she hasn't been faithful to you. I've seen her with so many men lately, it's a wonder she can remember all their names.'

"That was no lie, either. Reg was only the latest, and perhaps the most adventurous encounter. There had been many others I'd seen her holding hands with.

"My eyes met his and I saw fury dawning in them. I knew he had a temper, but in that moment he looked as though he might murder someone. I hoped it would be Edie.

"He didn't question my word. If I'd taken the trouble to go all that way to tell him about Edie, then it had to be true. He knew that.

"'I'm seeing her tomorrow,' he said. 'I'll get the truth out of her.'

"'It might be better if you didn't let on that you know. Let her do her bit and see if I'm right. I'd like to think I'm wrong, for your sake, but I'm sure I'm not.'

"Sam drained his cup and rose to his feet. He didn't look hurt, just angry, but I could find no comfort in that. The hurt would come later, when the anger had died.

"He said goodbye and left me to sit and finish my tea, deep in thought and hoping I'd done the right thing. For all I knew Sam might have preferred to remain in ignorance, to let Edie get him into bed and marry her, and never know that the child wasn't his.' She paused before adding wistfully: "Some people are like that, aren't they? When they love someone, really love them, they don't ever want to lose them, no matter what the cost."

Stella had the feeling that Aunt Bess had personal experience of what she said. She could see that her mind was elsewhere, not in a railway buffet with Sam at all. She didn't disturb her thoughts, just waited until she went on.

"A loud hiss from one of the engines made me jump and I looked up, remembering suddenly where I was. I had to get home. I didn't feel happy about leaving mother alone and I worried about her, even when I was at work. She had declined rapidly in the last few weeks, not only talking about Billy as if he were going to come back one day, but building a whole fantasy life for him, a life in which he had gone away to become an apprentice and would get himself a good job and take care of us all. That's where she believed her son was – apprenticed to a tailor up north. All memory of that place had vanished from her mind.

"The following morning, I watched Edie as she preened herself in front of the mirror, getting ready for her meeting with Sam. She'd spent ages brushing her hair to make it shine and now she was fiddling with her hat, trying to get it at just the right saucy angle. Her face was flushed and her eyes sparkled with nervous excitement. She'd never been this enthusiastic before, just because Sam was home.

"'Not long now,' she said suddenly. 'You'd better start saving for a wedding present.'

"'What makes you so sure he'll want to marry you yet?' I answered.

"I felt a bit guilty, seeing her so sure of herself, when I knew it wasn't going to work out the way she planned. I felt a little sorry for her, too, and it was on the tip of my tongue to tell her what I'd done, if only to save her the embarrassment of finding out for herself.

"'Why shouldn't he?' She replied. 'We've been engaged long enough.'

"'What about Reg?'

"She glanced at me crossly.

"'He was just a bit of fun, that's all. Forget about him. There's nothing to stop Sam and me from getting married right away.'

"Just a bit of fun? How could she dismiss it like that, when things had gone so far? Her careless remark chased away my little spark of sympathy.

"'Sam might think you haven't got enough saved,' I suggested spitefully.

"Her reply was an ugly glare as she went out, slamming the door behind her. I spent the time she was gone imagining the scene which was taking place between them, and recalling Sam's face when he'd left me at the station, how angry he was. I was half expecting her to come home with a black eye.

"When she did come back, she was in tears. She flung open the door and sent it crashing loudly into the table, then threw herself onto the bed.

"I felt a moment of remorse. Supposing I had been wrong? Then I looked at her and realised that her tears were those of frustration, not misery. Her little feet in their shiny leather boots were kicking at the mattress and her gloved fists were clenched in anger. She was just like a toddler, enjoying a temper tantrum.

"Mother flew to her side and gathered her into her arms.

"'Whatever's wrong, Edith?'

"'It...It's Sam,' she sobbed. 'Sam! He's finished with me. He says we can't get married and he's even taken back his ring!'

"Mother gasped.

"'Rosina, put the kettle on. Edith's had a terrible shock. She needs a nice cup of strong, sweet tea.' She turned quickly back to comfort Edie. 'There, there, child. If he's going to do this sort of thing, after all the time you've been engaged, he's not worth having. There's plenty more fish in the sea.'

"'But there aren't plenty more sailors,' I said cynically. 'Are there, Edie?'

"I was leaning against the edge of the table, my arms folded, prepared to enjoy the scene and the outcome, whatever it may turn out to be. Mother turned on me, her eyes blazing.

"'I don't know how you can be so hard, Elizabeth,' she said angrily. 'I never brought you up to be like that. Edith's heart is broken.'

"'That's not all that's broken,' I replied spitefully.

"'What's that supposed to mean?' Edie raised her head suddenly, glaring at me.

"'Bess, please,' Rose pleaded. 'Not now. Let her get over her disappointment.'

"'Don't you mean her tantrum, Rose? Let her get over the fact that her little scheme didn't work.' I leaned toward Edie, a grim line of contempt on my mouth. 'Why don't you tell mother what you're really crying about?'

"'I don't know what you mean,' Edie replied, sitting up. Her tears had stopped suddenly and her eyes were full of fear. She was beginning to realise that I knew something, and I was the last person on earth she wanted to know about this.

"'Tell mother the reason Sam refused to marry you,' I kept on bluntly. 'You did ask him, didn't you? You had it all planned, I expect. Get him alone, let him think he was the first, then demand that he marry you? Is that something like the way you planned it, Edie?'

"'It was you!' She gasped with sudden enlightenment. 'It was you who told him!'

"'Told him what?' mother demanded. 'What are you two talking about?'

"Edie looked up fearfully, but she couldn't keep the fury from showing in her taut muscles and her clenched fists.

"'I tried to stop him, mother,' she said, almost desperately, a little tear threatening to begin a new deluge. 'I tried, but he made me.'

"'Sam?'

"'No. No, not Sam. This bloke. He...he forced me. He was stronger than me, see and I couldn't stop him.' She began to cry again as her eyes met mother's. 'I'm two months gone, mother.'

"'Pregnant?' Mother asked in a terrified whisper, drawing herself a little away from her favourite daughter. 'You mean, this man...raped you?'

"I watched all this with fascination, wondering whether Edie had her story planned or whether she had made it up on the spur of the moment. I never did find out. Whichever way it had been, I was not about to let her get away with it.

"'Who's the father, Edie?' I demanded. 'Who was it forced himself on you?'

"Edie shook her head.

"'Well, then, we'd better notify the police, hadn't we?'

"'No!'

"'Don't be daft. You can't just let somebody go around raping young girls. If he's done it once, he'll do it again. It's not right.'

"When Edie made no reply, I leaned forward, peering straight into her eyes.

"'Was it Reg?' I asked softly.

"'Reg? Who's Reg?' Mother demanded.

"'Go on, Edie. Tell her about Reg. Or would you like me to?'

"Edie flung herself off the bed and ran to the door. Mother looked at each of us, her eyes bewildered, before she followed. I was weary of the whole thing by then and I just hoped that Reg would consent to marry my sister. The shame of a bastard in the family would easily be enough to tilt my mother over the edge.

"Nina had sat quietly, listening and watching the entire scene. She was trying not to make a noise, trying not to remind mother that she was still in the room. No one ever talked about things like that if she were listening and now she was wide-eyed with fascination.

"'Rose,' she said softly from where she sat before the cooking range, hugging her legs. Rose turned to look at her, a little gasp escaping her lips at the realisation that she had heard everything. 'How can Edie be having a baby? Did she get married?'

"'No, love. Edie's not married.'

"'But she can't be having a baby if she's not married, can she? Mother told me you had to be married to have a baby.'

"Rose looked at me and shrugged helplessly. She didn't know whether to tell the child the truth of make up some story. My mother would simply have told her she was too young to know.

"Rose was silent for so long, Nina went on.

"'How did the baby get there if she's not married?'

"Mother returned in time to hear the question.

"'You'll learn the big secret soon enough, my girl,' she snapped, then muttered to herself: 'and if that's the big secret, I don't think much of it.'"

CHAPTER SEVEN

"So you're telling me my grandmother maintained a lie all those years?" Stella asked incredulously. "That the story she told my mother, told me, was only part of the truth?"

"I wouldn't say that. Knowing Edie, she probably turned the whole thing round in her mind, made herself the injured party. Maybe she truly did believe I had no right to put my spoke in, no matter what the circumstances. Maybe she was right. It was her business, after all, wasn't it?"

Slowly, Stella shook her head.

"No," she replied. "If what you say is true, I owe you an apology."

"What for? It wasn't your fault, was it?"

"And she never forgave you, never spoke to you again?" Stella thought hard before she broached the next question. She had no wish to antagonise the old lady. "But are you sure you haven't got things mixed up? I mean, she loved my grandfather. They didn't marry simply because of the baby, did they?"

Bess lifted her eyebrows and her expression became enigmatic. Stella realised she would have to wait. Bess had more to say before her questions would be answered.

"There was an atmosphere in the room once mother came back," Bess continued with her story. "We were all dying to talk about Edie, but none of us quite dared, not with the way mother was glaring at everyone.

"After a while, I'd had enough and I went out. I saw Edie out in the street, standing under the faded 'Angel' on the pub's emblem. I thought how appropriate it was that she'd chosen that particular place to stand; she seemed something of a faded angel herself that day. She was dabbing powder on her face and peering into a little mirror. She always imagined nobody noticed she wore it, that we all thought it was her lovely complexion.

"She was seriously worried, I could see that. She was also seething with anger and disappointment.

"I went up to her and stood staring at her for a few minutes before she noticed I was there. She turned and gave me a look of pure hatred, but I didn't much care. She'd disgraced everyone with her behaviour, and in my opinion she deserved whatever she got.

"'I had everything worked out,' she snapped at me. 'And you had to go and stick your nose in!'

"'What else did you expect? I wasn't going to just stand by and let you foist someone else's kid off onto a decent man like Sam.'

"'It was none of your business, Bess,' she argued bitterly. 'I could always twist Sam round my little finger, always could get my own way with him. It would have been easy, after all the months he's been away at sea, without a woman in sight, to pretend to be crying out with love for him. I could have made him do it with no trouble; then he would have felt guilty and insisted on marrying me before he went back. He'd never have known the difference!'

"'And what was supposed to happen when the baby came?' I asked her. 'Even Sam can add up, you know.'

"She laughed contemptuously, the sort of laugh that told me it should have been obvious, even to me.

"'I can't see where there would have been any problem. All I had to do was move the kid's birthday and not tell him the news for a couple of months. He'd have been away so he need never have known.'

"She glared at me viciously as she spoke, and I wouldn't have been surprised to see her strike out, start a fight there in the street. She certainly was mad enough.

"'But you had to go and open your big mouth, didn't you?' She screamed. 'Why couldn't you just mind your own business? I'd have had Sam just where I wanted him if only you hadn't interfered! Just because you were going with him first, you seem to think you've got some right to decide what he does!'

"'I just thought he deserved to have all the facts before he made up his mind, that's all. It's not as if you love Sam; you never have. You've never loved anyone but yourself. You're just a little trollop, and that's all you'll ever be!'

"'I'll never forgive you for sticking your nose in where it doesn't belong. I'll get my own back, you'll see. I could have been content, married to Sam. Now I suppose I'll have to marry Reg. That's the only way out of this mess!'

"I had to smile. It never occurred to Edie that she wouldn't get her own way, somehow or other. Not even now, when she had lost Sam. But marrying Reg was the only alternative left to her. She couldn't have the baby out of wedlock. Nobody would speak to her, only whisper behind her back. No one would give her a job.

"'I have to find Reg,' she said sullenly. 'I have to tell him about the baby. And you needn't look at me like that. I know whose it is, in spite of what you or others might think. He's the only one I've been all the way with, so it has to be his, doesn't it?'

"'You mean you're going to wait outside the bank for him? He won't like that.'

"'Then he'll just have to lump it, won't he? This is his fault, and the sooner he knows it, the better.'

"She seemed very sure of how Reg would receive her news, but I couldn't help worrying about what would happen if he didn't react the way she expected.

"'Suppose he refuses to marry you, Edie?' I asked. 'What'll you do then?'

"She gave me a little smug smile, a smile which dimpled her cheeks flirtatiously.

"'Of course he'll marry me,' she said confidently. 'Why shouldn't he? He loves me and it's his kid. The trouble with you is you've never been loved like that. You don't know what it means when a man gets that special look in his eye.' She paused and arched an eyebrow at me, her mouth forming a line of malice. 'You want to take a long, hard look at yourself, Bess. You're nineteen years old and already you're well on the road to being a dried up old maid! Nobody's ever going to want you. That's why you've done this to me, isn't it? Because you're jealous!'

"I could have argued the point, but I didn't bother. She should have known about Daniel, just like Rose did. She was my sister, too. But Edie never did know about anything that didn't directly involve her. Besides, I didn't much care what she thought.

"'Do you want me to come with you?' I asked her. I don't know why, really. I can't deny that I wanted to see the look on his supercilious face when she told him. But I could tell from the insults she had thrown at me and the hysteria in her tone, that she was more distressed than I would have thought possible. I thought she needed some moral support.

"She stared at me for a long time before she answered, and I was sure she was going to refuse, to tell me I'd done enough, thank you very much. I was prepared to go back inside and to hell with her, and I was a little taken aback when she nodded.

"'All right,' she said. 'It'll do you good to see what love's all about, since it's the only chance you're likely to get! But you'd better hide while I speak to him. He won't much like having an audience for this little scene.'

"I couldn't be angry. Her insults meant very little to me at the best of times, but I was beginning to pity her. It wasn't like Edie to be really nasty, not like this. She was usually too wrapped up in her own importance to bother getting angry with anyone else. She was hurt by Sam's rejection, by my interference, and it was the hurt that was talking.

"We caught the tram, expecting a long wait until the bank closed and Reg emerged. We had little to say to one another as we rode into the city centre, so I suppose it was just as well that

London was full of suffragettes that day. I don't know how much you know about the suffragettes, but I can tell you they were all heated up with their cause. They were marching all over the road, waving their banners and chanting. The police were out in force, trying to hold them back, and some of those women got quite vicious. That was the day they smashed all the windows in the west end, and that's where they were heading while we were trying to get to the city to see Reg before he went home for the night.

"Because of the delay, we had to run when we got off the tram and Edie was somewhat bedraggled by the time we reached the bank. Her hat sat lopsided on her head and her hair was all mussed. She was just in time to see Reg as he came out of the main doors on his way home.

"I was hiding in the doorway of some offices and I saw him draw up sharply when he caught sight of her, a flash of anger crossing his already stern features. He stepped forward and grabbed her arm, so tight it must have hurt, and hustled her out of sight.

"I left the doorway and went to peer round the corner so I could hear what was said.

"'I told you not to come here,' he said testily. 'This is my place of business, for goodness sake. What sort of impression will it give my employers to have young women hanging about outside.'

"He hadn't even noticed the state of her, nor did he seem to think it odd that she wasn't at work.

"'I had to come Reg. I had to see you.'

"'Well, that's very flattering, I'm sure, but I have to think of my position.'

"'Can we talk?'

"'Not now, Edith. I am in a hurry, you know. I'll see you on Sunday, same as always.'

"She shook her head furiously.

"'Now,' she demanded, her tone leaving no room for argument.

"He sighed irritably.

"'Very well. But be quick, please.'

"Edith looked into his eyes for an instant, and I wondered how she was going to endure being married to him. He wasn't her type of person at all. It was a wonder they'd ever got together in the first place. Perhaps she never realised before just how pompous he could be, but now as he stood before her in his black suit, I could see the contempt in her eyes and I felt sorry for her again. And guilty, I felt that too. Perhaps I should have kept quiet. There she was, with her life falling about her ears, and he couldn't even be bothered to take a few minutes to find out what was wrong. Well, I thought, just you wait Reg Parrish! She'll soon wipe that superior look off your face!

"'I'm going to have a baby, Reg,' she said bluntly.

"His expression would have been comical, had the situation been less serious. Both his eyebrows shot up, his eyes opened wide and he took a step backward. Edith looked panic-stricken, probably afraid the shock would give him a heart attack before he could get around to marrying her.

"'Well, Reg,' she went on quickly, before he could speak. 'What are you going to do about it?'

"'What am I going to do abut it?' He demanded, with emphasis on the I. 'Are you saying it's mine?'

"She flinched. She was hurt by that, perhaps more hurt than she had ever been in her life, and I think she finally felt some of the shame that Rose and I were always telling her she should feel. As for me, I was furious. No matter how disgusted with her I was, she was still my sister and I wanted to run and hit him myself. She fought back her tears and tried to summon the anger that had brought her this far.

"'Of course it's yours!' She replied hotly. 'I've never been with anyone else, as well you know.'

"'Oh, but I don't know, Edith, do I?' He said and she frowned at him. I was puzzled, too, for a moment. We always thought that a man could tell if a girl was a virgin. 'After what your sister said, naturally I have my doubts.'

"Me and my big mouth! I couldn't believe that Edie was about to lose her last resort because of what I had said.

"'To hell with what my sister said!' She shouted at him. 'I'm in the club and you're the father. You'll have to marry me!'

"He cleared his throat, causing Edie to sigh irritably.

"'Come now, Edith,' he said with a little half curve on his lips. 'Let's be adult about this. It takes two to make a bargain, you know. I have my position to think of.'

"'What does that mean?'

"'Well, no disrespect intended, my dear, but as a head clerk I am expected to marry erm...' he paused and glanced at her furtively. 'Shall we say, a better class of person.'

"I was seething. Who the hell did he think he was? I should have expected it. After all, the man was obviously a pretentious little snob, but my heart went out to Edie. She had been through enough that day, after everything I had said to her, after the names Sam had called her – a thief, among worse things for spending all his money, or so she told me on the tram earlier. She hadn't expected to be insulted by the likes of toffy-nosed Reg Parrish!

"It must have really hurt to realise that the man she'd chosen to lose her virtue to, the man she'd thrown away everything for, had only been playing with her all along, even if she had been doing the same with him. And she'd believed that he loved her, when all the time he had thought of her as little better than a prostitute. I could imagine how damaged was her pride, and it must have been doubly humiliating to know that I was within earshot. But I got no satisfaction from knowing how she felt. I was only furious that someone had deceived and used my sister that way. He obviously intended to talk his way out of his responsibilities; he had no intention of marrying her, and what would that do to mother?

"She kept her pain in check until it turned to a need for vengeance. A malicious little grin crept over her mouth before she replied, almost spitting the words at him.

"'Lady Metcalf keeps her money in your bank, doesn't she, Reg?'

"'Your employer? As a matter of fact, she does, but I cannot be expected to discuss the bank's clients with you.'

"'Quite a few of Her Ladyship's friends keep their money there, too, I believe.'

"His air of confidence was beginning to crumble as he wondered where the discussion was leading, and he looked at her with suspicious dread. I could have told him where it was leading – blackmail, pure and simple, and for the first time in many months, I was proud of my sister.

"'I don't really see what our clients have to do with this, Edith.'

"'Don't you? Then you must be dafter than I thought. I wonder what Lady Metcalf will say when she finds out her parlour maid was got into trouble by one of her bank's clerks – and that he isn't honourable enough to face up to his responsibilities. She might decide you're not honourable enough to look after her money, either. The bank manager will have to choose then, won't he? Who do you think he'll choose, Reg? You? Or Lady Metcalf and all her wealthy friends?' She stopped speaking and smiled smugly. She had him now, and she knew it. 'I don't know about you, but my money's on Her Ladyship.'"

CHAPTER EIGHT

"This can't be right," Stella interrupted sharply. "My grandparents were always very affectionate, very respectful toward each other. You want me to believe he only married her under threat? I can't accept it! She was too proud, much too dignified to have blackmailed him like that!"

"I can't tell you what to believe," Bess replied quietly. "I can only tell you what happened. Edie might have been everything you say she was; I'm not saying no different. But you didn't know her when she was sixteen, and you can't understand the way things were, what attitudes were like then. She had to marry him; there was no other choice for her, and if that meant threatening to tell his bosses, then that's the way it had to be. It was her only weapon and she had to swallow her pride and use it."

Reluctantly Stella nodded. She could see what it must have been like, though she couldn't really understand it, couldn't really put herself in her grandmother's place and feel the desperation and panic that she must have felt.

"Go on," she finally urged. "What happened?"

"The wedding was arranged for the earliest possible date, just as soon as the banns had been read in church.

"Edie gave Lady Metcalf notice, explaining that she was to be married but not of course, telling her the circumstances. But the following Saturday when she came home, she was in a panic.

"'Lady Metcalf wants to see my wedding gown!' She declared frantically. 'What am I going to do? I can't tell her I haven't got a proper dress. I refuse to lower myself by telling her we can't afford one!'

"'Why does she want to see it, anyway?' Rose asked. 'I wouldn't have thought she'd be that interested.'

"'I think she's just trying to be kind.'

"Mother looked up from her lace, her hands resting momentarily upon the little cushion on which she pinned it.

"'What did you tell her?' She asked.

"Edie threw her hat and gloves onto the bed and bounced after them.

"'I said my sister was still making it,' she said, throwing me a reproachful glare. 'I couldn't think what else to say.'

"Mother got up from her chair and put her lacework aside.

"'If Her Ladyship wants to see a wedding gown, then we'll have to show her one,' she said decisively.

"We all stared at her suspiciously. Sometimes she came out with the most far-fetched notions and you never knew whether she was really lucid or not. Now we all thought she was in one of her unreal states, perhaps thinking we were rich and could go and buy whatever we wanted.

"'You needn't look like that,' she said crossly as she pushed her arms into her coat sleeves. 'I didn't get married in my petticoat and stockings, you know. If Edie must have a proper dress, she can wear mine.'

"'Yours?' We all said at once.

"It was the first any of us knew that she'd ever possessed such a garment, but she went off to collect it from her sister, who had been storing it for her for years.

"When she got back, we all gathered round the table to watch her unwrap the dress from its many layers of white muslin.

"It was a fairly simple arrangement, years out of date, of course, but that only made it seem quaint. It was made of silk, with piping at the front of the bodice, quite plain except for the sleeves and veil, which were lace made by mother's own hand.

"'I never thought I'd have to look at this again,' mother said with a bitter grimace.

"She fingered the lace thoughtfully, her mind wandering for a long time, perhaps racing back more than thirty years to when she was sixteen herself, living as she had always lived, in an elaborately painted Romany Vardo amid many other elaborately painted Vardos with her Romany family.

"George Shaw had come to sell her father some gold, a ring and necklace which his mother had left him. That was how they had met and she had fallen for him at once, seeing only a handsome face and never stopping to wonder what sort of man would sell his mother's legacy so casually. My grandfather, always a shrewd man, had disliked him on sight and had forbidden his daughter to have anything to do with him. That prohibition had only strengthened her attachment. George was sure the old man had money and, being uneducated, could be easily parted from it.

"He had been right in thinking that the Lees had money, but quite mistaken in believing he had the cunning to cheat them.

"She had put love and hope into every stitch of her wedding gown, love and hope that were quickly shattered.

"'Mother, it's beautiful!' I cried when I saw the exquisite sleeves.

"You've never seen anything quite as lovely as the lace my mother used to make, and I've always regretted not having kept any. Every scrap she made was sold; she couldn't afford to make anything just for us. Edie had the only sample, in those sleeves, and you'd know more about what happened to that than I would.

"Mother was slowly nodding her head.

"'Yes,' she said. 'But I'm not happy about Edie wearing it. It's unlucky, that dress. It won't do her no good.' She sighed heavily, with an air of giving in to the inevitable. 'If it has to be, it has to be. Anything's better than Lady Metcalf suspecting the truth. But I don't want her to wear it like this. I want it changed some way, so it doesn't look the same.'

"'Would you like me to embroider some flowers on to it? Perhaps on the skirt?'

"'Not coloured ones? I don't want anyone saying your sister was afraid to wear white.'

"'No, mother. Just some white flowers, and perhaps a few small pearly things to make them stand out.'

"I had a picture in my mind of what I planned to do and I knew she'd feel better about the gown once it was done. Besides, my fingers were itching to get started once I had the idea. I actually ended up taking the whole thing apart and remaking it.

"I worked late into the night on the wedding gown. For almost a week, I sat up till past midnight, a small oil lamp beside me, sewing with white silk thread and tiny white pearls. My eyes couldn't see straight by the time I went to bed, and I could see little round pearls in front of them all the time, but I enjoyed doing it and Edie seemed enchanted with it. I felt sure that all my efforts had brought about a truce. But I was exhausted, and I wished more than once during that week that I could make my embroidery pay better and stop working in the factory altogether.

"The day it was finished and Edie took it to show to Lady Metcalf, was the day my wish began to come true.

"Edie ran in full of excitement. She wasn't due home until Saturday night, but she'd been given special permission to pass on a message. She couldn't help being smug and self satisfied about it.

"'Lady Metcalf loved my gown!' She said at once. 'And the Countess wants to see you, Bess. She wants you to go and work for her!'

"I was sceptical, thought it was just Edie showing off.

"'Since when did countesses give audience to the likes of us?' I asked her.

"'It's the Countess of Hazelforth,' she replied impatiently. 'She's American.'

"'Oh. That explains everything.'

"'Really, Bess, I'm not making it up. She's not like other titled people. She wants to see you herself, she said, tomorrow morning at ten o'clock.'

"'Then she's going to be unlucky, isn't she? I can't have any more time off work. We need the money and I need my job.'

"'So what am I supposed to tell her?' Edie asked, vague panic creeping into her expression. 'You've got to go.'

"I looked at her, wondering whether it was worth the risk. For all I knew, Edie could be exaggerating the situation. The Countess might want a few daisies sewn onto some handkerchiefs and nothing more. No, it definitely wasn't worth risking my job for.

"'You'll have to explain,' I replied after a while. 'And tell her I'll come after work. About half past seven'

"She was unhappy with the errand. It was not her place to tell a countess, Her Ladyship's friend at that, that her sister was too busy to see her. Still, she was off at the end of the week, so why should she worry? It was my problem if I blew my chances, not hers.

"The following evening found me hurrying toward the American Countess' house in Regents Park. I'd never been there before; I had no reason to venture into that part of London. The only thing to be seen in the park was the zoo and the very thought of those beautiful creatures, locked up in cages, always made me want to let them all out.

"I never could bear to see anything in a cage, perhaps because I lived in a kind of cage myself. Oh, I could come and go as I pleased, there weren't any bars or locks to keep me in. But when your every waking thought revolves around keeping out of the workhouse, you can't get away from your own little universe. Without money, you can't go anywhere. If you're really poor, you're no better off than the animals in the zoo. Worse in fact, cos at least they know where their next meal is coming from. "I wasn't nervous at the prospect of meeting the Countess. I've always made a point of not being intimidated by anybody, certainly not just because they had a title and a lot of money, and if the job turned out to be a servant's position, I'd stick to the factory. I thought I was probably going to have a wasted journey. When countesses stipulated a time to come and see them, they weren't impressed to be told the time was not convenient. However, I had said I would go and I would and who knew? Perhaps the Countess would be so impressed with my work, I'd be able to make a name for myself. I'd be able to give up making boots for a living and give my hands time to return to the colour that God intended.

"I wasn't kidding myself, either. I knew I was good at what I did and there's never any harm in knowing what you're good at, provided you really are good at it and don't bore everybody to death.

"The house was so vast, it could scarcely be called a house at all. I've seen hotels smaller than that place and when I thought of the way we all crowded into one first floor room, I couldn't imagine what anyone would want with so much space.

"I went down the steps to the tradesmen's entrance, prepared to be told that the Countess had changed her mind. The door was opened by a footman, who led me through an enormous kitchen where about five women in aprons worked on various ingredients for the evening meal. None of them gave me so much as a glance as I followed the footman upstairs and into the main house, where he asked me to wait in the library, just like some important visitor.

"Now I was impressed. While I waited, my eyes roamed the bookshelves and I longed to just sit here until I had read every last page in the room. Books were a luxury that no one in my family could afford, neither could we afford much time to read them, though Rose liked her love stories before she went to sleep. The Bible was about the only book I had ever read, twice in fact, and while Auntie Ann took that to mean that I had a God-fearing soul, I was more inclined to appreciate its historical value. Apart from that, the best I could find in the way of reading matter were out of date newspapers found in the bar downstairs when one of Tom's customers left them behind.

"'Hello, Miss Shaw,' a feminine voice came from the doorway. I spun around, feeling slightly guilty for so much as thinking about touching the valuable collection. 'How do you do? I'm the Countess of Hazelforth.'

"The voice was very soft and very slow, and I found it extremely unattractive. I had no way of knowing that I was hearing a southern drawl.

"I couldn't bring myself to either curtsy or call this woman 'your Ladyship', as I knew were expected. Instead, I simply inclined my head.

"'I'm sorry I couldn't come this morning,' I said. 'I've got to go to work, you see.'

"'That's quite all right,' the Countess replied with a comforting smile. 'It was my fault. I should have realised.' Then, gesturing to a settee covered in blue velvet, she said: 'Please, do sit down.'

"I sat, perched on the edge of my seat, my hands clasped tightly in my lap. The Countess sat beside me, relaxed in her seat with her arm resting along the back of the settee.

"She was in her early sixties, much older than I had expected, but her hair was still blonde and it shone. It was piled high on her head and fastened in the centre of her crown with an elaborate, pearl-encrusted hairgrip. She was dressed in a gown of burgundy velvet, expensive but simple, and she wore no jewellery apart from her wedding ring.

"'Well, Miss Shaw,' she said at once. 'Let me tell you why I asked you here. I saw the embroidery on your sister's wedding gown. I've never seen anything like it. Exquisite! What I'd like very much for you to do for me, is some embroidery on my little granddaughter's dresses.' She paused to let the information settle in my mind, then went on slowly: 'What do you think?'

"I was relieved to have made the right decision in not risking my job. Edie had obviously been exaggerating; the lady wanted nothing more than a few bits of decoration, just as I'd suspected.'

"'I can embroider anything, Countess.' I let the word 'countess' slip out before I could retrieve it. 'But it'll take a while, depending on how much you need doing. I don't have a lot of time, you see.'

"'Yes, I see,' she said thoughtfully. 'Your sister tells me you made her gown, that you unpicked every stitch of your mother's wedding dress and remade it. Is that true?'

"'It's true,' I answered, feeling a little rattled. Was she calling my sister a liar?

"'Then you make clothes as well as you embroider them.'

"I allowed a little smile to creep into my defensiveness. It had been a long time since I'd had either the materials or the time to make anything from scratch.

"'I can,' I replied at last. 'Not that I get much time for it.'

"'A little proposition, then,' the Countess said softly. 'How would you feel about working for me full time? I am in need of a seamstress and I think we would suit each other very well. What do you think?'

"I was amazed, so amazed that I could find no answer to give. I hadn't really expected anything like this.

"'I thought ladies like yourself got all their clothes from them big fashion houses?'

"'Some of them,' she replied with a short laugh. 'But it's not for me so much as my granddaughter. She is, you see, a cripple. She is very shy and doesn't like to visit designers. Neither does she like them to come here. She feels they are patronising her because of her handicap. It would mean a lot to her, and therefore to me, if she had someone she could trust, who she knew, to make her clothes for her. And, when you're not too busy, you can still embroider for other people, as you have been doing. What do you say?'

"I was suspicious, as is my nature, and I still couldn't see why the Countess would want to pay someone full time.

"'What makes you think I won't patronise her?' I asked at last.

"'I don't really know that you won't,' she answered candidly. 'But I imagine you've seen worse things than a rich little girl in a bath chair. Belinda needs someone she can get to know, someone she can be herself with. Perhaps you'd like to meet her before you decide?' She got to her feet and moved toward the door. 'On the way, I'll show you where you'd be working. Then you can give me your decision.'

"The room she led me to was on the ground floor, overlooking the gardens at the back of the house. It had a deep, soft carpet in rose pink and pink silk flocked covering on the walls. There were three chairs and a table, on which rested a brand new sewing machine.

"I fairly pounced on it. I'd only ever seen one through a shop window before. I ran my hand along its shiny black horse shape, peeped apprehensively at the cylindrical bobbin. But it wasn't the machine itself, nor was it the longing to install myself in this wonderful, quiet room, that made me decide to accept the Countess' offer. She didn't look for gratitude; that's what made up my mind."

CHAPTER NINE

"The Countess didn't have a lot to do with my life, but she was the one got me out of the boot factory. It's funny how things work out. If Edie hadn't had to get married in such a hurry, I'd never have done that dress and I might have spent those early years stuck with the boots and the polish and the noise.

"Edie and Reg managed to settle their differences and had decided on a fairly amicable truce by the time the wedding took place. They both knew it was inevitable; there was no other choice for either of them. Edie didn't feel a trace of guilt over the way she'd blackmailed Reg, though I don't think she ever quite forgave him for not being Sam. They seemed to jog along all right, though I always got the feeling it was just show for other people. I was right, too, as it turned out.

"Explaining the hasty wedding to Auntie Ann, and a wedding to the wrong man at that, was the most difficult problem to cope with. She couldn't understand why her niece was not, after all, going to marry the good looking sailor she'd been engaged to for so long, and she didn't much like the look of Reg Parrish when she met him.

"She could see he had better prospects than Sam, but she didn't credit Edie with the guile to marry a man for his prospects. We all agreed that nobody would tell Ann the real situation. Nobody, that is, except a naive child who hadn't been deemed old enough to even know the secret, much less keep it.

"'I don't understand your sister, Rosina dear,' Ann said. 'Why did she give up a man she knew so well? Why does she want to marry this Reginald person? He doesn't strike me as though he cares nearly enough for her.'

"She had called to see my mother just a few days before the wedding. She wanted to make sure that mother had chosen all the right hymns for the ceremony. Ann thought that, not being a religious woman, she might get mixed up. It would never do to have a morbid hymn played by mistake.

"Mother wasn't in when she arrived, just me and Rose and Nina, who was busy with the kettle, heaving it onto the stove to make Auntie some tea. For the first time that I could recall, Auntie Ann hadn't brought Maud with her.

"Rose had no immediate reply to Auntie's question and she tried to drag the subject back to hymns, but Auntie wasn't about to let the topic go that easily.

"'Who knows how Edie's mind works, Auntie,' Rose said at last. 'Reg does have a good job, I suppose that might have something to do with it. And Sam was always away so much, perhaps she needs someone who's going to be there.'

"She hated having to lie. It wasn't in the nature of any of us to tell anything but the truth. Any of us except Edith, of course. To her, lying seemed to come as second nature. She resembled our father in more than just looks.

"'I know why she's marrying him,' Nina piped up suddenly. 'She's going to have a baby.'

"'Nina!'

"'What's wrong, Rose? I think it's lovely. I'm going to be an auntie, just like you, Auntie Ann.'

"Nina couldn't see any reason why Ann shouldn't be told. We never talked about these things in front of children those days. We never talked about them at all.

"Ann looked from me to Rose, her eyes round and startled.

"'Is it true?' She asked in a small whisper. Of all the motives she'd imagined for Edith's marrying her bank clerk, I think that was the only one which hadn't occurred to her. She would not have entertained the idea for one second.

"Rose nodded slowly, and her cheeks flushed with shame.

"'I don't understand!' Ann cried, a note of outrage in her tone. 'She was brought up decently, just like the rest of you. How could she do something like this?'

"'I don't know, Auntie. You'd better ask her.'

"'Ask her? Ask her? I shall never ask her anything, ever again! Never, in all my born days, did I expect her to do anything so wicked.' She got to her feet and began to gather up her things, oblivious to Nina's puzzled frown.

"'What's she making so much fuss about, Bess?' Nina whispered. 'My friend, Ivy's mother's having a baby soon, and nobody says she's wicked.'

"I couldn't resist a little chuckle.

"'That's because Ivy's mother is married, Nina, and Edie isn't. It's usual to get married before you get pregnant, not the other way round.'

"She looked bewildered. She was probably still wondering how, if you had to be married to have a baby, Edie had managed to do the latter first.

"'I'll be going now,' Auntie Ann said indignantly. 'And don't expect to see me, or Maud, at the wedding. Dreadful, sinful girl! Do you imagine that either one of us would be prepared to sit in that church, while she makes a mockery of a marriage before God? I'd rather die!'

"She stormed out of the room, and had intended to storm down the stairs, but the combination of the narrow, precarious staircase and her own bulk prevented her from venting her fury in that direction.

"Nobody was particularly sorry to see Ann and her friend absent from the ceremony. It was a very small affair and an embarrassment to us all, as there were not many among our neighbours who had failed to guess at the reason for the hasty arrangements. But we knew our discomfort would be short-lived. There was always plenty more to gossip about in the neighbourhood and everyone would soon forget Edie and her insignificant little secrets.

"Reg's contribution to the festivities was to provide a small gathering after the ceremony in the church hall. There were just a few neighbours, and his own parents, who obviously disapproved of the whole procedure. I can't say I was surprised. They wanted something better for their only son than us in our twice turned and patched Sunday best.

"I was sitting in the corner with a glass of sarsaparilla, listening to the little band and feeling bored, wanting the newly weds to be off on their honeymoon to Brighton so we could all go home to bed. Suddenly, I heard a familiar voice in my ear and my heart did a somersault.

"'I hope you've saved me a dance?' He said. 'It's the only thing I came out for.'

"'Daniel!' I laughed. 'What are you doing here?'

"'Your mother invited me,' he replied.

"His hand felt warm and comforting as he led me into the centre of the hall, and I couldn't wipe the smile off my face. My heart glowed with the pleasure of looking at him again.

"'Oh, she did, did she?' I answered.

"I could well imagine how her mind had been working, with all the talk of weddings in the air; probably thought she'd do a bit of quiet matchmaking. Oh, but it was good to have his arms round me.

"They were playing a waltz and we glided round the floor together so smoothly, it was almost as if there was some telepathic link between us. Daniel was a beautiful dancer.

"'Have you missed me?' He asked with a crooked smile.

"It was always difficult to know how serious he was being. He found humour in most every situation, even if that humour was at his own expense. And I had missed him, but I didn't think it right to tell him so, not when it couldn't lead anywhere. So I took the coward's way out and pretended I hadn't heard, though my heart was hammering so loudly, I'm sure he must have heard it.

"'Sorry,' he said. 'Was that an unfair question?'

"'Yes, it was.'

"'How do you know, if you didn't hear it?'

"'Blast you!' I cried, punching him lightly, but I couldn't help laughing. 'You always could read me like a book.'

"The music stopped and he led me back to my seat. But when I had sat down and looked up, he'd gone. I wondered for a moment whether he'd really been there at all, whether I'd let my mind wander so much with boredom that I'd imagined it. But I was sure I hadn't. I could still sense the warmth he'd left behind.

"He must have realised how I felt, and he knew it would do no good to hang around. But I was disappointed, just the same. Who knows how things might have turned out if he'd stayed? I might have been persuaded, we might have found some way to put all the doubts aside.

"That winter had been one of the worst I can remember, and I remember many, I can tell you. But that was the year of the coal strike and people had been dying from the cold. As April approached, there was a promise of spring and I was rather enjoying my journey to Regents Park every day to my new job.

"I still couldn't quite believe my luck nor that it was Edie, of all people, who had indirectly got me the job to begin with. But I didn't want to become too complacent. I didn't know the Countess well enough for that, and it was always possible that my employment was nothing more than a passing fancy that the lady might soon regret. But no matter how insecure I felt, I never could bring myself to be subservient. My family had never had much in life, but there had always been pride and I continued to address the Countess simply as 'countess'. The odd thing was she didn't seem to mind in the least. I sometimes wondered if she might even like it.

"Belinda was thirteen years old, a pretty little girl, blonde like her grandmother. She had fallen from a horse and broken her back two years before. I must admit I had expected a spoilt brat of a girl, perhaps one with an almighty chip on her shoulder because she spent her days in a bath chair. I could not have been more mistaken.

"Belinda was a very intelligent and kind child, shy and restrained, but always thoughtful.

"'This is gorgeous, Miss Shaw,' she said when I had finished the first thing I made for her. It was a white silk blouse, the first really grown-up garment she's ever had.

"'I'm glad you like it,' I replied, pleased.

"'How do you make these beautiful designs? Those little peacocks on the collar?' She fingered the silky stitches wonderingly. 'Could you teach me?'

"I laughed.

"'If I do that,' I replied, 'you won't need me any more, will you? You'll be able to make your own clothes and your grandmother's. Then the Countess will give me the sack.'

"She giggled.

"'Don't be silly,' she said. 'I shouldn't be able to reach Grandmother to measure her. Not from my racing car.'

"That's what she called her bath chair, her racing car. It was her most endearing quality, her total lack of self pity. It was just one of those things, she said, and sulking wasn't going to give her back her legs.

"'Will you teach me, Miss Shaw? Please?'

"'Well, all right. But only if you promise to call me Bess.'

"So I began to teach her to sew, every spare minute I got, and she learned quickly. She spent the rest of her time reading and writing her own stories, and when she learned that I had a young sister, she gave me some stories she'd written herself, for Nina's opinion. She also gave me some clothes that she had outgrown; Nina was thrilled.

"The money was the same as I was getting at the factory, but the hours I had to work were shorter and the conditions too far removed to even compare the two.

"I would have been happy to take up permanent residence in my sewing room, move my bed in. It was so quiet and peaceful. The trouble was, working all day in such a place made me realise just how dismal and shabby was our room in Shoreditch.

"When I first started working for the Countess, I was suspicious of the questions and confidences the lady initiated. I thought maybe she was one of those do-gooders who liked to tell the poorer population how they should live their lives. But after a while I just took these little conversations as another curious aspect of her personality. I came to believe that she felt slightly uncomfortable with the English aristocracy, not having been brought up to it, and that, having known hardship herself, she felt more akin to me than she did to them.

"The Countess often came in to chat while I was working. You wouldn't expect it, would you? But I think she really enjoyed my company. I know I enjoyed hers. She gave me some glycerine to soften my hands and some lemons, the juice of which was supposed to make the dye stains disappear.

"'We used to use it on our skin to get rid of freckles,' the Countess told me. 'The South Carolina sun is a devil to avoid, and a lady must keep her skin white at all costs.'

"I knew enough to know where South Carolina was and I wondered if she had seen anything of the civil war in America.

"'Were you a southern belle?' I asked her one day.

"'No, honey. I was too young. But my sisters had their share of young men calling.'

"'Did your family keep slaves?' I asked. I suppose it was a bit cheeky, but the subject of slavery always has fascinated me.

"'We did. All plantation owners kept slaves, or they would never have been able to run their plantations. Not and stay wealthy at least. I remember my mammy and a few others, but it was all a long time ago.' She turned and looked at me, a little frown on her brow. 'You know an awful lot for a girl who's had little education, don't you?'

"'I try to keep myself informed.'

"'Well in that case,' she remarked bitterly, 'you'll know what happened to us southerners when we lost the war. We all nearly starved.'

"I had to force my tongue to be silent. Auntie Ann said it was God's will, what happened to the confederates after the war, God's punishment for daring to own other human beings.

"'So I heard,' I said finally, unable to keep a note of cynicism from my tone. 'I only know what happened to our mill workers when the cotton couldn't get here from America. They starved.'

"'Touché!' She cried with a little smile.

"'Sorry. Not your fault, I don't suppose.'

"'I'd never try to defend slavery, Bess, but when you are raised to accept something as natural, it never occurs to you to question it. We always kept Negroes, treated them well mostly, too. It seemed the natural order of things. Now I look back, I can see it was wrong, but I'd never try to tell my father that, were he still alive. Not all of us recovered, either. Most of the great families lost everything, and it stayed lost.'

"'You survived, though.'

"'Sure, we did, but that was sheer luck. My husband was way down the line to become the Earl of Hazelforth; he never expected to have the title. Then half his family were wiped out in the cholera epidemic in Egypt, back in 1902. So here we are.'

"She watched me in silence for a few minutes, as she often did, and I couldn't fathom what was going on in her mind. She seemed to find me fascinating sometimes, though I can't imagine why.

"'Do you have a beau, Bess?' She asked suddenly.

"'A what?'

"She laughed.

"'A beau. A young man.'

"I only shook my head, but I bent my face low over my work to hide my expression. I didn't welcome her reminder of Daniel. I hadn't seen nor heard from him since Edie's wedding, and dancing with him then had churned everything up in me. I silently cursed my mother for inviting him and I didn't want to think about him now. But the Countess' careless question brought a picture of his smiling face into my mind, a picture so clear it seemed I could almost reach out and touch it. My heart twisted and I bit down hard on my lip to keep it from trembling.

"The sewing room was silent as the Countess watched me, realising that she had said the wrong thing.

"'I'm sorry, Bess,' she said after a moment. 'I shouldn't have pried.'

"She left without another word, left me alone to fill my mind with memories I'd fought hard to suppress, and I allowed myself to wonder seriously if it was too late. Could I change my mind and marry him? Should I do so? What if he changed, like my father had? But I couldn't convince myself that Daniel would ever do that. I turned the question over in my mind as I made my way home that night, a little dart of excitement making me tingle as I contemplated the possibility.

"By the time I snuggled beneath the covers that night, I had made myself admit that I wanted Daniel. Mother still clung to her belief in Billy's continued existence but, apart from that one delusion, she had got no worse. Perhaps she would never get any worse; perhaps I had been wrong to think that she would. All I knew was, the only thing left to decide was whether I would ever be able to do the things a married man expects, though even that didn't seem so dreadful when I remembered his handsome face and his laughing eyes.

"When I finally fell asleep, the choice had been made. As I drifted off that night, my thoughts were focused on the best way to tell him I had changed my mind. He would laugh at me; I expected that. I never changed my mind about anything once it was made up. But I saw his smile, how pleased he'd be, how he'd take my hand and gently try to allay my fears. He understood me so well, did Daniel.

"A loud and insistent banging woke me. I sat up in bed, my mind fuzzy from sleep and wondering if I had only dreamed the noise. Then I felt Rose stir beside me, and I looked about the room. It was too dark to see where the hands of the clock were pointing, but the shapes in the other bed told me that someone was missing.

"The knocking came again, more urgent than before this time, accompanied by a deep voice demanding that we wake up and open the door.

"Rose climbed out of bed while Nina and me sat rigidly, almost afraid to move. I couldn't see Nina's face, but I could feel that the child was terrified.

"The sight of a policeman in the doorway made my heart jump. The man was tall and broad and I couldn't see the small figure standing behind him until he reached for her, a hand on each of her shoulders as he pushed her forward.

"'Do you know this woman, Miss?' He asked Rose in a gruff voice.

"Rose could only nod dumbly. I slipped out of bed and crept up behind her, peering over her shoulder.

"'She's our mother,' I said evenly, making Rose start. She didn't know I was standing right behind her. 'What's happened?'

"Mother stood in her nightdress, her hair in a long plait down her back. Clutched against her chest she held a wad of papers.

"Rose reached out and pulled her inside.

"'Take care of her, miss,' the policeman said over his shoulder as he turned away. 'It's not safe for her to be wandering the streets at this time of night.'

"Rose closed the door while I guided my mother to the bed and wrapped a blanket around her shoulders, then sat beside her. She was icy cold. A glance at Nina told me the child had not moved an inch since she awoke. I prised the papers carefully from mother's hands, frowning at them as I passed them to Rose.

"'Birth certificates?' Rose's voice was trembling. 'Why, mother? What were you trying to do with all our birth certificates?'

"Mother's eyes met hers, but they were vacant, unseeing.

"'I know what they're all saying,' she said vehemently. 'I know how they're all talking about me, don't think I don't! Fifteen children and no husband! They all think I'm a bad woman.' She paused and looked about, her eyes suddenly taking on an intelligence they had previously lacked. 'But I'm not, Rosina,' she went on in a tiny, pleading voice. 'I'm not.'

"It was nearly four in the morning before we got mother to sleep and crawled under the covers ourselves. Nina had fallen asleep a long time ago, and the sound of Rose's even breathing soon came to my ears. But I could find no peace, not that night.

"I had been happy when I went to bed, full of anticipation about an imagined future, a future I had never envisioned before. My joy was shattered now. I was too practical not to see that, not to make myself look into that future and see how much care she would need. And there was no one else. Nina was too young, Edie too selfish. And Rose – Rose was too talented. And I refused to even think of saddling Daniel with a senile old woman. I couldn't be certain that I wouldn't make him miserable without adding that complication.

"Thank God I hadn't had a chance to see him, to tell him. At least I need never be tormented by the sight of him again.

"I was wrong, for the following Sunday, Daniel came knocking at our door."

CHAPTER TEN

"Clutched in his hand was a box, wrapped in brown paper and tied with string, but I didn't stop to wonder what it was. There was an unwelcome shuddering in my stomach, a stammer of excitement which was almost painful, and I told myself firmly to keep calm. My recent plans and ideas had already faded, for I knew they could never be, and I wasn't one to hanker after things I couldn't have. I did not want to love him and for some unaccountable reason, I imagined that would be enough to put an end to it. But you can't argue with your emotions, can you? No matter how much you'd like to.

"'I've brought a little something for Nina,' he said, when he had greeted everyone. 'I know her birthday's not for another week, but I shan't be here then.'

"I shot a glance at him. Shan't be here? I thought frantically. Where was he going? But I couldn't voice my question. I had no right to ask.

"Nina's eyes lit up and a huge smile spread across her face. Birthday or not, the child was unaccustomed to gifts; no one could ever afford much more than a box of hankies, homemade by me usually, and Daniel's parcel looked far more interesting. She got a knife and cut the string, then opened the wrapping as quickly as her little fingers would allow, while Daniel watched along with everyone else. Her smile of delight was thanks enough, for inside the box was a doll, a brand new doll, and that was something she'd never had before. It was a pretty doll, dressed in pink satin with lace edging, and its body and face were made of wax. It was obviously expensive.

"'Why, Dan!' Mother exclaimed delightedly. 'You shouldn't have spent so much.'

"'I wanted to Mrs. Shaw. Nina's my best girl, after all.'

"Nina threw her little arms around his neck and hugged him, while mother glared at me.

"'And after the way Elizabeth threw you over,' she said sharply, not even considering his possible embarrassment. 'Well, it just goes to show.'

"I looked at him with a plea in my eyes, tacitly apologising for her lack of tact.

"'I expect it'll be the only present she'll get this year,' mother went on. 'Unless Billy remembers to send something.'

"Daniel glanced at her quickly, but said nothing. He'd heard all about her delusion, and her words only confirmed the rumours. The sympathy in his eyes made me angry; I could never bear to have anyone feeling sorry for me.

"'Would you like some tea, Daniel,' Rose said quickly, before mother could say any more about Billy.

"'No, thanks, Rose. It's Liza I've really come to see.' He turned to me and gave me a gentle smile. 'Can we walk out for a bit?'

"I nodded once, then got my coat and followed him down to the street. A threat of rain hung in the air, and I buttoned my coat as I walked.

"'What's up?' I asked as soon as we were alone.

"'D'you know what?' He said. 'If anyone sees us together, the neighbours will have us married off before the week's out.'

"'I can think of worse fates.'

"'Can you? I must have got it wrong then. I thought marriage was a fate worse than death.'

"He spoke with a smile of mischief, perhaps laughing at himself as well as at me.

"'That's not very fair,' I answered quickly. 'Besides, I meant that I could think of worse fates than being talked about.'

"He already knew that, I could tell by the teasing smile he gave me.

"'Your mother's no better, then?' He asked.

"'What do you think? If anything, she's worse. D'you know what she did the other night? Took all our birth certificates, all fifteen of them, and went down the police station with them.'

"He stopped walking and turned to look at me.

"'What for?' He asked.

"'It seems she thinks everyone's talking about her, because she hasn't got a husband. She thinks they're all saying her kids are bastards, by different fathers. She took the birth certificates to prove them wrong.'

"'Oh, Liza, I'm so sorry.'

"'What have you got to be sorry for? It's not your fault, is it?'

"I didn't intend my voice to sound so harsh, but the battle being fought inside me was hard to keep buried. I had set myself firmly against this meeting, and only my treacherous emotions had allowed it. I should have stayed at home where I couldn't be alone with him.

"We went on in silence for a few more minutes, walking close together but carefully not touching. The tension began to settle over me as I fought the urge to reach out to him, to just hold his hand.

"'I've come to say goodbye, Liza,' he said at last.

"It was my turn to halt my steps. I looked up at him, my eyes searching his, feeling my mouth turn down.

"'Where are you going?' I managed to ask.

"'I'm going to sign aboard one of those big steam ships as barber. I'll be leaving for Southampton tonight.' He started to walk again and I ran to catch up with him. 'Unless you want to change your mind and marry me, that is?' He added as he glanced back at me.

"'Daniel, I can't.'

"'No. I didn't think you would. It's worse for you now, isn't it? You've got your mother to worry about.'

"I made no reply, only let my gaze rest on his face. He knew me so well, it made me shiver. We had come to a narrow, cobbled pathway and I followed him into it. There was no one about, not another soul in sight. Suddenly he stopped and turned to face me. His fingers firmly gripped my arms and there was a trace of unfamiliar impatience in his tone when he spoke.

"'Look, Liza,' he said. 'I'm not going to say this twice, so I hope you're paying attention. I love you, more than anything in the world. I want you to be my wife, and if that means putting up with your maidenly modesty, I'll be happy with that. I'll be happy with anything. I'd never hurt you; you must know that.'

"'Yes, I know, but...'

"'But you won't leave your mother?'

"Oh, how I wanted to say yes. I bit my lip to keep the treacherous word from escaping, while my mind considered the prospect of a future for us. I tried to imagine what it would be like, but all I could see was my mother, getting less and less coherent, taking up all my time, time that ought to belong to Daniel.

"It was no good. I knew it couldn't work, that she'd come between us. I couldn't ask Daniel to burden himself with my mother. I couldn't and I wouldn't. But I still sought desperately for some words, any words that would make him stay.

"'Perhaps later...' I began, not knowing where the sentence would lead.

"'Don't give me perhaps,' he interrupted. 'I'll wait, if you only say yes.'

"'Wait for how long, Daniel?' I asked miserably. 'Mother's not an old woman. She's barely fifty.'

"'And if I told you I'd accept your mother as well, if I had to? But I don't suppose you'd let me do that, would you?'

"I shook my head.

"'That's what I thought. I always said you were something special.'

"I knew I loved him then. All those nagging doubts were swept away on a tide of warmth and longing. The only words that sprang to mind were 'don't go!' But I couldn't say it. If I did, I'd have to give him some incentive to stay, and I had none to offer.

"He sighed heavily.

"'I'll say goodbye then, Liza. I hope your sister likes her doll. I thought it was time she had one, before she gets too old.'

"He offered me a weak smile then turned away, and I couldn't believe it was really that simple. I would probably never see him again, and he was going without so much as a peck on the cheek.

"'Daniel!' I cried after him.

"He turned back to me and I took one step toward him, wanting him to gather me up, like he'd done before. But he only stood there with his hands at his sides, until I could no longer stop myself from running into his arms.

"He kissed me then, but it was nothing like before, just a tender kiss of farewell for me to cherish in the lonely years to come. And the worst of it was, it was within my power to stop him – and I knew I couldn't do it.

"When Daniel went, I gradually came to realise how much comfort it had given me, just knowing he was in the same city. Now when I passed the barber's shop, I knew he wasn't there, behind the advertisements in the window. There was no longer any chance that I might bump into him in the market on Saturday evenings, or down the Lane on Sundays. I realised I'd been unconsciously hoping we would meet unexpectedly somewhere or other. Now I knew that wasn't going to happen and the strange thing was, I still couldn't keep myself from looking for him everywhere I went.

"I had never felt so alone; he had gone for good, and left an empty space in my life that nothing and no one else could fill."

CHAPTER ELEVEN

It was early afternoon. Bess had been talking almost continuously for hours, and still showed no signs of fatigue. Stella was amazed that someone who had lived for a century could have this much stamina.

She got up and went to the kitchen to make them both a cup of tea. She thought Bess needed something to stimulate her; she knew she did.

She handed Bess the cup for which she thanked her with a nod, then sat down to listen further.

"It wasn't long after Daniel left that Rose got herself discovered," she went on. "She always did have a voice like an angel and that was one of the reasons I had to stay with mother. I couldn't let Rose tie herself down, not when she could make something of herself.

"She'd been singing in the Angel for nearly a year and she'd got used to being the only woman in the bar, but still she felt nervous every time she started, afraid there might be someone there who didn't think she could sing. Sometimes, we'd gone with her, me and Daniel, but now there was no Daniel to escort me and mother would have had a fit if she'd known I was sitting in a public house by myself. Only the very worst sort of woman entered a pub on her own in those days.

"Rose never said very much. Unlike me, she believed in keeping her opinions to herself as much as possible. She was the type who would rather only face trouble when it became unavoidable, while I believed in meeting it head on, or even seeking it out if necessary.

"Everyone thought she was the sweet and gentle one, but they didn't know her like I did. She was as self-motivated as everyone else; she just preferred not to show it. And I knew she had always secretly fancied herself on the stage.

"You never know, do you, when you turn down one of life's avenues, just what lies at the end of it? None of it would have happened if she'd never gone on the stage, but she couldn't know that then and I doubt if it would have stopped her if she had.

"That night, after the regular customers had left the pub, Tom called her over and introduced her to a man she'd never seen before. He told her he was the manager at the Alhambra Theatre and he was looking for new talent for his music hall. I could see how nervous she was when she realised she'd been singing before such an important audience, but she had lived in the East End too long to be easily convinced. He invited her to attend an audition at the theatre the following week, and though she saw no reason to doubt him, she didn't let herself get too excited where he could see.

"Alfred was there that night, as well. He often used to come to the pub to watch her sing and he'd sit there telling everyone she was his girl. It annoyed me no end but she seemed to think it was funny.

"This particular night, he had charged himself with the chivalrous duty of sitting with me to stop anyone from gossiping. I suppose I should have been grateful, but I suspected him of trying to butter me up so I'd put in a good word for him with Rose.

"He sat there listening to her conversation with the theatre manager and when she came over to our table, all flushed with excitement, he folded his arms and said smugly:

"'So, my girl's going to be a star. Just wait till I tell 'em down at the factory.'

"'Don't you dare!' She said crossly. 'I don't want anyone to know about it. I haven't even made up my mind to do it yet.'

"'Course you'll do it,' he said. 'There's a few bob to be made out of this, you mark my words.'

"'Well, if there is,' she snapped, 'it'll be my few bob, not yours. So you just keep your big mouth shut, okay?'

"That was typical of Alfred. You could almost see the pound signs in his eyes, like on an old fashioned cash register.

"It was very late when we got upstairs and mother and Nina were both asleep, snuggled down together in the bed. The other mattresses were on the floor, made up ready for Rose and me, and she waited until we were both tucked beneath the covers before she spoke. She was so excited, it warmed my heart to see it.

"'Bess,' she said. 'You will come with me, won't you?'

"'Leicester Square? Of course, if you want me to.'

"'I do. I'd be too nervous to go by myself.'

"'You've got nothing to be nervous about. You'll knock 'em dead.'

"'Do you really think so?' She asked timidly. 'I mean, there'll be a lot of other girls there, a lot of competition. Do you really think I'm good enough?'

"She always was too modest for her own good. She'd been attracting more customers for Tom on Saturday nights than he saw for the rest of the week put together, and from upstairs we could hear the enthusiastic cheers from the men in the bar.

"'It's not like the pub, Bess,' she went on. 'I mean, working men in a pub, they're happy with anything. This is the real music hall.'

"'You'll be fine,' I assured her. 'How many girls do they want?'

"'Half a dozen. Why? You going to have a go, too? We could do a double act.'

"I laughed at that. My voice would have scared away the rats and we both knew it.

"The Countess was away with Belinda, staying with friends in Yorkshire, so it was easy for me to get the day off. No one would miss me at the house, but Rose felt guilty about the money she was losing, having time off from the factory. She had never had a day off since she started working there when she was twelve, except Christmas and times like that. But she still managed to feel guilty, especially as she hadn't told mother. She left home at her usual time and waited for me up the road, so that mother wouldn't know where she was going. She wanted to surprise her if things went well, but she didn't want her to know if they didn't. Mother would have made some comment about her getting ideas above her station.

"When I met her on the corner of our road, she was looking ruefully down at her skirt and blouse. It was the best she could find to wear, but the skirt was old and patched, and the collar of the blouse was badly frayed.

"I wish I had something decent to wear,' she told me. 'I feel like everyone's poor relation in this.'

"I studied her, only then taking the trouble to notice her clothes. We were so used to seeing each other in worn and patched garments, we never took any notice. Now my eyes swept her up and down and I had an idea that brought a little smile of mischief to my lips.

"'I'll find you something to wear,' I said. 'I know just the very thing.'

"We went first to Regents Park, where I had been putting the finishing touches to a simple day dress for the Countess.

"It was the first time Rose had seen my sewing room and I can't deny I was proud to show it off.

"'Bess!' She cried, her eyes roaming around in awe. 'Is this really where you come to all day? I had no idea it would be like this. No wonder you were in such a hurry to leave the factory.'

"'It's wonderful, isn't it?' I replied as I opened the wardrobe where I hung the clothes I'd just finished. I pulled out a primrose colour gown, made from fine Irish linen, and held it up against her. 'You're about the same size,' I told Rose. 'I'm sure she won't mind if you borrow it.'

"Her eyes widened in horror.

"'Of course she'll mind,' she protested, recoiling from the dress. 'I can't borrow the Countess' frock. You'll get the sack.'

"'She'll never know the difference,' I insisted, and my fingers fell over themselves trying to undo the hooks on her skirt before she could wriggle away. 'I'll put some green leaves or something on it afterwards, then it won't be the same frock. And if you don't stop arguing and get a move on, we'll be too late for the audition.'

"'No, Bess!' She argued. 'I'm nervous enough, without having to worry about spoiling the Countess' frock!'

"'Trust me,' I answered. 'It'll be all right. This is important.'

"She insisted on washing her hands before we left. She was afraid to touch the dress, afraid even to move, in case she left a mark on it. She had never worn fabric like that and she didn't suppose she ever would again, but she would have gladly denied herself the opportunity on that occasion.

"I hustled her out of the door before she could take the dress off again.

"'I wish I'd never mentioned it now,' she said miserably. 'I'd have been happier with my patches.'

"When we arrived at the theatre, there was already quite a queue of women outside and all their heads turned when they saw us. The shade of the Countess' gown suited Rose's dark colouring, and she was wearing a big bow perched on top of her piled up hair, like a butterfly. I'd fashioned it quickly from a piece of linen left over from the gown, and I told her not to move too much as I had no time to sew up the edges. Looking back, I can see that all this carefulness was turning Rose into a gibbering idiot, but I didn't notice at the time. I was almost as excited as she was.

"When loose, Rose's hair was long enough to sit on and it sometimes took days to dry properly when she washed it. She often thought of having it cut, but she never did have the heart. We used to joke that if money got really tight we could always sell Rose's hair to the wigmakers. It nearly came to that once or twice, I can tell you.

"The women in front of us were of all ages, all classes, but they each had one thing in common: a little fanatical gleam in their eyes. Rose had it too, though she was unaware of it. There was not much noise among the group, they were most of them deep in thought, imagining themselves wowing the theatre managers with their extraordinary talents, I expect.

"As more women joined the group behind us, Rose cursed her own conceit for thinking she might be good enough to compete with them all. She whispered to me that she should just forget the whole thing and go to work.

"'Will you shut up,' I told her, not unkindly. 'You're getting on my wick, keeping saying you're not good enough.'

"'But there are so many of them, Bess. How am I going to stand a chance against this lot?'

"'How do you know any of them can sing? Or dance? Or do anything else for that matter. Remember how Auntie Ann sings in church?

She obviously thinks she's a budding Marie Lloyd, but we know different, don't we? This lot might be kidding themselves as well for all you know.'

"'Well, I expect they've all been invited, just like me.'

"'So what? Doesn't mean they're any good, does it? Perhaps your manager thought he might as well make the most of it while he was opening up anyway. He came all the way to Shoreditch to hear you; he'll be disappointed if you don't show up.'

"'I suppose you're right,' she replied and buried her chin in her collar, stamping her feet to keep the circulation going.

"It was an hour before we reached the stage door. The queue behind us stretched almost to Piccadilly Circus and two street sellers had been along the line twice selling tea and jellied eels. One was selling peace pudding as well, but he had few customers. The yellow pudding was very messy and all the women were afraid of getting stains on their clothes, though none as much as my sister, decked out in the Countess of Hazelforth's new gown.

"We had bought two cups of tea each, but nothing to eat. Our stomachs were too delicate from fluttering nerves to risk anything solid. Even though I wasn't taking part in the audition, I felt almost as nervous as Rose. She deserved to succeed, and if there really was a God up in Heaven, I knew He'd see to it that she did.

"I was allowed to stand in the wings when Rose went on. I didn't want to sit facing the stage because she'd be put off her performance if she could see me. I saw her begin to tremble when the pianist asked her what music she'd brought.

"I...I'm sorry,' she stammered. 'I didn't realise.'

"'That's all right, love,' the man said kindly. 'If you're going to do something well known, I've probably already got it.'

"Rose turned round to look at me, standing in the wings, and I could see she was terrified. She hadn't even thought about what to sing.

"I started to wave my arms up and down, like a bird, to give her a hint.

"'Only a Bird in a Gilded Cage,' she said promptly.

"'Oh, good,' the pianist remarked as he sat down at his instrument. 'We haven't had that one yet today. If I hear one more mutilation of "After the Ball" you can book me a bed in Colney Hatch.'

"His sarcasm annoyed me, but when I considered how many people he'd had to play for that day, I couldn't blame him. It must have been a frustrating business, if they all chose the same song.

"Rose sang. She put her heart and soul into each word, a song that was popular at the turn of the century, all about a beautiful girl who married an old man for his money and found herself nothing more than an ornament for his amusement. I wanted her to sing that one because she could make a person's heart break when she sang those words.

"The theatre was hushed as they all listened and I saw that Rose had her eyes firmly closed. If she couldn't see anything, she could pretend she was in the pub where everyone knew her, and she wouldn't be so nervous.

"As the last note faded, the manager and the other men sitting in the front row of the otherwise empty theatre applauded; so did the pianist. I felt a little lump of pride in the back of my throat. It was a wonderful moment, one I have always remembered vividly.

"'You're in, beautiful,' the manager said with a smile. 'How long is that hair?'

"I never heard her reply. I was too happy to listen, but as I waited outside, I saw many of the women who had been standing close to the door turn to leave. There was a lot of disgruntled muttering among them, but they knew they were beaten. They only wanted half a dozen girls and Rose had been the sixth one chosen. There was no point in hanging about in the cold.

"She emerged from the theatre, her face alight with sheer pride.

"'Oh, Bess! They want me!' She cried.

"'Of course they want you. They know what they're doing.'

"'But, Bess, they want me to wear a man's suit, like Vesta Tilley.'

"It was the first shadow to fall over the day.

"'Mother's not going to like that,' I said.

"'No. I don't think she will, either.'

"Suddenly, I smiled and linked my arm through hers.

"'Never mind,' I reassured her. 'We'll cross that bridge when we come to it.'

"We came to it on our arrival home, when Rose had explained everything to mother. She looked thrilled to bits until Rose mentioned the man's suit.

"'I'm not having that!' Mother exploded. 'I'm not having no daughter of mine parading round a stage in trousers. It's indecent!'

"I've often wondered what my mother would have said had she lived to witness today's fashions. I expect the shock would have finished her off.

"'Vesta Tilley wears men's clothes, mother,' Rose argued.

"Mother turned her black eyes on Rose, who shrank back under the glare.

"'I don't suppose she's any better than she should be, either!' She spat. 'You can forget it, Rosina, d'you hear me? I won't have it.' She turned away and collected her washing from the table where she had left it. 'I've got work to do, even if you haven't. You'd do better to get to the factory, my girl. You've lost enough money today playing music hall stars!'

"She slammed the door as she went out, leaving us to look at each other thoughtfully.

"'Well,' I said. 'What are you going to do?'

"'There's not much I can do,' she replied ruefully. 'I'll have to go round to the theatre and tell them I can't do it.'

"'You must be mad, girl! I wouldn't turn down a chance like this for anyone.'

"'But, Bess, you heard what mother said. She'll never forgive me if I go on that stage in trousers.'

"I walked across the room, slowly, and sat down on the bed beside her. I looked at her thoughtfully for a long time, wondering how I could persuade her. She was just as stubborn as the rest of us once her mind was made up.

"'It's your life, Rose,' I said finally. 'Do you really want to spend it putting boots together in some noisy smelly factory? Look at your hands; they're worse than mine were. You've got talent and you know it. Didn't you hear how they all clapped? You can't turn down a chance like this, just because of her old-fashioned ideas. It's not right.'

"Rose didn't say so, but I could tell she'd been thinking along the same lines herself, and was only waiting for someone to persuade her. She was, after all, free, white and over twenty-one, as they used to say. It was up to her, wasn't it? She didn't relish the idea of upsetting mother, but on the other hand, was it really any of mother's business?

"'I'll do it,' she declared after a minute. 'Who cares what she thinks? Who cares what anyone thinks? As you say, Bess, it's my life.'

"As luck would have it, they changed their minds about Rose wearing a suit. They decided she wasn't really suited to comedy, and quite right, too. She was always much better at the sad songs. That didn't stop mother from refusing to talk to her, though. She couldn't forgive her eldest daughter's intention of defying her and going on the stage like Vesta Tilley anyway. She'd have expected it of me, she said, but not Rosina. Rosina had never done anything to upset her before and she suspected it was my fault for leading her astray and filling her head with far-fetched notions. That didn't bother me too much, though. Mother and I often rubbed each other up the wrong way.

"Rose and me had fun, that first week in April. Whenever I could, I'd go with her and watch the rehearsals, and I swear she could sing better than any of the others. And everyone liked her; everyone always liked Rose.

"But my little bit of carefree respite wasn't to last long."

CHAPTER TWELVE

"I've always had a sort of sixth sense. I told you how I always know when someone close dies, though that's a sensation I haven't felt in a long time. There's no one close left, you see. Well, I could always tell when someone was in danger, too, and I've even had the odd foretaste of the future. Nothing definite, just a hazy image. That's a fact, whether anyone believes me or not. I know they all think I'm a dotty old woman whenever I mention it now, but it wasn't like that then. People who knew me, my family in particular, they all knew about my so-called gift. I always considered it more of a curse than a gift, myself.

"It was just before dawn when icy cold water hit me in the face, waking me up with a gasp. It was like a great wave hitting me full on, taking my breath away. My hair was stuck to my shoulders and neck, my nightdress clung to my body. I was soaked through and shivering, with goosebumps all over me, and I could taste salt water in my mouth.

"As my eyes shot open, I could hear Daniel's voice, calling my name, his own special name.

"'Liza!'

"I sat up, wondering where the water had come from, but as I hugged myself, I realised I was still dry. I ran my fingers through my hair. It was clammy with perspiration, but certainly not wet. My heart was hammering fiercely, loud enough to shut out the sleeping sounds of my mother and sisters.

"Fragments of a dream returned to me, a great ship on a dark ocean, people screaming.

"Rose stirred beside me and she sat up, too.

"'What is it, Bess?' She asked.

"'Daniel,' I said, and my voice struggled through a gasp. 'Something's happened to Daniel.'

"I didn't have to wonder if it was just a nightmare; I knew that I'd seen what was happening, that his ship had gone down in that dark, distant ocean – that his last thought had been of me.

"Rose could only stare at me. She was well aware that I sometimes knew things, before anyone else did. She'd seen it happen too many times before to question it now.

"I couldn't stop shivering; I was fighting for every breath, and I was so frightened. I don't think I had ever been so frightened in my whole life.

"'He's drowning,' I said through long breaths. 'He's drowning in the cold sea and there's nothing I can do about it.'

"I began to sob, uncontrollable, gasping sobs that threatened to tear me apart and leave me helpless. I felt my sister's arms around me, drawing me close, but I could not control the awful sobs.

"'Bess, Bess,' she murmured, trying to comfort me.

"'I...I c...can't help it,' I stammered.

"I was still shivering, cold right through to my bones and sure I would never be warm again. I was enveloped in fear, a dread fear that I, who always faced whatever life chose to throw at me, had never felt before nor since. But worse than that, beneath the terror, there lay a shadow of grief for something I had lost. No, I recognised bitterly, something I had thrown away. Daniel would never have been on that bloody ship were it not for me.

"The papers were full of the news the next day. For the first time in my life, I went out and bought a newspaper, spending some of the precious money I had managed to save.

"There it was, the proof that it had been more than simply a bad dream. Not that I needed any proof. I knew the difference between a dream and whatever it was that gave me insight into personal tragedy.

"Even so, it was a few days before they got it right, before the full horror was officially known. There were only about seven hundred survivors, but I didn't bother to search the lists. I knew that Daniel wasn't one of them.

"I'd sit staring at the newsprint for hours, while Rose tiptoed silently about, making tea. It seemed to her to be the only useful thing she could do.

"'Fifteen hundred people, Rose,' I muttered, still shocked to the core by the sheer volume of the deaths. 'Fifteen hundred people drowned on that ship. And they said it was unsinkable.' I looked up at her, feeling bewildered. 'How can that be?'

"There were no words that could make a difference and Rose knew it. Nothing she could say would bring any comfort.

"'Strange, isn't it?' I said. 'I didn't even know the name of his ship. If I was like everybody else, I could be reading this and just shaking my head, thinking that no one I knew was on that ship.' I threw down the newspaper angrily and it bounced off the bed, rustling and cascading onto the floor. 'Why can't I be like everyone else?' I demanded, as though it were her fault. 'Why do I have to know things?'

"Rose was beside me, her arm about me shoulders, pulling my head onto her shoulder.

"'What can I say?' She said soothingly. 'You wouldn't want to go through life kidding yourself, would you? You wouldn't want to doubt that Billy's dead, for instance, like I do sometimes. Like Nina does. Would you?'

"My eyes met hers.

"'I didn't know,' I whispered. 'I didn't know you thought...' My voice trailed off and I took a deep breath. I couldn't think about Billy then; I didn't want to. 'He is dead, you know. Billy, I mean. I'm sure of that.'

"I picked up Nina's wax doll from where it rested against the brass bedstead and began to fiddle with it. I stroked its hair, looked into its eyes as if searching for something, something of Daniel.

"'Daniel bought her this,' I said unnecessarily. '"When he came to say goodbye.'

"'Please, dear, don't torture yourself.'

"'He asked me again then, you know. He asked me if I'd changed my mind. He wouldn't have gone if I'd agreed to marry him.'

"'Bess, please. It's not your fault.'

"'It is my fault!' I insisted viciously. 'Who else's fault is it? He'd still be here if only...'

"'But you didn't want to marry him, remember?' Rose interrupted sharply. 'I suppose you'd rather have spent your life regretting that you'd married someone you didn't want? Well, would you? Even if you'd known what would happen, it wouldn't have made any difference.'

"'But I did want to marry him, Rose,' I cried bitterly. I'd never told anyone that before. 'When he came back, I really wanted to say yes.'

"'I don't understand. If you wanted to marry him, why did you send him away?'

"I searched her eyes, wondering if I could ever make her understand, wondering if I would ever understand myself. I wasn't going to tell her it was mainly mother's approaching senility that had stopped me. She'd have felt responsible if I'd told her that and I didn't want his death on both our consciences. One of us was enough.

"'I don't know,' I answered at last. 'Perhaps because I've never wanted to get married. I could never see myself as anybody's wife. Look what happened to mother.'

"'That's a bit different, you know.'

"'Is it? Why is it different? D'you think she didn't love our father once? She must've thought he was something special when she married him. Look what she gave up for him.' I looked down at my hands, embarrassed to meet her gaze. 'I s'pose I was afraid that Daniel might change, too, after he'd got the ring on my finger.'

"Rose made no reply. I think I'd given her a new idea, that it had never occurred to her to think that any man could turn out to be like father, least of all Daniel. She'd always thought I was lucky to have him and I had the feeling she thought it was a bad mistake to give him up.

"I carefully placed the doll on the pillow, wondering how I was going to tell Nina. That poor child had lost a brother already that year, and Daniel had been like a brother to her too. She must have thought nobody lived to grow old.

"I got to my feet wearily. I felt that I could never shed enough tears to wash away the grief. I had seen countless babies, small brothers and sisters, leave this world before they had even had a chance to sample it. I had watched my father disappear from my life – though I never considered that to be much of a loss. And Billy. Billy had died; and I had seen days, even weeks on end when we hadn't known where the next penny was going to come from. But none of it had meant very much to me. Not one thing, not one loss I had ever suffered had left me feeling like that. Life must go on, I had always said. There was no point in brooding about what you couldn't change. Get on with things, put it all behind you. That had always been my philosophy.

"But not this time. This time I felt that to die myself would be a blessing, would be the only relief I could ever find.

"There was a memorial service at the end of that week, in St. Paul's Cathedral, for all the victims of the disaster. I was one of the last to find room inside before they closed the doors, it was so crowded with mourners. But I think I only went to assure myself that I wasn't alone, that there were many, many others whose loved ones had gone the same way. When the service ended and the doors opened, I had to fight my way through the crowds outside. There were hundreds of them, all wanting a part in the farewell to the dead.

"There was an eclipse over London that week, too. I wondered if it was Daniel saying goodbye, and I knew I had to pull myself together. That's just the sort of fancy I'd have scoffed at before.

"Mother chose to believe that I'd got it wrong, which surprised me because she always loved a tragedy.

"'I don't know why you insist that Daniel was on that boat,' she said. 'You didn't even know the name of Daniel's boat.'

"'Mother,' Rose interrupted. 'I told you before. Bess knew; she knew when it happened. It was as if she was with him.'

"Mother ignored her. Mother had ignored her ever since she gave up her job and started rehearsing at the Alhambra. She would not give in on what she called a point of morality and nothing that Rose could say or do was going to change her mind.

"'I know, Mother,' I said. 'Like Rose says, it was as if I was with him.'

"'Like who says?' Mother asked pointedly. Rose simply sighed impatiently. 'You're imagining things, Elizabeth,' mother went on. Her terror of the supernatural would never let her accept that I had some sort of insight. 'And you're dramatising. I suppose you think if everyone believes Danny's dead, it'll stop them nagging you about why you wouldn't marry him? Is that it? That's a wicked thing to do, my girl. He'd never have gone away if it hadn't been for you.'

"She could be a cantankerous old cow, sometimes, my mother and what she said really hurt me. I don't think she'd ever succeeded in really hurting me before and normally I'd have given as good as I got. But I just couldn't bring myself to get mad, because I knew that what she said was true.

"'Mother, stop this!' Rose shouted at her. 'Bess feels bad enough without you telling her it's her fault.'

"Mother stared at her, but made no reply. She had found her answer and that was all she needed. She was never content unless she could tell people where they'd gone wrong.

"'Anyway,' she said triumphantly, 'this sixth sense you think you've got doesn't always work, does it? I mean, you think Billy's dead, but I know he isn't. Why, I wrote to him only last week.'

"I felt my fists clench involuntarily, as though they had a will of their own. I knew very well that mother had written to Billy. That place had sent the letter back to Rose, just as they sent all mother's letters back. And she still believed she was writing to some tailoring firm. I couldn't find any sympathy for her delusion just at that moment, and I only felt angry that she couldn't accept facts when they stared her in the face. How much easier it would have been if I could have pretended that Daniel was never on that ship, but that luxury wasn't mine.

"In the silence that followed, a small bird chose to hurl itself against the window pane, making mother start. She shook her head slowly and her forehead creased into a worried frown. She knew at least a hundred superstitions and bad omens and she believed them all implicitly. A bird hitting the window meant death.

"She looked at me and her expression softened, showing a sympathy which was seldom revealed.

"'I'm sorry, love,' she said gently. 'I think maybe I was jumping the gun a bit.' She paused and took a deep breath. 'Mind you, I still say you should have married him when you had the chance.'

"I've always wished I'd followed my instinct to go and see Daniel's parents, give me my condolences. Although we'd never had much time for each other, he was their only child and I thought a lot about visiting them. But because I blamed myself for what had happened, I was sure they'd do the same. They'd slam the door in my face. My life could have been a whole lot different had I put aside my pride and visited. A whole lot different.

"Most of the victims were buried in Nova Scotia, so there wasn't going to be a funeral and I was thankful for that. I couldn't have endured seeing him put into a box in the ground.

"Results of official enquiries kept making their way into the newspapers, but the last thing I wanted to know what that it need never have happened, that there weren't enough lifeboats, not nearly enough for the number of people on board the ship. None of the enquiries and conclusions were going to bring Daniel back, and knowing that the accident had been entirely preventable wasn't what you might call a comfort."

Stella knew, of course, which ship the old lady was referring to. One of the most famous ships, the most famous disasters in history.

"The Titanic?" She whispered.

Bess nodded.

"I'm so sorry," Stella said. "It must have been awful, all these years, having to listen to all the speculations, all the films made about it. And they were talking about retrieving the wreck too, weren't they? I can imagine how you felt about that."

"They won't do it, though," she replied. "That wreck's a grave; they'll leave it alone." She paused then added slowly: "Belinda's parents were on that ship as well. Her father was something to do with the American Embassy and they seemed to spend most of their time flitting across the Atlantic, while the Countess looked after their daughter."

"Were they killed?"

She nodded.

"I don't know why," Bess said. "Most of the first class passengers managed to get themselves rescued, the women at least.

"I sent Nina round with a message for the Countess, telling her why I wasn't there, and she sent back to say she'd lost her son and his wife and she needed me.

"There were lots of people coming to the house to give her their condolences and she gave me the job of answering the door and taking their visiting cards. She had a butler and maids to do that sort of thing and she was only really trying to give me something to do to keep my mind off things.

"Late in the afternoon, I opened the door to Viscount Hartford. He was a young man, in his late twenties, and I noticed him particularly, partly because he smiled and spoke to me pleasantly.

"'Do give the Countess my condolences, won't you,' he said. 'And dear little Belinda, of course. Poor child. Tell them I'll call again in a few days. Thank you so much.'

"But there was something else that struck me as soon as I saw him, something that made me wary. His face stayed in my mind, though there wasn't much room there for anyone's image but Daniel's. I can't explain it, but I felt certain we'd meet again, that he would somehow play a major part in my life.

"As the weeks went on, as May came and brought a breath of fresh air to our grimy little road, the newspaper reports gradually petered out, diminished to nothing more than a few lines on the middle pages. But I was still numb from it all when Nina got ill.

"She came home from her lace selling early one afternoon and by the time I got back she had taken to her bed and was burning up.

"'She's getting ideas about her own importance, now,' mother snapped. 'Coming home half way through the day with a whole basket of lace still unsold. I don't know what I'm slaving away for, wearing out my fingers. Perhaps she'd like me to go out and sell it as well as make it. Time was when children helped out.'

"She was sitting in her chair, her bobbins flying about, and her expression sour. I took no notice of her ramblings.

"'Oh, Bess,' Nina said croakily. 'I feel so sick. What's wrong with me?'

"I didn't have the answer to that. There were a hundred nasty diseases you could get in those days, particularly being so overcrowded, the way we were. I felt her forehead and the heat coming from her almost burnt my hand. I opened the buttons at the front of her dress and I saw a nasty red rash on her neck and chest. I knew what it was, but I didn't know what to do about it.

"I spent that night soaking her down with cold water and the next morning I went to the Countess and told her my sister had scarlet fever, and I was afraid of spreading the infection to Belinda.

"When I got back, I found a well dressed little man sitting on Nina's bed. She was delirious, moaning incoherently.

"'I'm Dr. Fraser,' he announced himself.

"'I can't afford you,' I said abruptly. 'Did my mother send for you?'

"Mother had these queer ideas sometimes, thinking she could afford things like doctors. He shook his head and smiled kindly.

"'No, my dear,' he replied. 'Her Ladyship, the Countess of Hazelforth asked me to call and it's just as well I did. Your sister is very ill.'

"If anyone but the Countess had done that, my pride would have rebelled against the proffered charity. But she was different and I felt pleased that she'd been so thoughtful.

"He stayed for about twenty minutes, measuring out medicine for her, and all the while my mother just sat with her lace, grunting occasionally. Suddenly, she put her work aside and stared at us.

"'If she's in pain, it serves her right,' she declared. 'Perhaps she'll think twice in future about bringing shame on this family.'

"Dr. Fraser looked at her sharply, then glanced up at me, but he said nothing.

"'It'll be a blessing if the child dies,' she went on. 'What sort of life is it going to have, being born a bastard? Just answer me that.'

"The doctor paid more attention this time.

"'Miss Shaw,' he said, 'is your sister in a delicate condition? It could make a difference to the treatment you know. You should tell me.'

"I shook my head.

"'Take no notice, Doctor. It's just mother getting mixed up again.'

"'There's nothing mixed up about me, Elizabeth!' She cried. 'Don't pretend your sister's innocent. We all know different and it'll come out sooner or later, whether you like it or not.'

"'Doctor, Nina is only twelve years old,' I said. 'Mother's been a bit strange for a while now. Please don't listen to her.'

"He gave me the medicine and instructions then turned toward the door.

"'If she's no better in a week or so, Her Ladyship will call me out again,' he said, then he glanced at mother as he was going out, lowering his voice to a whisper. 'Try to keep your mother quiet and away from your sister. The child needs peace and comfort, not condemnation for imaginary sins. I've seen it happen before; your mother will get worse very quickly. She could even become violent.' He paused and gave me a sympathetic smile. 'I'm only warning you, Miss Shaw, so that you'll be prepared.'

"I knew he was right; I'd known it from the beginning and it became a terrible strain, never knowing if she was going to be herself from one day to the next. Nina had grown frightened of her but she was my mother, and I had nothing else to do now but look after her."

CHAPTER THIRTEEN

Stella hadn't notice the ornate, wooden chest beside Auntie Bess' chair until she reached down to open it. It was an old, oak casket with a design of lilies carved into the lid. She bent forward and opened it awkwardly, her brow creased with effort. She drew out a rolled up poster, not unlike the ones that cover the walls of teenagers' bedrooms all over the country.

The poster was very old, but well-preserved, and it announced the debut performance of Rosina Shaw, among other, more famous names. Rosina Shaw? The name seemed familiar, if only vaguely, but Stella decided it was merely because Bess had been talking about her.

She started to speak again while Stella was still studying names such as Marie Lloyd and Harry Tate, with a sense of wonder.

"Edie hadn't been home since her wedding day. Part of the reason lay in her inability to appear content with the marriage, and I knew she would rather never see any of us again than admit to the mess she had made of things. But the main reason, I suspected, was her husband.

"I didn't find out till later, of course, but life with Reg had proved to be even more tedious than she had expected. He was eternally correcting her behaviour, telling her she must live up to his standards. I remember my own opinion of his standards when I'd caught them together that Sunday. He had bought a house in Potters Bar and said that he would commute to London. He couldn't simply say he'd go on the train, could he? He had to say he would 'commute'.

"The day after that appeared," Bess said, nodding toward the rolled up poster in Stella's hands, "Edie turned up at our room. It was a Saturday and I was washing the front windows, trying to get off some of the soot and grime that had gathered over the winter. I saw her coming down the road.

"Auntie Ann was visiting that day, with Maud in tow, and while the little woman sat silently with her eyes darting about the room, the two sisters had spent the past hour shaking their heads over what mother liked to call my 'personal heartache'.

"I was relieved to see Edie coming. I didn't particularly want to see her, but I was glad that her visit would give them something else to talk about.

"She was wearing loose dresses by then. She was one of those women who burst out early on in pregnancy so she looked a lot more than the four or five months gone that she actually was. There was something obscene about seeing my little sister with her stomach bulging out like that and it wasn't considered seemly for a woman so far gone to be out in public. But none of that stopped me from noticing that her dress was brand new. It looked quite expensive, too. Well, I thought, she seems to have landed on her feet.

"As she drew nearer, I noticed that she had that sulky look on her face. It was an expression she'd often worn in the past when things weren't going her way. I suppose she'd come to cheer herself up, but I was annoyed because the dress she wore was bright mauve and my mother wouldn't have mauve in the place. She thought it was terribly unlucky and Edie should have known that.

"I watched her turn down the alley beside the pub, then I crossed to the back window to keep my eye on her. She was talking to Tom in the yard and after he went inside, I watched her disappear through the back door. It must have been a good five minutes before I heard her tread on the stairs and I thought she was probably getting her breath back, having a rest to prepare for the exertion of hauling her extra bulk up the narrow staircase.

"She was sweaty and out of breath when she got upstairs. I expect she had forgotten how grimy it could be in the city once the weather warmed up, especially now she was so heavy. It really wasn't decent, her wandering about on her own like that with the baby so big inside her.

"She was clutching a letter in her hand, which Tom must have given her. The post for all the building was delivered to him and he'd bring ours up later. Edie's other hand was buried in the big patch pocket of her frock and she handed the envelope to mother awkwardly because of it.

"I could see she was disappointed to find me at home and annoyed that Auntie Ann was with us. And Maud, of course, but she was always so silent you could forget she was there.

"Edie had an affected smile on her face as she started straight in about her new house and her select neighbourhood and she went up to mother expecting a great hug of delight.

"Mother's furious eyes swept her from head to foot.

"'Oh,' she said angrily, 'so you've remembered you've got a mother then? About time you showed up. And haven't we got enough troubles without you bringing that unlucky colour in here?'

"Edie looked down at herself and comprehension dawned in her eyes.

"'I'm sorry, mother,' she said. 'I didn't think.'

"'You never do, not about anyone but yourself at any rate.'

"Edie was taken aback.

"'Well, that's nice, I must say,' she said. 'I come all this way to see you and that's all the thanks I get. I might as well turn round and go back to Hertfordshire.'

"'Ooh! Hertfordshire, is it?' Mother mimicked her. 'I s'pose the likes of us aren't good enough for you now, eh? We were certainly good enough when you got yourself up the spout, weren't we?'

"'Are you going to bring all that up again? I told you what happened.' Edie took a deep breath and shot a warning glance my way. 'It was just lucky for me that Reg was good enough to marry me, after I was attacked.'

"'You must think I was born yesterday, my girl! I've been hearing a few things since you took off, none of them good, I don't mind telling you.'

"'Who's been saying things about me?' Edie demanded.

"'Just about everyone. They all know round here what you were.'

"'And you believe them, do you? You believe a lot of strangers instead of your own daughter!'

"Mother's lips formed a thin, hard line and her eyes blazed furiously.

"'I know truth when I hear it. And if it's not true, why haven't you shown your face before this? Just tell me that?'

"'We've been busy, that's all. Trying to get the house straight and get the room ready for the baby.'

"Mother grunted, folded her arms and fixed her gaze out of the window.

"'Mother,' Edie went and sat beside her. 'I came all this way to see you. You might at least ask me how I am.'

"'I know how you are. You're in the pudding club, stuck with a toffy-nosed bank clerk who you don't give tuppence about and you think the best thing to do to make you feel better is to come here and tell us all how well you've done for yourself.'

"I couldn't help grinning but Edie's cheeks went bright red. She hadn't expected mother to see through her so easily. She had always supported Edie, stood up for her against the rest of us, and it must have come as a shock to realise that mother no longer thought the sun shone out of her backside.

"Mother pressed her face close to Edie's.

"'Well it won't wash, Edith,' she said. 'D'you hear me? Your sister's gone on the stage, wearing men's clothes if you please, like some trollop off the streets.'

"'Now remember, Rebecca,' Auntie Ann spoke for the first time. 'Rosina did say that they don't want her to dress like that any more. They said she wasn't any good at comedy songs.' She paused and grunted, shifting her considerable weight. 'Not that that makes much difference, mind. Being on the stage at all is a wicked thing to do. We pray for her every Sunday in church, asking the Lord to show her the way.'

"'I should've thought she'd found the way, Auntie,' Edie replied. 'I mean, singing on the stage could earn her a lot of money. It's got to be better than working in a factory.

"Auntie Anne gave her a withering stare.

"'I was unaware,' she said imperiously, 'that I was speaking to you. Whatever your sister's done, it's nothing to the shame you've brought on us all. There is only one future for sinners like you, Edith. Hell! Damnation! You must repent your sins, before it is too late.'

"By the look on her face and from what I've found out since, I don't think there could have been anyone on earth more repentant than Edie was. Having to spend the rest of your life with Reg Parrish must have been the greatest penance known to man.

"'P'raps you can tell me, Ann,' said my mother suddenly, 'what I ever did to deserve two such wicked children? If it weren't for Bess working so hard, I don't know where we'd be.'

"Her statement hurt Edith more than she would have admitted. I could see that by the way she looked at mother. She had always been the favourite and as far as she could tell, the old girl had never cared much for me. We fought all the time and she must have wondered why mother had decided to elevate me, of all people, in her estimation. I have to admit, I'd have wondered that myself if I hadn't known how my mother loved a tragedy.

"'Bess!' Edie exclaimed. 'Since when was Bess such a favourite?'

"'She's got a broken heart,' mother answered in her best mournful tone.

"'Bess?' Edie scoffed. 'Bess hasn't got a heart, broken or otherwise.'

"'Daniel's been killed,' she said quietly. 'Drowned on that boat that went down in April. Something you'd know about if you hadn't been too high and mighty to bother with your own family.' She added mournfully: 'She'll never get over it.'

"It had been over a month since the disaster, but mother was still milking it for all it was worth. She had always thrived on doom and gloom but she was getting worse. And how I wished she'd shut up about Daniel.

"Edie frowned for a moment, as though she were trying to puzzle something out, then I noticed a little smile on her face as if what mother had said was in some way amusing. I was furious.

"'And what, may I ask, are you smiling at?' I demanded.

"'Oh, nothing,' she said quickly. 'I was just laughing at mother, calling a huge great ocean liner a 'boat'.'

"Auntie Ann heaved herself to her feet.

"'Come along, Maud,' she said. 'I think it's time we went home. I've no wish to hear any more of Edith's nonsense. Goodbye, Elizabeth. Try not to brood, dear.'

"'I'll come down with you,' Mother said. 'I want to see if Nina's coming. She shouldn't be out so long; she's still weak from the scarlet fever.'

"As soon as the door had closed behind the three women, Edie let out a long and angry sigh. 'This is all Reg's fault,' she muttered. 'He had no right to take advantage of me.'

"'You didn't seem to be protesting all that much when I saw you,' I said.

"'It's your fault, too,' she retorted. '"Why couldn't you keep your nose out of my business?'

"'If you want someone to blame, look in the mirror. I can't be bothered with you.'

"The back window was open and I suddenly hard my name being called from the yard. I poked my head out and my heart sank. There was my mother, her grip firm on Tom's shirt front. She was shouting at him.

"'Why, George? Why did you go and leave me with all the kids? Haven't I been a good wife to you? Just tell me why!'

"I was rooted to the spot for a minute. Tom's face had gone pale and he had hold of her wrists, trying to loosen her grip on his shirt.

"'Bess!' He called again.

"I turned toward the door.

"'You'd better come and help me,' I said to Edie. 'Trust you to come here in that frock and set her off. You know how she feels about that colour.'

"'So it's my fault, is it?'

"'Well, you haven't exactly helped matters, have you?'

"That's when I started to look into the future and what I saw depressed me almost as much as losing Daniel.

***

"Rose soon found she was making enough money to buy a small house a little farther out in Dalston.

"'It's only one of those Victorian terraces,' she told me. 'But it's got three bedrooms and a parlour and even an indoor bath. Honestly Bess, we won't know ourselves.'

"I felt a spark of excitement I hadn't known since Daniel went away. It was going to be heaven a whole house to ourselves. Rose thought a change of scene, a proper home for us all, might help mother to see reality again. But mother would have nothing to do with it.

"'If you think I'm going to benefit from your ill-gotten gains, my girl, you're very much mistaken,' she declared.

"'But I bought the house so we could all have a bit of space,' Rose protested. 'I thought it would be nice for Nina, too, to have her own room.'

"'You leave Nina out of this,' mother retorted. 'She's quite happy where she is. It was good enough for you, wasn't it?'

"Not really, I thought, but I didn't say so. Neither did I point out that no one had actually asked Nina if she was quite happy.

"Although mother had begun to talk to Rose again, she was still determined to disapprove of her career as a music hall artiste. Her disapproval was regularly fuelled by Auntie Ann, who insisted on praying for Rose's redemption whenever she got the chance. Maud had gone one better. Not being family, she felt no obligation to continue her visits and she would have nothing more to do with us while one of our members chose to display herself. Christian tolerance was apparently not one of her most pressing beliefs.

"None of these things mattered to Rose. What did matter was that mother refused to allow her to take Nina to live with her and even refused to let the child accept any presents from her.

"Once she was settled into the house herself, she decided to have one more try. She arrived at the same time as me and we walked upstairs together, only to find Nina in floods of tears. She was hugging the wax doll that had been Daniel's parting gift.

"Both windows were wide open, but the room was stifling and little beads of perspiration broke out all over me as soon as I went in. It was summer, but mother had a roaring fire going in the range. We were accustomed to doing without a hot meal in warm weather, because the heat from the range made the little room like a turkish bath.

"'Whatever's wrong?' Rose asked at once, crouching on the floor beside Nina.

"'It melted!' Nina wailed. 'It's face has all gone!'

"Rose turned to look at mother, who was sitting in the solitary chair, staring out of the window.

"'Mother? What happened to Nina's doll?'

"Mother looked back at her and shrugged.

"'Oh, that,' she answered. 'Silly girl left it in front of the range. It's wax, isn't it? It melted.'

"'Didn't you notice?' Rose demanded. 'Didn't you tell her what would happen? And why did you light it at all?'

"'How else am I supposed to cook your dinners? P'raps you'd like to breathe on them – you certainly talk enough hot air! Besides, I've got more important things to do with my time than worry about a doll!' Mother got to her feet and started to tidy things up, making an effort to be busy. 'I've got enough to do, bringing you lot up, without having to worry about a doll getting burned!'

"'There's only Nina, mother.'

"'Only Nina? What about the rest of you? I can't just leave everybody to fend for themselves, can I? You all need looking after.'

"Rose said no more on the subject. Mother was apparently having one of those days when she thought we were all still children, still dependent on her. Nina was hugging the doll, rocking back and forth in time to her sobs.

"'Let's have a look, love,' I said softly. 'Let's see if we can't do her hair to cover up the marks or something.'

"Nina shoved the doll at me, tears streaming down her cheeks. We saw at once that it was hopeless. The doll's face had completely melted away, leaving two grotesque blue eyes wandering aimlessly about inside its head.

"'I'll get you another doll,' Rose told Nina. 'Just don't tell mother.'

"Nina looked at her gratefully, but she wasn't satisfied.

"'Daniel bought me that doll,' she cried miserably. 'It's the only thing he ever bought me and now he's dead. Can you buy me another Daniel, too?'

"Rose drew her close. No amount of money could replace Daniel.

"'Don't worry, Rose,' the child said against her shoulder. 'I'm too old for dolls, anyway.'

"'It's her own fault,' mother said. She was standing staring down at them with her hands on her hips. 'Fancy leaving a wax doll in front of a fire? Stupid girl!'

"'How was I to know she was going to light the range?' Nina protested. 'I sat the doll there and when I came back she'd made it too hot for her.'

"Rose gave her little sister a last squeeze and got to her feet, then started to cross the room to the door.

"'Don't walk there!' Mother demanded imperiously.

"Rose looked about the floor, bewildered, wondering if she had trodden in something nasty.

"'What?' She said.

"'I said don't walk there. The King and Queen's just walked there!'

"Mother turned away to stare out of the window again, as though she were waiting for something.

"'He's late,' she muttered. 'I can't stand this waiting. George has got to come before father gets back, or he'll stop us from going.'

"'It's all right, Rose,' Nina whispered. 'She'll be all right with us.'

"Rose nodded. Perhaps the child was right, I thought. Perhaps she was too old for dolls."

"During the next few weeks, mother grew steadily less coherent. She was spending more and more time in the past, thinking we were still children, sometimes thinking she was still a young girl living in her father's vardo. I suppose that must have been the happiest time of her life.

"She insisted on telling everyone that she had met and spoken to Jack the Ripper, though how she survived that encounter she never said. She also told us that she had known King George V when he sold bootlaces down Petticoat Lane.

"And she spent a lot of time watching from the window and asking why Billy didn't come."

CHAPTER FOURTEEN

"At the beginning of August, everything was to change.

"Mother started getting ready to go out, but she put on her heavy coat and bonnet. The morning haze was hovering over the rooftops and you could see it was going to be a scorcher.

"'It's a little warm for a coat, isn't it mother?' I suggested.

"She turned her sternest glance on me.

"'What would you know?' She said. 'It might look bright, but it's chilly. I need my coat and so do you.'

"She lifted my coat down from the hook and began to put me into it, as though I were a child. She stood in front of me to button it up.

"'Where are we going?' I asked.

"'Shopping of course.'

"'Can't I stay here?' I asked carefully. 'I could be doing a bit of cleaning for you.'

"She looked startled, then outraged.

"'I'm not one of those women who go off and leave their children on their own,' she declared. 'We might have to live beside scum, but we don't have to live like them.'

"I allowed her to carry on; there seemed to be little point in arguing and besides, I realised it wasn't a good idea for her to go off on her own. She'd had moments before this of thinking we were all still children, but she'd never gone this far.

"Once outside, she held my hand. The heat hit me as soon as we emerged and I wondered how long I'd be able to endure wearing the coat. We attracted some curious stares as we went down the street, both dressed in warm, winter clothes and my hand clasped firmly in mother's. She made me stop at the kerb.

"'Now then, Elizabeth,' she said. 'When you're older and you're out on your own, always remember to stop and look both ways before you cross a road. Horses can't stop in a hurry, you know, and if you get in the way of one of them, you could be killed.'

"There was a motor car coming along the road, but it was a long way off and she didn't seem to see it. They didn't go very fast in those days and we had plenty of time to cross, so I started forward. She yanked me back and I turned to see that her eyes showed sheer terror.

"'What's wrong, mother?'

"'That carriage!' She cried. 'Look at that carriage! The horses must have got loose! It's running away down the road and all those poor people inside will be killed!'

"'It's all right,' I tried to assure her. 'That's a horseless carriage. Don't you remember. It doesn't need horses to draw it.'

"'Don't talk nonsense to me, when there are lives at stake!' She screamed. 'I've got to do something. You stay here.'

"Her hand slipped out of mine as she spoke and though I tried to grab for her, I grabbed only air. I ran after her, calling her back, but she took no heed. She was running toward the motor car, yelling to passers-by to come help her. Couldn't they see what was happening? People just stared, not understanding. I couldn't keep up with her, and all I could do was scream for help, but it was too late. Mother had thrown herself in front of the car, grabbing the headlights at the front.

"Everyone had seen what had happened, but they couldn't believe it, any more than I could. It almost looked as though she had wanted to commit suicide, and if it had been a runaway carriage as she believed, how on earth had she thought that she could stop it anyway? The answer to that is something I've never been able to fathom.

"The motor car had rolled right over her before it managed to stop and it had to be pushed back before anyone could get near mother. I was still standing in the road, staring like an idiot. I didn't need to see her dead face to know that she was gone.

"And you know what I was thinking as I stood there, watching the little group which gathered about my mother's body? I was thinking of myself. I sent Daniel away because I thought I'd have to spend the next twenty years looking after her and less than four months after I said goodbye to him, mother was dead.

"Auntie Ann paid for the funeral. Mother wouldn't have liked that, would have called it charity, but she'd had everyone insured except herself. She'd have liked even less to lie in a pauper's grave and if her sister couldn't give her a decent burial, then who could?

"All Ann's latent maternal instincts seemed to come out at the funeral. It was as though she wanted to take her sister's place, for she kept fussing round us and putting her arms around me. I'd never seen her behave like that before. She'd always been a little stand-offish, keeping herself aloof. That day, she even had a kind word for Rose, despite her disapproval.

"'I think Nina should come back with me,' she suggested quietly. 'After all, a child that age needs a mother. Maud and I would be happy to care for her.'

"I glanced at Nina and saw her eyebrows climb up, her dark eyes widen in alarm.

"'That's very kind, Auntie,' I replied tactfully. 'We'll have to discuss it.'

"Of course we never did, but it was the best deferring tactic I could think of. I was in no mood to decide anything that day.

"Mother's death left me in a sort of void. I'd had no doubt what my future would be. I'd accepted it, even if it wasn't what I wanted, and now that future had been snatched away. I should have been relieved, but all I felt was cheated.

"'You'll come and live with me now, won't you?' Rose asked. 'You and Nina?'

"'I don't know,' I answered. 'We have the place to ourselves. Perhaps it's best if we don't rush into anything.'

"'Whatever you like. You're always welcome, you know that. What will you do now?'

"'Yes, Bess,' piped up Edie. 'You must feel a bit lost without mother to worry about.'

"She shouldn't have come you know. She was about eight months pregnant by then, the sweat was dripping out of her bonnet from the heat, and she could barely move. But do you think Reg had put in an appearance on his wife's behalf? Not likely!

"'Life goes on, I suppose,' Stella replied quietly.

"I couldn't say what I was thinking. I didn't want them to know, but Rose had her share of Romany blood too.

"'You're thinking of Daniel, aren't you?' She asked. 'It was because of mother that you turned him down, wasn't it?'

"'How did you know?'

"'I guessed. You should have told me, Bess. I would have done my share.'

"I took her hand and gave it a little squeeze. I didn't need words to explain it to her. She knew.

"'If the good Lord had to give me this cursed gift,' I said, 'He might at least have let me see that this was going to happen. Daniel would have waited, if we'd only known. I could have married him, couldn't I? But it's too late; it's all too late.'

"Edie moved quickly away to gather up her things.

"'I best be getting back,' she said, as she made her way to the door. 'Reg'll be worried.'"

***

The old lady's story had moved Stella. She sat watching her, feeling remorse for all the contentious things she had believed about her in the past. She knew now that they were, if not outright lies, distortions of the truth.

The old lady was quiet, contemplative and Stella thought, don't stop now! There were too many things she wanted to know. Why had she never heard before of this mysterious older sister? It couldn't be simply her choice of career that had kept her existence hidden from Stella's mother and her. Who was she, that Bess had been so anxious to reveal her secrets?

The answers were soon provided but they were not satisfying; they merely gave her more to wonder about.

Auntie Bess brought another poster out of her chest and handed it to Stella.

"Rose got to be very famous," she said. "That one was put up in 1913, when she was the star of the show."

Stella unrolled it carefully, afraid of damaging something so old and precious. She recognised the words immediately. They leapt out at her, emblazoned across the white and gold skirts on the artist's portrait of a beautiful, dark haired girl.

"The Romany Princess?" She asked.

"That's what they called her. They went in a lot for nicknames in those days – the Swedish Nightingale, the Divine Sarah. You know the sort of thing."

Stella stared at her and she knew what she meant her to know. There was no mistake, no coincidence of names. Her eyes were clear and steady, waiting for Stella to make the connection. Suddenly, Stella was furious.

"Is that what this is all about?" She demanded angrily. "Is that what you brought me here for, to tell me that your sister, my grandmother's sister was a criminal almost as infamous as Crippen? I don't believe you!"

"I see you've got over thinking you mustn't argue with a sweet old lady. Edie always gave as good as she got. I knew there had to be a streak of her in there somewhere."

"Even my mother doesn't know anything about this. Grandma made sure we never knew, for our own good. Did I really need to know this? Don't you think I'd have been happier without this knowledge?"

The old lady leaned toward her with unexpected determination.

"This isn't about you," she said sharply. "I see there's a lot of Edie in you after all. She always thought of herself first, always wanted to know how things were going to affect her."

"What is it about then?" She demanded. "Is it some sort of retribution for the past? Because your sister never forgave you for causing her fiancé to break up with her?"

"Is that what she told you?" She asked quietly.

"Yes. Are you telling me it isn't true?"

"You'll find out, if you listen. Or would you rather go now and keep your little illusions?" She waited while Stella tried in vain to calm herself. "Well? You know where the door is; why don't you use it?"

Good question – why didn't she just walk away? She knew she couldn't do it. Bess was ancient, she was dying, she wanted to tell her story and it would have been morally wrong to deny her. And she wanted to hear that story; she wanted to know the rest.

"I don't believe any of this," Stella said at last. "You've painted a picture of someone sweet and kind. How am I supposed to equate that with a murderess?"

"What did you expect her to be like? Myra Hindley? Or some Nazi war criminal? It's not hereditary, you know. You're not going to go out and bump someone off because of bad blood."

Stella sank back into the chair, staring at the poster in her lap. She wanted to rip it to shreds and throw them in her face, but she was too stunned to move.

"Rose was one of the gentlest, nicest people I ever knew," she went on. "They lied about her at the trial. None of it was true. That's what I want you to understand."

Stella saw compassion in her old eyes and she felt ashamed. Bess was right, wasn't she? This wasn't about her.

CHAPTER FIFTEEN

"The next time I saw Edie was at Auntie Ann's funeral – her first funeral, that is."

Bess' eyes twinkled with mischief and Stella knew she wanted her to question her statement.

"First funeral? How can anyone have more than one funeral?"

"One day," she went on, "Maud came to our room. We heard her running up the stairs, as though the Devil himself were after her, and she hammered on the door and threw it open almost in one movement. She didn't wait to be invited in, either. She just ran into the room and headed straight for me, grabbing me by the arms and shaking me. I was amazed. I'd never seen so much animation in the little woman before.

"'She's dead!' She cried. 'Ann's dead!'

"Now that I didn't believe. I always knew when someone close died, and I had felt nothing.

"'She can't be dead, Maud,' I answered, though as I tried to soothe her, I felt a sense of wonder that in all the years I'd know Maud, this was the first time I had ever heard her speak.

"She looked at me as though she didn't quite know who I was or where she had run to, and then she sat down, nodding her head. She just kept nodding her head.

"Eventually, I managed to get the story out of her. It seemed that she had been unable to wake Auntie Ann that morning, so she had called in the doctor. He had pronounced her dead, probably of heart failure.

"All the time she was talking, I was thinking she had gone mad. I just couldn't believe that someone in the family had died and I hadn't felt it. Perhaps I've grown out of it, I thought; I hoped. It was never a pleasant gift to have, you know, always knowing when someone went, always knowing before anyone told me.

"I went with Maud back to the house, to see for myself, and sure enough there was Ann, still in her bed, white and rigid with no pulse, no sign of life.

"I had to accept it, didn't I? The doctor had confirmed it, so who was I to argue?

"They never used to wait too long to bury people in those days; we had no refrigeration like today and bodies went off quickly and started to smell. The funeral was arranged for a couple of days later and that's when I saw Edie again. We were all there, and I couldn't help thinking of mother. Ann was our last link with her and I felt the loss, even though Auntie had driven us all mad with her preaching and quoting of the scriptures.

"Reg didn't show his face at her funeral, any more than he had at mother's. There was some excuse about pressure of work and I don't know who she'd found to look after the baby. She'd had a little girl a year before, your mother, Mary. Just like them to name their child after the Queen.

"We were all at Auntie Ann's, waiting for the funeral carriage to come and take the coffin which was lying open on the table in the parlour. I was sitting in the corner, watching Edie. She was dressed in black like the rest of us, except that her clothes were brand new while ours were old and dyed for the occasion. She was standing at the mirror, fiddling about with her bonnet and she had her back to the coffin. She could see the reflection of it in the glass.

"'I don't think it's right, having that lying open in here,' she complained. 'It gives me the creeps.'

"'What's the matter, Edie?' I replied. 'Scared of ghosts? Frightened the old girl'll come back and haunt you? Auntie Ann never hurt anyone when she was alive, I don't see why she'd want to start now.'

"'She hurt me, didn't she?' She said bitterly. 'She wouldn't come to my wedding and she wouldn't speak to me after I married Reg.'

"I laughed.

"'She wouldn't speak to you after you got yourself in the club, is what you mean.'

"'Bloody old hypocrite!' Edie snapped viciously. 'Going on about Christian charity and God, then ignoring me all these months. And she tried to turn mother against me; I know she did!'

"I wasn't looking at her and I was only half listening while I tried to suppress some of the dread I was feeling. I wasn't happy about Auntie Ann being buried.

"All my life I had known when someone I cared about died. Sometimes it was the only way to know whether I cared or not. Ann had always managed to get on my nerves, but just the same I'd believed myself fond of her. If she were really dead, I'd either lost the curse or I hadn't cared about her at all. Either that, or they were making a terrible mistake. You can see how that idea frightened me, can't you? I could hardly tell the undertaker not to bury her because I didn't believe she was dead. They'd have carted me off in a straightjacket.

"I looked up sharply when I heard Edie scream, and I saw what had frightened her.

"In the mirror, she had seen the body begin to move, then sit up. I must admit I was more than a bit shaken myself when I saw the old girl sitting up, dead straight, in her coffin and I'd been half expecting it. It must have been an even greater shock for Edie. She stood stock still for a minute. Suddenly, she wrenched the bonnet off her head and threw it at the figure on the table. Then she fled.

"I laughed so much I nearly split my corsets and I was still laughing when I went to Auntie and put my arm around her. The relief was indescribable.

"Edie had caught the first train home by the time all the fuss had died down and I didn't see her again until well into the war."

"I don't understand, Auntie Bess," Stella said. "How did your aunt come to nearly get herself buried if she wasn't dead?"

She shrugged.

"It wasn't all that uncommon in those days," she replied. "We never had all these machines like they have today, to measure brain waves and things. If the doctor couldn't hear a heartbeat, then as far as he was concerned, the patient was dead. It was catalepsy Auntie Ann had. That was quite common then, still is as far as I know. It makes your muscles go rigid and it looks for all the world as though you are dead. And bodies were never left around long enough for them to start to rot, so we couldn't tell like that."

"So...she was lucky, then. There might have been a lot of people with this disease who actually were buried alive."

The old lady gave Stella a sinister grin.

"'Course, dear," she said. "Where d'ya think Edgar Allan Poe got all his stories from? It wasn't all that unusual for someone to get themselves buried before their time, not then. Some people who could afford it had a bell put up over the grave with a string going down into the coffin, so they could ring for help."

The image her words conjured up filled Stella with horror. Then she saw that her eyes were twinkling again and she wondered if Bess had been having a little joke at her expense.

"I'm sorry," Stella said quickly. "Please. Go on with your story."

"Nina left school and went to work at the boot factory. Rose was still a great success on the stage. The people loved her and I only wished I had more time to go and watch her. She always got me free tickets. But we had drifted apart a little over the months, what with us both being so busy.

"One night, I decided it was time I went down to the theatre and watched the show. I bought my ticket that time, because I didn't want her to know I was going to be there.

"I scarcely recognised her, standing up there all dressed in pale blue satin with long, white satin gloves covering her hands and arms, and an enormous hat, trimmed with ostrich feathers, perched on top of her piled up hair. She looked so beautiful and so happy, it made me proud. I felt my sacrifice hadn't been in vain, after all, for I knew that if I'd been engaged to Daniel when her big chance came along, she'd have turned it down. Chances like that don't come along twice in a lifetime.

"It was hard to believe that less than two years had passed since she'd stood trembling on that very platform, dressed in the Countess' primrose linen. Now, she walked about the stage, smiling and flourishing her hands, full of confidence, a real professional. I had to fight the urge to tell everyone near enough to list: 'that's my sister up there.'

"She ended her performance with 'After the Ball' and half the audience were in tears when she had finished. Most people only know the chorus nowadays, but then it was still a popular song and ever so sad. It was about a man who lost his only true love because of a mistake.

"I was dying to see her and I had no trouble getting backstage. The staff there knew who I was from the other times I had been and I was thrilled to bits to find they'd given Rose her own dressing room. She'd been sharing with several other girls before and this was really a step up.

"The first thing I noticed was the absence of Alfred. Every time I'd been before, I'd found him hanging about outside the dressing rooms, waiting for her to come out. I was pleased to think he'd finally given up, that is until I learned the reason for it.

"'Bess!' She cried when I opened the door. She got up from the dressing table and threw her arms around me. 'Were you in the audience? And you never told me you were coming!'

"'Thought I'd surprise you,' I said. 'Don't let me hold you up. You just carry on with whatever you were doing.'

"She sat down at the mirror and started to put cream all over her face to wipe off the stage make-up. Her hair had grown even longer and it was hanging down below the stool, nearly reaching the floor where she sat. Her eyes were shining and her cheeks were pink with excitement and I had never seen her look so lovely. And she was lovely, was Rose. She had the sort of face and figure that made people turn around and look as she passed them in the street.

"I remember watching that night and feeling really happy that she wasn't going to be wasted in a little room in Shoreditch and a boot factory. It might have been better for her if she was.

"There was a sharp tap on the door and a man entered, only his dark wavy hair visible above a huge bouquet of red roses. As he lowered them and turned to close the door, I caught a glimpse of a handsome face with even, aristocratic features. He had a small moustache above his lip and he was expensively dressed in evening clothes.

"I recognised him at once and my heart missed a beat. Of all the people who had come to pay their respects to the Countess that day back in April 1912, I had known there was something special about him. I shivered.

"Rose caught a glimpse of his reflection in the mirror and she turned and smiled, a really delighted smile.

"'James,' she said, rather shyly. 'I'm glad you came tonight. I want you to meet my sister.'

"She ran across the room and stood in front of him and when she turned to face me, she was holding his hand.

"'Delighted,' he said, giving me a gracious bow. 'Wasn't she simply magnificent tonight? Did you notice how many people were weeping, actually weeping, when she sang?'

"I didn't answer. My head was in a whirl and I didn't like the feeling one bit. The man had a very precise English accent, he was obviously very well educated and, if his clothes were anything to go by, extremely well off. And I knew who he was; I just couldn't put my finger on his name.

"It came to me suddenly.

"'Viscount Hartford.'

"'That's right,' he confirmed with a smile, showing white, even teeth. 'Have we met?'

"'No,' I said. 'But I've seen you before at Countess Hazelforth's house.' I paused and watched him thoughtfully before I added: 'I'm her seamstress.'

"I was hoping to let him know precisely where Rose and I stood in the scheme of things, but my words seemed to fall on deaf ears.

"'I do beg your pardon,' he said. 'I'm afraid I don't remember you. However, the next time I visit the Countess, I shall make a point of nipping in to say hello.'

"Don't bother, I thought and I was about to say so, but I thought better of it. I looked at Rose, who was standing beside the mirror, nervously wringing her hands. Surely she hadn't been stupid enough to let herself fall for someone like him? I thought. Oh, I didn't doubt his good intentions and he was more than likely a very nice man, but it could never work. I knew it and I couldn't believe that Rose did not.

"'I've booked a table,' he said quietly, 'at that little restaurant in Soho. I'll wait for you outside, shall I?'

"As he left the room, Rose slipped behind a little dressing screen and began to change her clothes.

"'I s'pose he won't see anyone he knows at a little restaurant in Soho,' I commented sourly.

"'I knew you wouldn't approve,' she said. 'I suppose you think he's just playing games with me, is that it?'

"'You said it.'

"'Well, you're wrong. We've been seeing each other for months and we've been to lots of places. He even took me to the Savoy last month.' She stepped out from behind the screen and turned her back so that I could hook up her dress. 'I love him, Bess. And he loves me.'

"'Oh, I'm sure he means what he says,' I answered slowly. 'But he'll change his mind when his family get to hear about it. He'll never marry you; surely you can see that?'

"Rose turned and faced me, drawing a deep breath. She must have known this wouldn't be easy, which was why she'd never mentioned him.

"'I never took you for a fool before,' I said. 'How d'you think it's all going to work out, eh? Has he mentioned marriage? Can you see yourself as Lady Hartford?'

"'I know you've got my best interests at heart, Bess,' she answered evenly, 'but I'm not asking for your approval, so please don't spoil it.' Her eyes met mine and she reached out and gripped my wrist tightly. 'Please.'

"There didn't seem to be any argument to that. She opened the door, admitting the sound of far off laughter from the audience in the theatre, then she looked back at me, her eyes sparkling, and I knew of no way to save her from the disaster into which she was heading. I could see what the attraction was. The Viscount was charming, and very handsome, but he was strictly forbidden to the likes of us. Why couldn't she see that?

"I was worried. I couldn't see any future for them, no matter how much he said he loved her. And when I got to know him better, I really believed he did. But his family would never allow it; we all knew that, even him.

"A few weeks later, I called to see Rose at her little house and James was there. So were his suitcases, piled up beside the stairs.

"Now, I know I've said it before, but in those days you simply didn't live with a man if you weren't married to him. You were ostracised for such a thing, outcast. And the vast gulf between his class and ours meant that everyone would think of my sister as nothing more than a little whore he kept in a house in Dalston. It wouldn't matter to them that the house was hers, nor that she had her own money. There was simply no other way of looking at it.

"I had a key to Rose's house. She had given it to me when she first bought it, and I had been in the habit of just opening the front door and walking in. I did the same that day; I wasn't expecting to find James in residence.

"'James has told his family that he wants to marry me,' Rose said as soon as I appeared in the doorway.

"They were sitting on the settee together, holding hands, and looking as if they hadn't a care in the world. He squeezed her hand tighter and turned to face her.

"'I don't care what they say!' He declared. 'And neither must you. We'll manage, won't we? Or is it just my title you're after?'

"He said this last with a playful little smile, which she answered with a chuckle. I couldn't help wondering what the pair of them thought they had to laugh about.

"'Well, Me Lord,' she said pertly, emphasising her cockney accent, 'I really don't know 'ow I'm going to get along without a title. After all, it's what you get used to, ain't it?'

"He laughed and hugged her, almost as if he were afraid she might melt away and I could see that he really cared for her. But that didn't make me feel any better.

"She went upstairs, saying she was going to make some room for his things, but I'm sure she only wanted to leave us alone for a while. It was important to her that I got to know him, but I could only feel angry with him for coming into her life and changing the course of it, and not for the better.

"I caught up with her in her bedroom, where she had turned down the bed and was moving things about in her wardrobe.

"'Can't you see how this will look?' I demanded.

"Then I glanced about and saw that some of his things were already scattered about the room. I was incredibly naive. I really thought they would have separate rooms and here was the evidence that the relationship had already been consummated. I felt my cheeks flushing.

"'Aren't you afraid, Rose?' I asked softly. 'Suppose you get pregnant? What happens then?'

"She smiled serenely, a smile filled with confidence.

"'Supposing I do?' She replied. 'He'll stand by me.'

"I hurried downstairs and into the parlour. I stood looking at him for a long time, where he sat with his legs crossed and his fingers intertwined on his knee. Such fine hands he had, meant for playing the piano and for gesturing in meaningful conversations. I went and sat beside him, leaning forward earnestly.

"'Is it true, then, My Lord?' I asked him and I had to force the title from my lips. 'Will you marry my sister?'

"'It's James,' he answered quietly. 'You don't approve of me, do you?'

"'No. I don't think you've got any business messing about with Rose's feelings. You know you'll never be allowed to marry her. Why can't you just leave her alone to find someone of her own kind?'

"He gazed at me thoughtfully for a moment, then a dart of anger glowed in his dark eyes.

"'Is that what she wants?' He demanded. 'Because if it is, I'll go now. Or is it what you want?' Suddenly his hands shot out and gripped mine tightly. 'You have no idea what it's been like for us. When I realised how much she had come to mean to me, I tried to break away. I knew if my father found out he would try his damnedest to marry me off to some suitable lady. But I couldn't stop thinking about her and I know she was miserable, too. We belong together. I've given up everything for her and I shall be just as much an outcast as she will, but that was our decision to make, not yours, not anybody else's. She needs you on her side, don't you see that?' He released me and fell back into his seat. 'All I know for certain is that I love her; I adore her. So don't interfere, please. You don't have the right.'

"He had frightened me a little and I couldn't think of anything to say. His eyes met mine then and he smiled.

"'Rose told me about your Daniel,' he said gently. 'Don't you think you would have done the same for him, if you had to?'

"I couldn't get away from that one. The answer had to be yes and I had to understand, if nobody else did.

"They lived happily throughout the summer, playing house like two children, but though he tried to hide it, I could sense the dread that emanated from him. I grew quite fond of him, despite my own misgivings. He tried so hard to fit into what for him was a different world, and he was doing it for her. I could hardly blame him for that.

"But he had been raised for the higher things in life and he found it difficult to give them up. His income had ceased abruptly and he soon realised he had been trained in absolutely nothing of any use. James had been raised to one day inherit his father's title and there wasn't much demand for earls in East London.

"None of her old friends would have anything to do with Rose now. She was living in sin and there was very little likelihood of the couple ever marrying. Nina never met him, never even laid eyes on him. Rose wouldn't let her visit. She was afraid the scandalmongers would take it out on her and Nina didn't have the experience to stand up to them. I was the only one who kept in touch with her, the only one who went to make sure she was all right. But then, I never have much cared what people think.

"'It can't last,' I declared angrily one day when I went to visit. 'I can't see any future in it, for either of you. I only wish I could.'

"It wasn't the first time I had said it and I didn't expect it would be the last.

"Rose's next words silenced me as swiftly and permanently as a steamroller.

"'I'm sure you're right, Bess,' she said with a soft smile.

"'I am?'

"'Of course you are! Have you really got such a low opinion of me that you think I can't see that?'

"I shook my head. I wanted to shake her, but I didn't think that would do much good.

"'I don't understand you,' I cried. 'If you know it isn't going anywhere, what the hell d'you think you're playing at?'

"She fingered the large, oval locket which hung about her neck. It had been a gift from James when he first moved in with her, a family heirloom destined for the wife of each first born son, down through the generations.

"'I'm just grabbing a little happiness while I can, that's all. I know it's difficult for him and it's fast become impossible. He can't find any work that he's skilled to do. Can you see him down the boot factory, for instance? He'd blend in very well with the likes of Alfred, wouldn't he, with his Savile Row clothes and his Eton accent. I couldn't bear for him to have to do that. He misses the money and he misses his family, though he won't admit it.' She paused and gave me a direct stare. 'Before he told his father about me, he asked me to marry him. He hasn't mentioned marriage since and I know he's wondering if he can live like this. His savings have almost gone and soon we'll be living off my money.'

"'So what?'

"'Come off it, Bess. You know that any man worth having is going to feel he's got to support his wife. I'm not sure I'd want to marry him under these circumstances, not when it's breaking him up like this. He'd love to be able to support me, to be able to say "give up the stage". Not that I'd want to give it up, but you know what I mean.'

"I left her house with a new point of view. Just watching the two of them together made me envious. They were always touching, always exchanging secret little smiles and most of all, they were always laughing together. Perhaps Rose was right. I found myself wishing I'd had the sense to grab a little happiness with Daniel, while I'd had the chance.

"James kept trying to find work. He even got a job in a shipping office, but it didn't last long.

"'What is one to do,' he asked me, 'when one's employer is a fool?'

"I had to laugh.

"'One is supposed to put up with it,' I told him. 'If one doesn't want to be out on one's aristocratic ear'ole.'

"He sat at the oval, mahogany dining table, fiddling with its lace tablecloth. Rose was in the kitchen, preparing the dinner. She had already said her piece – that he didn't have to work at all. Now he sank down into an armchair and sighed.

"'You know, Bess,' he said, 'I've never thought of myself as useless before.'

"'You're not useless, James. You just don't fit, that's all, any more than she'd fit into Mayfair and Buckingham Palace.'

"'But if I could earn some money, we could be married. That's all I want, for us to be man and wife. I hate her having to live like this.'

"'So marry her.'

"'I can't. I won't live off my wife's earnings. I have to find something useful to do.'

"On August 4th of that year, Britain declared war on Germany and James finally found himself something useful to do.

CHAPTER SIXTEEN

"London was abandoned by most of its male population, as thousands, young and not so young, volunteered to go and fight for their country. Feelings were running high all over with prejudices against Germans living in Great Britain which forced the government to round them up and settle them in camps for their own protection.

"Nina left the boot factory and got a job in one of the munitions works that were opening up. They were recruiting female workers at a much higher rate of pay than she would have got elsewhere but it worried me, her working with all those explosives.

"It was a great time for the suffragettes, though. They loved every minute of it. There weren't many men left to do the work they'd always done and the jobs had to be done by women.

"They were driving ambulances, conducting buses, working on the farms, doing everything that the men had always done and doing it just as well too. The sight of a woman in trousers became a familiar one and I laughed to think of the fuss mother had made about it not so long before.

"Can you imagine what it was like, seeing all the men disappear like that? The only young men we saw were in uniform. But it was exciting too, in its way. At least it was for the women; I don't think all those poor soldiers thought there was anything exciting about it, fighting and killing total strangers, up to their waists in mud and blood.

"For Nina and me the greatest shock came when our landlord decided to join up. He came upstairs one night where there were only us two left and knocked on our door very timidly.

"'I'll come straight to the point, Bess,' he said as soon as he was settled on the solitary chair. 'I'm joining up. I'm going to have to get someone in to manage the place, if I can, and I can't be too choosy, either, not with so few men about. What I'm trying to say is that you and your sister might have to go. Whoever I get, he might not be happy with just my two rooms downstairs. If he turns out to be a family man, he's going to need this room too.' He looked down at his hands for a minute and his face went a little scarlet. Then he got up and walked toward the door. 'I'm just warning you, Bess. Just in case.'

"We were stunned. It had never occurred to either of us that the war might make us homeless. We hadn't expected Tom to come over all patriotic, and I privately thought he was a little past the age of adventure. He must have been well into his forties by then.

"'I'm a single man,' he went on. 'I've got no real ties and it just don't seem right for me to stay at home, all cosy like, when there's other men my age and older out there doing their bit. You do understand, don't you?'

"My mind was too busy looking for a solution to answer him. We could go and live with Rose, of course. She had enough room with James away, but it didn't seem fair somehow. It was her place. She'd earned it and it didn't seem right to invade it.

"The idea that came to me wasn't very practical, but it had formed itself into words before I could properly consider it, or reject is as untenable.

"'I'll run the place, Tom,' I said.

"He looked at me as if he thought I was going the same way as my mother. He was probably right.

"'You, Bess? I don't want to get personal but what do you know about running a pub? You're a woman, for Christ's sake! You know as well as I do what sort of women run pubs.'

"'That was before the war, Tom,' I said. 'Nowadays, women are doing everything the men used to do and you know it. And you're not going anywhere right this minute, are you? You can show me what to do.'

"Nina stared at me and her mouth dropped open in astonishment. It wouldn't be easy, working for the Countess and the other clients I'd acquired, then coming home to stand behind the bar all evening. I'd have to do the ordering as well and keep the drunks and trouble makers under control.

"Well, why not? I thought. It was certainly better than not having a roof over our heads wasn't it?

"Tom spent the next fortnight teaching me the ropes, but I got the feeling he had only agreed because he felt responsible for us.

"As soon as he'd left we moved into his old living rooms behind the pub. For the first time in our lives, Nina and me, we had two rooms to ourselves. It was real luxury to us I can tell you.

"But I had ideas of my own too. I wanted to do the place up. Not change it, just give it a face lift you know. It was only a small pub; the front door faced the bar, and there were about half a dozen little square tables to the right as you came in. Behind the bar was a small storage room and behind that were the stairs that led up to our old room. Access to Tom's rooms were through another door next to the bar. The pub didn't hold many people, but still it would take money to decorate and there was only one person I knew who might have some.

"Rose gave me the money – she refused to lend it, saying she didn't think it was going to work and if I was going to throw money away she would rather it was mine than hers – and I gave the place a real birthday.

"And it was a success, once I'd put a few blokes in their place and let them know I wasn't their usual type of landlady.

"Of course, all the men could talk about was the war. There were soldiers waiting for their orders so they could get on their way to the fighting. There were men too old to go; they'd spend their drinking time recounting their adventures in the Crimea and imparting words of wisdom to the young. We got all sorts, all convinced it would be over by Christmas.

"But Christmas came and went. We'd lost a hundred thousand men by then and there was no sign of it letting up.

"That Christmas was special to me and Nina. It was our first Christmas, the first one that hadn't passed over us with nothing more significant to show for it than a dinner at the local mission.

"Christmas 1914 saw us with a bit of money for presents and some mistletoe and even a small tree in the bar. The troops in France had called a Christmas truce and we thought if they can do that, then the least we can do is drink a toast to them.

"But my best and most regular customer was Auntie Ann. The most peculiar change came over her after she recovered from the catalepsy and the shock of waking up in her own coffin, dressed in a shroud. She never set foot inside a church again.

"She never told anyone why; she simply refused to talk about it. But I always believed she'd seen something, had some sort of experience when everyone thought she was dead. She took to gin, mother's ruin we used to call it. Maud walked out; we never saw her again. But every night, from opening to closing, there Ann would be, sitting in the corner with her bottle of gin, muttering incoherently about her mother and father or about the man she'd wanted to marry. Some nights she was unconscious when I went to close up so I just left her there. I couldn't lift her and she'd never have got home in one piece anyway.

"By the summer of 1915 when the war was almost a year old and we had grown used to the changes it wrought upon our lives, nearly all my customers were soldiers, home on leave, but they were the ones who were willing to spend the money. They wanted to get drunk and meet up with a pretty girl for a few nights before they went back to the fighting, not knowing whether they would ever see home again. We had the upper class toffs in, as well, the officers who had come home to see their families, only to find that their families simply did not understand. In the Angel they found other soldiers, other fighting men like themselves who'd been through the same horror.

"I was clearing away early one Monday night. There was no one else there but me and the sound of gentle snoring from Auntie Ann's corner so I thought I might as well put things in order so I could get to bed as soon as we closed.

"I was down on my hands and knees, scrubbing at a beer stain under the counter when I heard the door open and I could see through the gap between the counter and the floor, a pair of army boots and the bottoms of those khaki trousers. It was a familiar sight.

"'I'll be with you in a minute,' I called out.

"The soldier didn't answer, just stayed where he was, which I thought was odd, you know. He didn't move to a table or even up to the bar; he just stood there, a few feet inside the door. My heart began to beat a little faster. It was getting late and it could be a lonely spot when there was nobody about. I began to imagine all sorts of things. Perhaps he had come to rob the place or he might be desperate for female company, if you know what I mean.

"For as long as I could, I delayed the moment when I'd have to get to my feet and face him. I hoped he'd go away if I stayed out of sight long enough, but the longer I left things, the harder they became. My lips were trembling when I finally drew a deep breath and took a bottle of beer from the shelf beneath the counter as I got up, intending to use it as a weapon if I had to defend myself. I straightened up slowly, carefully, not wanting him to see I was afraid. Then my mouth dropped open and the bottle slipped out of my hand, shattering glass all over my nice clean floor.

"It was Daniel."

CHAPTER SEVENTEEN

"Daniel?" Stella repeated, bewildered. "So he wasn't on the Titanic after all?"

"Oh, yes, he was on there all right. He just hadn't drowned and I was too shaken by the experience I'd had, by the vividness of it, to stop and wonder if he might have survived. I'd been too numb with shock, you see, too overwhelmed by so many unfamiliar emotions to realise what I hadn't felt – that emptiness that told me someone I loved was no longer in this world."

It was the first ray of hope Stella had felt from her story, and she smiled, experiencing a little dart of pleasure to know that he'd come back. But Bess had never married. Stella prepared herself for more calamity to come.

"You can imagine my shock," Bess said. "Anyone would be shocked, wouldn't they? I just stood there, gaping. I really believed I was looking at a ghost.

"You know, you read about these things, don't you? How someone's spirit will come and visit their loved one at the moment of death? Well, that's what I thought at first and then I thought 'but that can't be right. Daniel's already dead; has been for more than three years'. I just stared at him, my heart hammering in my chest like it would choke me.

"Then he spoke and I knew he wasn't no ghost.

"'Liza?' He said slowly.

"I was round that bar and in his arms so fast, my feet barely touched the ground. I was so confused. I knew something had happened to him; my little psychic sense had never let me down before.

"But it had this time. He was standing there, right enough, hugging me against him as if he was just as bewildered as me. And there were tears in his eyes. As for me, my face was soaked with them. We must have stood there for a good twenty minutes, clutched together as though we were moulded from the same flesh. I was afraid he'd disappear if I let him go, like in all those dreams I'd had about him, only to lose him all over again when I opened my eyes.

"At last he moved away a little and put his hand on my cheek and kissed me.

"'Liza, Liza,' he said softly. 'You don't know how good it is to see you.'

"'To see me?' I asked. 'How d'you think I feel? I thought you were dead!'

"He gave me a puzzled frown.

"'Now why on earth should you think that?' He asked.

"We moved over to one of the tables, still holding hands, and sat down together. Part of me still expected to wake up at any moment.

"'I had a dream, Daniel,' I started to explain. 'Just after you went away. Except it was more than a dream, it was like a vision. I heard you calling me and I woke up and I knew you were…you were drowning.'

"He caught his breath and a little smile crept over his mouth.

"'So you heard me?' He asked, clearly amazed. 'I didn't expect that. I don't even know why I called your name; I knew you weren't near enough to help, but I thought I was going to die. I really believed I was going to die and it was a natural reaction to call your name. I'm sorry you had to suffer, too. You don't know what it was like, when the ship went down.'

"'Oh, yes, I do. I felt it, every damn freezing wave that came over you, I felt. I was shivering and gasping for breath and I heard you call my name. That's why I thought you were dead.' I looked up at his face, searching for some logic to it all. 'And why aren't you dead? They said there weren't enough lifeboats. They said nearly all the survivors were women and children. How did the ship's barber come to escape?'

"'That shall remain one of life's mysteries,' he replied with a little smile. 'It was terrifying, getting everyone on to the lifeboats. Women who didn't want to leave their husbands, we had to push into the boats. Then there were men who thought they ought to go first, simply because they were wealthy. And other women, older ones mostly, who refused to go, refused to leave their menfolk. I'll never forget those women, standing on the deck, adamant and dignified. They certainly put those wealthy men to shame.'

"'But what about you?' I urged.

"'I went down with the ship, just like you saw me do. It was sinking ever faster and we didn't have time to fill up the lifeboats before we had to lower them. Then the ship tilted backwards and threw everyone over. A great wave came and gobbled me up.' He was trying to make light of his experience, but he wasn't fooling me. His hands had begun to shake. 'I remember floating about, sure I'd freeze to death if I didn't drown first, then someone pulled me into a lifeboat full of women.

"I watched the ship go down, all its lights still blazing and the band still playing. A hymn it was. Nearer my God to Thee. I'll never be able to listen to that hymn again.' He drew a deep, shuddering breath. 'Then the ship tilted up, completely vertical and a great roar came from it.' He shivered and gooseflesh broke out on his neck. 'We watched until there was nothing left but bits of shattered furniture floating about in the water.' He halted abruptly as his voice began to break. 'I don't want to talk about it any more, Liza. I still have nightmares about it.' He studied me for a moment, and I saw the worry in his eyes. Then he said: 'This must mean you didn't get my letter.'

"I hadn't had any letter from him. But it was all right now, wasn't it? It didn't matter, did it, because he was there and I knew now that he was still alive.

"'I never saw any letter, Daniel,' I said after a minute. 'It must have got mislaid, lost in the post.' I snuggled against him. I was so happy in those few moments, I thought my fairy godmother was watching over me. 'I wish you'd never gone, Daniel,' I said. 'It was my fault you went away. I should have married you when I had the chance, instead of being so stubborn.'

"'Oh, Liza!' He cried. There was a little catch in his voice and he pulled himself away from me. 'Don't say that now, please!'

"'What's wrong?' I asked.

"He was leaning forward with his head in his hands and I put my arm around his shoulders. I couldn't understand what he was so upset about. He straightened up, his eyes meeting mine and I knew he was going to tell me something I didn't want to hear.

"'I wrote to you, Liza,' he said after a minute. 'I wrote to you when I got to New York and I told you I still wanted you to marry me. I'd have come back if you'd said yes, but you didn't answer. I should have known you'd have written to me, if only to refuse me again. I should have realised the letter never reached you.'

"'It was nobody's fault, Daniel,' I said. It seemed an awful lot of fuss to make over one missing letter. 'You're here now.'

"He shook his head.

"'No, Liza, I'm not. You see the uniform.' He looked down at his clothes then up again at me. 'I only came to see how you were. I couldn't come half way across the world without seeing you, and my parents. I've been in New York all this time, but when I realised the war didn't look like ending any time soon, I had to come back. England's still my country.'

"'Of course it is. I'm proud of you.'

"I hugged him, but he didn't respond.

"'You don't understand, Liza,' he went on, then paused to take a deep breath. 'When I didn't get any reply from you, I thought it best if I try to forget all about you and make a new life for myself. That's one of the reasons I didn't come back. I left the shipping company – I was too scared to get on another bloody ship – and I got myself a job in New York.'

"There was so much I wanted to say, but I kept quiet. He hadn't finished, hadn't got to the worst part and I didn't want to make things any harder for him, or for myself. Besides, by then I had sort of guessed what he was going to tell me.

"'You know what I'm going to say, don't you?' He asked. I didn't even nod my head. 'I'm married, Liza. Just a couple of months before the war started, I got married.'

"It was like when I thought he had died. That awful grief engulfed me all over again, only this time it was worse, if that were possible. This time it was all mixed up with feelings of anger and jealousy. I had gone from euphoria to devastation in the space of an hour. Daniel was alive; he was alive and he belonged to somebody else. And it was all my fault, wasn't it? Never mind that I hadn't received his letter. I had thrown away three chances to marry him and now it was too late.

"I realised something else as well – I hadn't looked farther than the immediate future when I'd refused him. I'd never been in the habit of looking very far ahead and this had been no exception. What had I expected him to do? Just because my life was tied up with mother, or so I thought, didn't mean his had to come to an end, did it? I was a fool not have seen it.

"I clung to him then, like I'd wanted so badly to cling to him when I thought he was dead. As I held him I heard an echo of James' voice, asking me if I wouldn't make the same sacrifice for Daniel as Rose had made for him. And I knew that if Rose loved her viscount even half as much, she had every right to keep him with her as long as she could and to hell with what everyone else said about it.

"'I'm sorry, Daniel,' I said. 'I'm so sorry.'

"'What have you got to be sorry for?' I felt his fingers on my chin, lifting my face up to look at him. 'That you put me and my welfare before everything else? You were so afraid of letting me down, then you were afraid of saddling me with a senile old woman, you never really listened to me. You wouldn't understand that I wanted you any way I could get you. You're special, Liza, very special. That's nothing to be sorry about.'

"'Don't say any more, Daniel, please. You're only making things worse. Is she an American?'

"I don't know why I asked him that, but I regretted it as soon as the words left my mouth.

"He nodded.

"'Yes, she's...'

"'No. Don't tell me,' I interrupted, putting my fingers to his lips. 'While I don't know her name or anything about her, I can pretend she isn't real, that she's just another bad dream.'

"We sat together in silence for another hour or more. There didn't seem to be anything to say. I couldn't tell him what I'd ached to tell him for three years – how much I loved him – could I?

"'I have to go, Liza,' he finally said. 'I have to report. I'll be leaving for France in the morning, so wish me luck. I'll ask them to let you know if anything happens.'

"I had to laugh at that. I could just see their faces, all those very proper officers who kept the records, when he gave them my name as a contact as well as hers.

"'I won't need to be told if anything happens to you, Daniel. I'll know.'

"I locked the door behind him, wondering if I'd ever see him again. And I wanted him, you know. For the first time in my life, I knew what it was all about, and I wanted him so much I thought I'd die of it."

CHAPTER EIGHTEEN

There were tears in the old lady's eyes. There were tears in Stella's eyes, too. How must she have felt, living all these years with the knowledge of what might have been?

Bess pulled a tissue from her sleeve and used it to dab at her eyes.

"Look at me," she said. "Blubbering like a baby at my time of life."

She started to get stiffly to her feet and Stella moved forward to help her, but she stopped her with a raised hand. She tottered, swaying unsteadily before gaining her balance, then moved to the old-fashioned sideboard and took from its surface a framed photograph, one of the really old sepia photographs in shades of brown and beige that were always printed with a postcard on the back. Stella took it from her and found herself looking at a young soldier with attractive features and curly, fair hair. The subjects of these sort of photographs taken long before the fashion of saying 'cheese' for the camera, always looked stern. But this young man had a little smile playing about the corners of his mouth, a mischievous smile, as though he couldn't really bring himself to take the procedure seriously.

"The writing at the bottom right hand corner was faded; she had to bring it close to her eyes to see that it simply said: To dearest Liza, from Daniel, with love.

"I never expected to get over it," Bess was saying as she settled herself back in her armchair. "And I was right. But life must go on, as they say, and there were lots of things happening to distract me.

"I'd got a lad in to run the pub for me during the day, so I could carry on working for the Countess. He was nineteen and had been turned down for service because of a club foot.

"She was a lovely lady, the Countess and she was having a lot of fun at her friends' expense. Nearly all the aristocracy had lost most of their servants, the men to the war and the girls to the munitions factories. It was only the very old ones, who'd been with them for years, who stayed on. They'd had to close down part of their houses and economize on food and clothes.

"Countess Hazelforth thought it was very funny, the way they made so much fuss about it, because she'd never had any servants to speak of until she came to England. She'd been used to hardships as a girl after the American civil war, and she thought it would do the English nobility a lot of good to shift for themselves for once.

"I didn't see Rose for a while after Daniel's visit. I knew I'd end up telling her and I couldn't bring myself to go anywhere where I'd have to talk about him. I didn't even tell Nina he was still alive, and that was really selfish because I knew how happy she'd be to know. But when Rose wrote, telling me that James was home on leave, I couldn't miss the opportunity of seeing him.

"I sat listening to his tales of adventure, though neither Rose nor I really believed in them. He was exaggerating the excitement while playing down the dirt and disease, the bad organisation. It was a filthy war and half the men weren't even sure what they were fighting for.

"I hadn't said anything beyond 'hello' since I'd arrived.

"'You're very subdued, Bess,' he said suddenly.

"He looked so concerned, I felt I could tell him all my troubles. As if he didn't have enough of his own.

"'Something's happened, hasn't it?' Rose asked.

"I nodded.

"'It's Daniel,' I said, almost inaudibly. 'He's alive.'

"Rose sprang to her feet, a smile spreading across her face, but James could see there was more to it.

"'You don't seem too happy about it,' he said. 'Do you want to tell us the rest?'

"I sat staring at my hands for a long time. I didn't think I'd be able to put it into words, didn't know if I could keep my voice steady. Eventually, I looked up and saw that his eyes were gentle, ready to understand.

"'He's married,' I said bluntly.

"'Oh, Bess,' Rose cried. She was beside me in an instant, her arms around me.

"'It's my own fault, though, isn't it? I could have married him, but I didn't. So why do I feel so betrayed? Why do I keep thinking he shouldn't have done it, when it was me who sent him away?' I turned to James for an answer. 'Would you have done that? If Rose sent you away, would you marry someone else?'

"He moved to sit down on the other side of me and took my hand.

"'Probably,' he answered gently. 'It wouldn't be so good, and it wouldn't be what I wanted, but I expect I'd find someone else. So will you.'

"I shook my head vehemently. I knew I'd never want anyone else.

"'I wish I'd carried on believing he was dead,' I said bitterly. 'At least when he was dead he was still mine.'

"James put his arm around me and kissed the top of my head, as though I was really his sister as well as hers, and I came home that day thinking how lucky she was to have him.

"And I said a little prayer for him. The lists of fatalities were already so long, we began to wonder where they were all coming from. I'd never realised there were that many men in the country and now there were so many being killed. Would James survive? Would Daniel? I had a sense of foreboding that wasn't exclusively mine, that was shared by everyone who had menfolk at the front.

"Rose grew more popular as the war progressed. Soldiers home on leave were an even better audience than the usual crowd. They had to enjoy every minute, in case it turned out to be their last. And she was always so happy when James was home. I understood now, like I never thought I would ever understand, but it took a lot for me to admit to myself that I'd have done the same in her shoes. I only wished I had the chance.

"Just before Christmas, she came to see me, her eyes dancing with excitement.

"'Oh, Bess,' she cried, catching my hand. 'Can you keep a secret? Of course you can! Silly question!'

"I had no idea what she was so pleased about. Perhaps they've run off and got married or something, I thought.

"'I'm going to have a baby,' she announced. 'Isn't it wonderful?'

"'Is it?' I asked, astonished.

"'Of course it is! don't you see what this means? We'll be married, whether he can earn a living after the war or not. And I'm going to give him a child, Bess. You can't imagine how that makes me feel.'

"She was right there; I couldn't imagine. There was a time when Rose had worried about the opinions of people, but her love affair had put a swift end to such minor concerns. I'd have thought she'd be panic stricken, like Edie was, but of course she loved James and she knew what he was likely to do better than I did. The first thought that entered my head was: 'what will his family say about this?'

"James was the sort of son every parent would want and I thought they were putting themselves through unnecessary torment, staying on bad terms with him. His chances of coming home from the war were about as low as every other man's and if he was killed, then how would they feel?

"As the new year of 1916 opened, Rose began to make plans for the future offspring. She couldn't wait to see James. She had written several letters and torn them all up before she was satisfied with the result, and she waited for every post to receive his reply. Her elation was contagious; I soon found myself looking forward to James' return almost as much as she did.

"The knock on the front door was loud and insistent, like someone demanding entry, and it reminded me of the night the police had brought mother home. It was the same sort of sound, arrogant and forceful. Our eyes met and I was sure the same memory had come to her.

"She put down her cup and got up to open the door. A lot of music hall people kept a maid, but not her. She always said she wouldn't know what to do with one, that she'd feel awkward having a total stranger in the house.

"I heard his voice in the hall and I jumped up. I thought it was James. The timbre and the accent were very like his, but when Rose came back, she wore an angry frown and she was followed by a tall man with iron grey hair and a defeated stoop to his shoulders. I knew who he was straight away; he looked so much like his son.

"No introductions were made. She was very nervous and I thought perhaps he'd heard about the baby and had come to try to buy her off, offer her money to leave his son alone.

"She asked him to sit down and he perched himself on the edge of the chair as though he might need to escape in a hurry. Rose didn't say anything, just waited for him to speak, and I think she was ready for an argument; she seemed on the defensive. When he finally spoke it was with a broken voice, and he wouldn't meet her eyes, just kept looking at his hands where he had them clasped in his lap.

"'I am here,' he said, 'because it is what my son would have wished.'

"Ominous words 'what my son would have wished'. He didn't need to say any more.

CHAPTER NINETEEN

"Her very substance seemed to crumble and melt, reminding me of Nina's wax doll. The Earl left, so quietly that neither of us even noticed he had gone until much later.

"I sat with her for the rest of that day, then I had to go and open the pub. My thoughts were full of plans for the coming birth, though I didn't mention them to Rose. I tried to sort out in my mind what was her best course of action, perhaps a move to the country where she could pretend to be a war widow. Lord knows, there were enough of them about. She always suspected it would come to an end some day, and I knew from bitter experience that it was better for her this way than having him alive and married to someone else. But she was so completely devastated, as though her own life had come to an end. Perhaps I had looked like that to other people; who could tell? But I'd managed to put it behind me, after a fashion, and I thought she would too.

"I grieved for him as well. I hadn't known when James died; we were never that close and I was surprised to feel his loss, feel it as other people felt loss, with no foreknowledge to harden me. Perhaps it was only the awful sense of waste, that such a man, so young and vital and kind, was no more.

"She carried on with her shows, just like always, but people kept asking me what was wrong, why did she keep singing more and more morbid songs? I didn't tell them; it was none of their business.

"I locked up the pub one afternoon and went round to her house. When I got there, I let myself in, same as always. She was just sitting, staring into space, like she'd been every time I'd seen her since we got the news. Except that day, the curtains were drawn in every room and she was sitting in the dark, all dressed black.

"'The funeral's today,' she said, not even looking at me. I should have guessed. People always used to close their curtains when there was a death in the house. They don't seem to do it so much now. 'They've had his body brought back,' she went on. 'That's what's taken so long. But I can't go, can I? I can't even go and tell him goodbye.'

"I didn't know what to say to comfort her. There wasn't any comfort to be had in words; I knew that better than anyone. But the next thing she said shocked me.

"'I wish I were dead, too.'

"Now, that's something people often say, without really meaning it. What shocked me was that she did mean it. I could tell by the determination in her, the hard glitter in her eyes.

"'Don't talk daft, Rose,' I said. 'James wouldn't have wanted that, would he?'

"'I'm past caring what James would have wanted. I'd like to think of myself for once, but I can't do it, can I? I've got the baby to think of. I've got no right to decide the child's fate, have I?' She turned to me and took both my hands in hers. 'Wherever he is, he's watching me. I can feel him here, in every room, can almost hear his laughter.'

"She'd have felt better if she could have done something, something to make things final. That's what funerals and memorial services are all about really, isn't it? A way to say goodbye and start living your life. She never had that comfort; she had to keep herself in the background.

"Then Alfred popped up again. I can't describe what I felt about him, except to say that his mere presence offended me. I thought he had a damned cheek, hanging about after my sister. She was so beautiful, you know, and although we never had much, compared to him she was a real lady.

"I found myself with a lot of time on my hands as far as the Countess' work was concerned, with most of my skills donated to the war effort, so I used the time to make myself a new coat. It was February and still cold, so I thought I might as well get some wear out of it before the spring came. It was the first brand new coat I'd ever owned, royal blue it was, and I was very proud of it. Skirts had crept up by a few inches and I'd made my coat with a hobble skirt, which was the fashion. It had a fitted waist and black edging and buttons.

"I'd never made an outdoor coat before and I thought I'd show it off to Rose, perhaps cheer her up a bit by telling her how many times I'd had to unpick it before I got it right. We could always have a laugh together, me and Rose. I didn't hold out much hope, but you never knew. I thought I might be able to take her mind off James for a couple of hours.

"But when I let myself into her house, I found Alfred sitting in her parlour, drinking tea. At first I thought he must have forced his way in. I could never see her inviting him there. She always treated him with a sort of indulgent amusement, even when he was turning up at the stage door every night. He'd never brought flowers or anything. He seemed to think his presence was enough.

"'Hello, Bess,' he greeted me.

"I gave him one of my withering glares.

"'What are you doing here?' I demanded.

"He grinned at me, all smug and self-satisfied, while Rose just sat watching us. Her face was devoid of any expression, as though she was in some sort of trance. She had been that way for weeks.

"'Your sister invited me,' he said, putting his cup down on her polished walnut side table instead of in the saucer where it belonged.

"'Why?' I asked. I turned to look at Rose but she didn't seem to have heard. 'Rose?'

"'You remember Alfred, don't you Bess?' She said slowly.

"'Of course I remember him. But why is he here? And why isn't he in uniform?'

"'They wouldn't have me in the army,' he said quickly. 'Old ticker not so strong, you know.'

"'There's nothing wrong with you that a day's work wouldn't cure,' I told him. 'Wriggled out of it somehow, have you?'

"'I do my bit,' he protested. 'I've got myself into the munitions now. The money's a lot better.'

"'God help us all if they're letting the likes of you handle explosives.'

"He didn't answer, but he grinned at me again and that made me mad. I couldn't stand to be in the same room with him a minute longer. He was up to something, I knew that, but I couldn't stay to find out what. I told Rose I'd be back when she'd got rid of him and I left. I'd always disliked him, and when there's a war on a healthy man should be in the forces; I wasn't the only one who thought so.

"I still had Nina to think about. She was at a very impressionable age and I didn't have too much experience at playing parent to an adolescent. She had got herself involved with the suffragettes and was out every weekend marching through London with banners. I was frightened she'd get herself arrested. They treated those poor women like scum in Holloway, force feeding them and bullying them. She'd got some idea in her head about going to France to nurse the wounded if the war lasted until she was old enough. She might have been safer there than running around with the suffragettes.

"Then one night she came home and told me about the poster she'd seen outside the theatre.

"'It was in letters a foot high,' she said. 'Romany Princess – final performance. What's going on with her, Bess?'

"I hadn't told Nina about the baby. Rose had been only a few weeks gone when James was killed and she was only just beginning to show. With careful dressing, she could still manage to cover it up and I could only guess that she was giving the stage a rest until after the birth. It was the 'final performance' bit that worried me.

"'I wish I knew. What on earth does she think she's playing at? Throwing everything away, just when she needs to work to take her mind off things.'

"Nina shrugged.

"'Search me,' she said flippantly. 'That Viscount of hers must have been quite something.'

"It was only a superficial remark on her part, but she couldn't have guessed the image it had conjured up. I saw James clearly, his dark hair, his kind expression, and I could scarcely believe that he wasn't coming back.

"'Yes, he was,' I murmured, half to myself.

"'There was a bit in the paper about him. Did you see it?' I shook my head while she rummaged in her chest of drawers and brought out yesterday's paper. 'Here it is,' she said, reading it out. 'James, Viscount Hartford, posthumously awarded the Victoria Cross. Then there's a paragraph about his war record.'

"The medal meant as much to me as this bloody telegram I got this morning. What good was it? She gave me the paper so I could see for myself, but I only glanced at the article. I never read newspapers if I could help it, especially with the war on. Everything in them was so depressing, but Nina liked to keep herself informed.

"It sounds awful to say, but mother dying had been the best thing that could have happened to Nina. She'd had to grow up in a hurry, but at the same time she'd developed a confidence that she never would have had. When mother was around, always snapping and acting mysterious when she asked questions about life, then later not even knowing who Nina was half the time, the kid had been like a frightened rabbit. Now she seemed to like herself more and the suffragettes were partly responsible. She'd found herself a cause, something she thought worth fighting for, and she'd got a personality all her own out of it. Mother would never have allowed her to get mixed up with them and I think it's fair to say that she rather enjoyed the war years.

"It was a good thing I had that young lad to look after the pub, or I might never have seen that last performance.

"She sang a song about a girl who hanged herself because her sweetheart left her. I can't remember the title, but it was a miserable song. Rose always liked a sad song, but nothing as miserable as that, and she sang it as though she wasn't really there, you know. There was no feeling behind the words like there usually was with her singing.

"I went backstage to see her and who do you think I saw going into her dressing room? Alfred. I had half a mind to go home instead, but I couldn't just leave things.

"She looked ill. There were dark circles around her eyes and she was so thin, it must have been weeks since she'd had a proper meal. Alfred was sitting beside her at her little dressing table, watching as she cleaned her face.

"'Hello, Bess,' he said as I opened the door. 'Nice to see you again.'

"'I wish I could say the same,' I answered.

"I felt instinctively that it wasn't a good idea to antagonise him, but I couldn't hold my tongue. He'd obviously managed to worm his way back into her life and I had a feeling that to offend him was to offend her.

"'Would you mind, Alfred?' I said, as civilly as I could manage. 'I'd like to speak to my sister alone.'

"He shot her a glance and when she said nothing he looked up at me with a frown.

"'Anything you've got to say to her, you can say in front of me,' he said.

"I don't know how I kept my temper.

"'Listen Alfred,' I said, leaning toward him threateningly. 'Rose and I have many, many secrets that you'll never be a party to, no matter how close you think you've got. I'm her sister and I've got a right to speak to her in private. So push off.'

"'Rose,' he said, turning to her. 'Are you going to let her speak to me like that?'

"She looked from one to the other of us languidly, as though she hadn't heard a word we'd exchanged and wouldn't have been interested if she had.

"'It's all right, Alf,' she said at last. 'Let Bess have her say. It won't make any difference to us.'

"He got up and left, slamming the door behind him; but what was all this 'us' business?

"'Rose,' I said firmly, 'you will get over James, you know. You'll never forget him, but you'll reach a point when you can remember him without feeling so bad. And hanging about with that character is only making things worse.'

"'Why's that, Bess?'

"'Why? Because he's so awful he makes James seem even better than he was.'

"'Alf's not that bad,' she said quietly. 'I wish you didn't dislike him so much.'

"'Why not? Why should you want me to like him?'

"She gave me a no-nonsense look, as though she was daring me to argue with what she said next.

"'Because I'm going to marry him,' she said firmly. 'And it's no good you complaining. The date's set, it's all fixed. I don't have any choice.'

"'What do you mean, you don't have any choice?' I demanded.

"'You know very well what I mean,' she answered calmly, too calmly really, as though nothing really mattered. 'I've got to marry someone, and Alf's the only one available at the moment.'

"I was furious. How could she throw herself away like that? She hadn't cared what anyone thought when she was living with James, so why now?

"She got up and went behind her screen to change, so I could see nothing of her but the top of her head, couldn't read her expression as her voice drifted out to me.

"'I can't have the baby out of wedlock,' she went on. 'James would have married me, had he lived, in spite of all the difficulties. But he's gone and I have to think of the child now.'

"A child born illegitimately was better off dead. I've even known people pray for the poor kid to be born dead, rather than be born a bastard. And their lives weren't worth living, as though it was somehow their fault. I don't think much of today's standards, but that's one change I thank God for. I could understand why she was doing what she was, but that didn't stop me from trying to find another solution.

"'Does he know?' I asked her.

"'Yes.'

"'And just what sort of man is he, to marry a woman knowing full well she's carrying another man's child?'

"She stepped out, struggling to fasten her gown and I had the strangest impression that this was a stranger standing before me. I couldn't get close to her, I no longer shared her secret thoughts and wishes.

"'Not a very good one, apparently,' she answered glibly, 'as I'm sure you were about to point out. But he wants something from me, too.

They're not calling up married men, so it'll keep him out of the war.'

"I already suspected he was a coward, but he was worse than I thought. And when I thought of Daniel, coming all the way home to help defend his country, when he could have stayed safe in America, I could cheerfully have strangled Alfred.

"'And you're quite happy to marry someone like that, are you?' I demanded.

"'Not happy, no,' she answered mournfully. 'But the child has to come first.' She paused, staring dreamily into space. 'It must have happened that last night, before he went back to France.' She was remembering their last night together, I was sure, but I hadn't the experience to imagine what it was like and I felt a sudden surge of resentment because of that lack. 'I can't let James' only child be known as a bastard,' she went on. 'It doesn't matter who I marry, so long as they give the poor little mite a name.'

"'There's got to be another way, Rose,' I said, clutching her wrist. I was frantic to find her a way out. Having Reg as a brother-in-law was bad enough, but Alfred made him look like St. George. 'Why don't you go away,' I said. 'Find yourself a little place in the country, or at the seaside, where nobody knows you. You can tell people you're married to a soldier and when you kill him off, nobody will be any the wiser.'

"She laughed then, but it was a bitter laugh, a laugh I'd never heard from her before.

"'And what am I supposed to tell the child when it grows up and asks about its father? The same tale? The same lie?'

"'But Rose...' I couldn't think of anything else for a moment, then inspiration struck. 'What about the Earl?' I said. 'This is his grandchild; he might want to help.'

"'The Earl?' She spat venomously. 'You think I'd ask him for anything? If it weren't for him, we'd have been married months ago and I could hold up my head as the widow of a war hero. My child will never know his father died for his country. Because of the Earl, he'll grow up believing his father's a snivelling little coward who was too scared to risk his precious neck. Because of the Earl, James had to spend his last days before the war shamefully for him, living off my earnings. I'll manage without his Lordship, thank you very much.

"There was no point in arguing with her. I had half a mind to tell him myself, but I knew she'd never forgive me.

"She managed the last hook on her dress, then sat down at the dressing table and picked up her hairbrush. She pulled her hair forward and began to brush it with determined strokes.

"'There's one thing you can do for me, Bess,' she said, interrupting my half made plans. 'Before I marry Alfred, I'm going to sign my house over to you and transfer all my money into your name.'

"I just stared at her. She was quite well off by then; not rich, but comfortable.

"'What d'you want to go and do that for?' I demanded. 'You're going to need every penny yourself.'

"'I thought you were the one who was so wise and all knowing, you could tell me and everyone else how to run our lives,' she said spitefully, then she saw the shock on my face and she took my hand. 'I'm sorry,' she said. 'I shouldn't have said that. I don't know why I did, really.'

"'Perhaps because it's true. Perhaps because you've always thought of me as an interfering know-all.'

"'No,' she said, shaking her head. 'I've always thought you were too quick to judge, but that's a common enough fault. And you don't always give people credit for knowing their own minds. I love you, Bess. You and Nina are the only people I do love, but you've become very bitter since that business with Daniel. I'm not stupid. I've thought of the only way out, and this is it.'

"I hugged her. She was right, of course. I had become bitter; I'd weaved a solid shell of self-sufficiency around myself so I wouldn't have to care about anyone, ever again. But I was seeing that same change come over her, seeing her become hard and self-centred and it didn't suit her.

"'So why do you want to give me all your money?' I asked.

"'Because I don't want Alf getting his hands on it. Once we're married, he'll be entitled to everything I own. He thinks he's marrying property and money, and I don't see any reason to tell him otherwise, not until I have to. If anything happens to me, I want my child to have the house and the money, not Alfred.'

"Her words sustained me as I sat and listened to the vicar joining them in holy matrimony. It was the only thing that kept me from fleeing the church in disgust, knowing that she'd gone into it with her eyes open, that while he thought he was using her, it was actually she who was using him.

"She wore cream for her wedding. It was a plain silk dress with a simple lace veil and the colour set tongues wagging for weeks afterwards.

"Even during the service, she was calm and serene, as though nothing could touch her ever again, and she still had that hard glitter in her eyes. It broke my heart to see her walk down that aisle with her arm linked through Alfred's, and him walking beside her where James should have been. I missed him that day more than ever, but I don't suppose I could have missed him half as much as she did. I couldn't have done it myself, married someone else. I admired her courage, for she was doing this for James' child, but if I couldn't have Daniel, nobody else would ever do, not even for the sake of his child.

"They didn't bother with a reception, didn't even have a few drinks at home for the family. She didn't tell Edie and Reg until it was all over. There was just me, Nina and Alfred's spinster sister from Southend.

"Alfred was insufferably smug about it, kept referring to the house as his and I think he harboured ideas about giving up the factory and living off her money. That was ironic, when you think that she'd have been happy to work for James, but he was too much of a gentleman to let her do it.

"If he hadn't been, she might have lived to receive a fancy telegram from the Queen.

"Alfred didn't know that she had no intention of going back on the stage after the baby came, and he didn't know that she'd given all her money to me. I never touched it, not then. I kept it in the bank, in a separate account, in case she needed anything. But the only things she bought were clothes and equipment for the baby, and later on more clothes as he grew bigger.

"She wrote and told Edie about the baby once her and Alfred had been married a couple of months. I was the only one who knew the child wasn't his, though I wish she could have told

Edie that its father was a viscount. Edie wrote very smugly because her beautiful sister, who she'd always envied, had ended up married to Alfred.

"Just to rub salt in the wound and make herself feel more superior, Edie sent Rose all those loose dresses she'd worn when she was expecting Mary. I was helping Rose sort through them, a great pile of them, far more than she could have needed in those few months. I'd only seen Edie a couple of times when she was wearing these sort of clothes, and one of them was that day she'd come up to see mother. I recognised the dress she'd been wearing at once. You could hardly miss it; I thought it was quite hideous with its big collar and I'll never forget mother's face when Edie walked in dressed in mauve. Even without mother's peculiar superstition, the dress was far too conspicuous for someone in the family way, but just like Edie's taste.

"'Oh, dear,' said Rose as she pulled the dress out of the parcel. 'I don't think I dare wear this, do you? Not after all the years of hearing how unlucky the colour is. Still, it's a shame to throw it out. It's good quality. What do you think? Shall we give it to the mission?'

"'Best way,' I replied absently, as I ran my hand over the pockets to make sure there was nothing in them. It would be just like Edie to leave a dirty hankie, hoping Rose'd wash it and return it to her.

"What I found instead was an open envelope, with the letter still inside. I've still got that letter; I think you're entitled to see it."

She rummaged in the wooden chest once more. Stella had given up speculating by then. Everything she did and said came as a complete surprise.

"Here," she said, handing her the faded envelope.

The letter inside was so old, had been folded for so many years that each crease was split and Stella had to open it very slowly, to avoid tearing it even further.

Liza, the neat handwriting read, *I am staying in New York. I can't face another sea crossing, but I thought I'd write in case you had been thinking the worst. I still want to marry you, even if I have to cross that bloody ocean again to do it, but I know you won't thank me for asking a third time. It's up to you now, Liza. If I don't hear from you, I'll have my answer. Love you, Daniel.*

It was dated April 1912.

Stella tossed the letter into the old woman's lap, almost as if she were afraid it might burn her fingers.

"So I knew what had happened to Daniel's letter," Bess said as she placed the ancient document back in her chest. "It hadn't got lost in the post at all."

"She'd taken it from the landlord," Stella suggested, wanting to supply any explanation but the real one, "and forgotten to give it to you. That's what happened, isn't it?"

Bess gave her that knowing look, but made no reply.

"Seeing the dress brought that morning graphically back to mind," Bess went on. "I recalled how I watched her as she walked toward the Angel, the sullen expression on her face. I saw her in my mind's eye, talking to Tom in the yard below, coming through the back door. And I remembered how long it had been before I heard her tread on the stairs. I knew what she'd been doing now, didn't I? She'd been reading my letter down there, deciding how she could use it to her own advantage.

"What I didn't know what why she had kept it, why she had said nothing about it.

"I could see us all, sitting in our room discussing Daniel's death, and I found it hard to believe that Edie had kept it to herself that she was the only one who knew he was alive. It wasn't like her. She always liked to be first with the news.

"I must have sat there for ages, on Rose's bed, just staring at Daniel's neat handwriting, and I could feel the anger and bitterness mounting inside me. Here was Daniel's letter, here in my hands, four years too late. And all because of Edie.

"'Bess? What's wrong?' Rose asked, taking my hand.

"Her voice startled me, made me jump. I'd forgotten where I was, or that there was anyone with me. I stared at her for a minute, wondering whether the shock would do the baby any harm. But I couldn't care very much about her or the baby or anything else. Finally, I handed her the letter.

"Her eyes skimmed it swiftly.

"'Oh, Bess!' She cried. 'Wherever did you find this?'

"'In Edie's pocket,' I answered bitterly.

"I was so angry, I could barely put a sentence together, but at the same time I wanted to cry."

CHAPTER TWENTY

"I'd never been to Edie's house before. Reg wouldn't have wanted the neighbours to know about her family, I don't suppose. We were clean enough, but our clothes were old and out of date and our accents weren't up to scratch, either.

"Well, he was the last person I was worried about that day. I got the train out to Potters Bar, then asked someone the way to her street. It wasn't far from the station, as it happens, and I was quite prepared to sit on the doorstep and wait if she wasn't in.

"She lived in a tree-lined avenue, in a terraced house with lace curtains at the windows and red and cream paintwork on the frames around the sash windows.

"I opened the little wooden gate and marched up the path, not knowing whether I was going to kill her or simply burst into tears.

"Her face was a picture when she opened the door and saw me standing there. Her eyes and mouth were round and startled, and her face drained of colour.

"'Bess,' she said. 'What are you doing here? Has something happened to Rose?'

"'A letter would be good enough for you if it had,' I snapped as I pushed her aside and made my way into the house. I took Daniel's letter out of my coat pocket. 'This is what I've come about.'

"I waved the envelope in her face as I spoke and she frowned at it. She must have forgotten all about it, otherwise she'd never have left it there for me to find.

"'What's that, Bess?' She asked, genuinely puzzled.

"You could always tell when she was lying – her face would flush and she couldn't meet your eyes if she was lying.

"'It's a letter, Edie,' I replied. 'A letter addressed to me, except I've only just received it, by way of a pocket in a gaudy mauve dress.'

"Recognition came over her face suddenly and two bright circles of red appeared on her cheeks, like clown make-up.

"'Keep your voice down, Bess, please,' she said. 'I've just got Mary off to sleep.

"As she shut the front door, she gave a quick glance up and down the street to make sure no one had heard me, no one who would tell Reg about it.

"'Well,' I demanded. 'What've you got to say for yourself!'

"She turned away from me and walked down the hall and into a small parlour containing an abundance of shining brass, green velvet and heavy fringe. Everything was spotless, as though it were a showroom in a furniture shop instead of a home. She sat down on a big, upholstered settee and gestured for me to sit opposite.

"I hadn't planned what I was going to say to her, that was never my way. But as I sat watching her, with every hair perfect in her elegant hairdo and the latest fashion adorning her skinny body, I wondered if I could actually tell her what she'd done without more of those damned tears falling. The thought of weeping before her, of having her know how much she'd hurt me, was almost worse than the reality of it. It was a facet of Edie's warped personality that she'd probably find it funny that Daniel had gone and married someone else.

"'Well,' I demanded again. 'Are you going to deny that you kept this letter from me? Left me thinking Daniel was dead all this time?'

"At least she had the grace to look shamefaced about it; I suppose that was something, but I knew it wouldn't take her long to try and turn the tables, try to blame me. That was always her way.

"'I'd forgotten all about that,' she said at last.

"'Why, Edie?' I asked her, and I struggled to keep my misery in check. 'Why did you do it?'

"A nasty laugh escaped her, full of bitterness and contempt.

"'Why do you think I did it?' She cried, leaning forward. There was a grim little line on her mouth that spoiled what little beauty she might have had. 'You were the one who interfered in my life, remember? You were the one who went to meet Sam and told him all about Reg. I told you then I'd get even with you for that, and when I saw that letter, I had my chance.'

"I couldn't quite comprehend what she was saying. It hadn't occurred to me that she still harboured a grudge against me, not after I did all that work on her wedding dress and went with her to see Reg. I can see now that having me witness his reaction that day only made her even more resentful toward me. But I didn't see it then, and I thought the whole thing had blown over long before her wedding. Perhaps it had. Perhaps it was the aftermath, her experience of life out in the sticks with her boring little house and her boring little husband. Her resentment must have been fermenting all those months. She was too young to give up her youth and she blamed me for it. Edie always had to blame someone.

"'You silly cow!' I shouted. 'You think there's no difference between what I did then and what you did, letting me think Daniel was dead? You got married, didn't you? You've got a nice house in a nice neighbourhood. It doesn't look to me as though you've done too badly for yourself.'

"She leaned back in her seat and stretched her arm out along the back of the settee, resting her chin on her clenched fist as she stared through the lace curtains. There was a bitter line across her mouth and loathing in her eyes. Suddenly she turned back to me.

"'Look around you,' she said, her voice rising as she gestured with her hands. 'Do I really fit so well into this setting? I'm trapped, Bess, trapped with the endless tea parties and perfect manners and having to watch every word I say. And it's so quiet here. Reg never meant anything to me, you know that! I didn't even like him much; I still don't. And he hasn't touched me since that one time. He won't either. He just turns up his nose like I was dirty or something. Just one time, Bess, that's all. Just one mistake and I'll have to pay for it for the rest of my life. And it's not fair! It wasn't my fault, either. I was always told you couldn't get pregnant the first time. Everyone I knew told me that – and it was a lie!'

"That was one of the old wives' tales we all believed then, like having a bath when you were pregnant would drown the baby, that was another one.

"'So just because you couldn't get your own way, you thought you'd spoil it for me, did you? I demanded.

"'You didn't want Daniel, anyway!' She argued, her voice coming out in a small shriek, as it always did when she was trying to justify herself. 'You'd turned him down twice. How was I supposed to know you'd changed your mind?'

"She wasn't going to make me feel guilty again, even if what she said was true. Whether I wanted him or not wasn't the point.

"'What about at mother's funeral?' I said. 'You heard what I was saying to Rose.' I frowned as the memory suddenly returned to me. 'That's why you left in such a hurry, wasn't it? You were afraid you'd give yourself away by going all red in the face, weren't you?'

"'I was half a mind to tell you then,' she said. 'But then I saw how you and Rose and Nina were all so chummy, and Auntie Ann fussing round you. I'd lost a mother, too, you know, but she didn't care about that. You'd have thought I was just an acquaintance, the way you were all carrying on. So I changed my mind and I went home.'

"Was she right? I was too mad to even think about whether we might have hurt her feelings, much less regret it.

"'You don't know how I felt that day, the day I saw your letter,' she went on. 'I'd had a lecture from Reg. He didn't know I'd gone up to London to see mother. He'd have gone mad if he knew. That's the only reason I went, really, to get back at him, to do something he wouldn't approve of. And I wanted to be with proper people, just for once, to be myself and not have to pretend I was something better. How would you like it stuck with a pompous, sanctimonious snob like him when I could have had Sam if you hadn't interfered.

"'I was so excited when I stepped off the train, so pleased to be back in London again. But I knew I couldn't stay there, that I'd have to come home and live this life that he'd mapped out for me. That made me angry enough, but when I saw that letter from Daniel, saying he still wanted you, I was so jealous.

"'I didn't know what it meant at first, didn't know what he was doing in New York to begin with. Then, when I realised you all thought he'd gone down with the Titanic, and mother was so nasty, I thought it would serve you right if you carried on thinking he was dead. I knew you'd find out eventually.'

"Oh, I found out all right,' I spat, leaning close to her so that my face was almost touching hers. 'Just last summer, I found out.'

"She gave me a nervous little smile.

"'Well, then,' she said. 'That's come out all right then, hasn't it?'

"I shook my head, as much in disbelief as in denial.

"'No,' I answered menacingly. 'No, it hasn't come out all right. Because you never gave me his letter, because he never got an answer, he went and married someone else. That's the result of your interference and I just hope you can live with yourself. I know I couldn't.'

"I marched out of the house and slammed the door behind me. I knew I'd woken her little girl up; I could hear her start to cry as I hurried down the path and I was gratified to see several of the neighbours standing in the street, looking toward the house. I suppose they wanted to know what all the shouting was about. I'd given them food for gossip for weeks to come; Reg was bound to find out.

"I knew I'd never speak to her again, and I never did."

***

Stella felt ashamed of being so presumptuous, of meeting this remarkable old lady with her mind already made up about her, about what she had done to Stella's grandmother. There were two sides to every story and she'd been raised on just one of them.

"So this is what the argument was really about?" Stella asked. "It wasn't your fault at all, was it? It was Grandma's."

Bess smiled reflectively.

"Who knows?" She replied. "Perhaps it was my fault. If I hadn't interfered with her, she wouldn't have interfered with me and I'd be a widow now instead of an old maid. Mind you, 'old maid' implies an aged virgin, doesn't it? So I wouldn't be that, either."

Stella guessed that her romantic notions of unrequited love were about to be dispelled, but she wasn't going to ask. Bess'd tell her if she felt like it. That was one thing she had learned about her during that long day.

"She had no right to open your letter, Auntie," Stella said. "She certainly shouldn't have kept it. It was a nasty thing to do. She must have seen how important it was."

"Oh, she did. That's why she kept it, as she said, to get even. But when I told Sam about her, I believed I was doing the right thing. When she kept my letter from me, she knew damned well she was doing wrong. I've never been able to forgive her for that, even after all these years. I expect she felt the same about me, when she sat there in her fancy parlour and imagined what life would have been like with Sam. I daresay she'd have been just as miserable with him, but she wouldn't have seen that. She'd have painted a lovely picture and told herself that I'd kept her from it. That's what she was like. Still, I didn't ask you here to tell you about Edith, remember. Perhaps I shouldn't have mentioned it, but I had to really. It's part of the story."

"You want to tell me about Rose," Stella prompted. "I can't imagine what you want to tell me. There isn't much that anybody can't discover for themselves."

Stella heard the note of peevishness in her own voice, but she could do nothing about it. She was still vexed to learn that this early century murderess was so close a relative.

"That's where you're wrong, Miss," Bess snapped. "There's nobody knows the truth about her, not now. Nobody except me and I can't let it stay that way. I'd turn in my grave if I thought there was no one left who knew. That's why you're here.'

CHAPTER TWENTY ONE

"There isn't much to say about the rest of the war, except that it went on. We lived from day to day, same as we always had, hoping to put enough food in our bellies to keep body and soul together. There were Zeppelins bombing London as well as the coast, but it wasn't like the second war, when the Krauts were dropping bombs on us and we had to spend most nights in the underground station.

"It was at the end of May, in 1916, that little Jimmy was born and that was the day I found out what Rose had really let herself in for.

"I was woken up one morning before dawn by someone hammering on the front door of the Angel. It took a while for the knocking to penetrate my sleep and when I finally got a shawl round my shoulders and opened the door I found a little boy of about ten standing there. He was breathing erratically, as though he couldn't have run another step if his life depended on it, and there were tears making channels through the dirt on his cheeks.

"'You've got to come, Missus!' He cried, swiping at his wet eyes. I hadn't got a clue who he was. 'She sent me to get you. All the way from Dalston I've run, so you will come, won't you?'

"I didn't ask questions. There was only one person who could have sent him.

"He followed me through the pub and waited while I pulled on some clothes. We ran all the way down the street together, until I saw and stopped a passing hackney and we both climbed in. Any other time, I might have felt the luxury of such an act, never having been in one before, but I was too alarmed to even realise it. I finished dressing the cab, buttoning my shoes and hooking up my dress as I questioned the boy.

"'Now then,' I said. 'Who are you and what's been happening?'

"'I live next door,' he answered. He'd managed to get his breath back, but panic still shone in his eyes. 'Me mum 'eard 'er banging through the wall. Woke 'er up, it did, then she called me and told me to come and get you. That's all I know. I don't know what's wrong with 'er. She won't die, will she?'

"'Of course not,' I said quickly.

"I wished I could be as certain as I tried to sound, but there was no telling. All I could think was, where was Alfred?

"When we got to Rose's house, I sent the boy home and let myself in. She was lying upstairs, making little moaning sounds that scared the life out of me. There was no sign of Alfred. I sat on the bed and took her hand.

"'Thank God,' she mumbled. 'I wasn't sure you'd come. I wasn't sure he'd find you.'

"The room was freezing and I shivered. Then I realised that all the windows were open and the night air was blowing in, making the room into an icebox. Rose was wearing a thin, cotton nightie and she was covered in goosebumps. I pulled the blankets over her then got up and closed the windows and the curtains.

"'What's going on?' I demanded. 'Where's Alfred?'

"'He went out last night,' she replied in a hoarse whisper. 'When the pains started. Said he wasn't going to stay around to watch someone else's kid being born.'

"Then she screamed. I had no time to voice my disgust with Alfred; there was suddenly too much to do. She must have been in labour for hours before she could make the woman next door hear her, because it was only half an hour or so later that the baby was born.

"I did all the things I thought you had to do, I delivered him and I must admit, I felt quite chuffed with myself. She called him James, but everyone soon shortened it to Jimmy.

"I hadn't seen as much of her as I'd have liked, so when the dawn broke and I sat watching her as she slept, I was shocked to see a massive bruise on her arm. As I pulled away the bedclothes and looked under her nightgown, a feeling of dread rose up in my stomach. I found more bruises, some old and yellowing, others fresh and purple. I didn't need a degree to work out where they'd come from.

"I'd always considered Alfred to be an ignorant layabout, someone who thought the world owed him an easy life. It hadn't occurred to me that he could be violent but I realised now that he was just the sort who would turn on a woman. He'd never dream of taking on a man.

"It was noon when I heard his key in the door and I ran downstairs to meet him, though some of my fury had died. There really wasn't going to be much point in trying to prick his conscience; I knew that.

"'What the hell are you doing here?' Was his greeting.

"'Helping my sister,' I replied. 'I suppose you realise she could have died.'

"He laughed. I could scarcely believe it, but he actually laughed.

"'Don't dramatise,' he said. 'Women in Africa and places like that, they have babies then go back to work in the fields straight after.' He pushed passed me and went into the parlour, where he sprawled himself out on the settee. 'So she's had the kid then? I suppose that means I'll have to get my own dinner.'

"'What's wrong with you? Why did you go out and leave her on her own?'

"'Not my kid. I suppose you might as well get my dinner, while you're here.'

"'Oh, I wouldn't eat anything I've cooked if I were you, Alfred,' I warned him. 'Arsenic stew's about all you're likely to get from me.'

"I stayed at the house until she was on her feet again. Alfred wasn't there much, once he found out no one was going to wait on him, but I wasn't happy about leaving her. She still had that hard glitter in her eyes, but that didn't stop her from putting up with his abuse.

"To tell you the truth, it upset me too much to see Rose after that. She just wasn't the same person any more. She had been so lovely, you know, so talented and spirited in her own way and now I couldn't fathom what went on in her mind. She cared for the baby, looked after him and kept him clean, but even he couldn't cheer her up.

***

"The government had been making a big effort to clamp down on drinking. The King had banned all alcohol from Buckingham Palace and they'd actually made it illegal for a man to buy his mates a round of drinks in a pub. He got fined £100 if he was caught, and that was a year's wages to some of my customers. It was done to try and stop the arms workers from drinking too much, because it slowed down production.

"I don't know about anywhere else, but in the Angel we managed to devise a secret code for buying a round. After all, most of my customers were soldiers and they were entitled to let themselves go a bit when they came home on leave.

"It was a hard time, but in spite of it all, I wouldn't have cared if it went on forever, because Daniel spent his leave time with me.

"He didn't have very much leave, and it was too far to go back to the States. So he came to me. The first time was a couple of years into the war. He turned up one night, late, after I'd closed up.

"I heard knocking round the back and I came through to see what all the commotion was about. I thought it was a late customer, hoping I'd give him a drink after hours if he came up with a good enough story, but when I called out, it was Daniel who answered.

"'It's me, Liza,' he said. 'I've just got back. Can I come in?'

"I tore those bolts open.

"He hugged me to him and kissed me, as though there had never been any talk of a wife in America and I didn't find it too hard to forget about her, I can tell you. But he looked thin and drawn, not like his usual self at all. He was shaking slightly and there were black circles under his eyes.

"'I've only got a week,' he said when we were settled in the parlour. I made him some tea and sat beside him, just wanting to look at him, to assure myself that he was really there. 'I know it's a bit of a cheek, but I was hoping you might put me up. I've nowhere else to go.'

"'What about your parents? Won't they be expecting you?'

"He was quiet for a moment, just looking at me, puzzled.

"'I thought you knew,' he said. 'Mother was killed in a Zeppelin raid on the coast. My father's out in France, driving ambulances. I'm all alone now.' He gave a little derisive laugh and looked down at his hands for a minute before meeting my eyes. 'I thought perhaps I could sleep upstairs, in your old room. I'd give you rent, of course.'

"I made up my mind then. I think I already had it made up really; I was just waiting for a chance. And when I looked at him, how grey and fragile he looked, I realised with a horrible wrench that this might be my only chance, that he might return to France and catch a bullet. It wasn't worth messing about, was it? I leaned forward and kissed him, my hands on his face. I wanted him so much.

"'There aren't any beds upstairs any more,' I said softly. 'You'll have to sleep with me.'

"His eyes met mine and widened in surprise, then I saw that familiar little mischievous smile as he answered.

"'You're sure?'

"I nodded slowly.

"'Oh, yes, Daniel. I'm very sure.'

"His arms went around me and he pulled me close as he sat back and sighed softly.

"'I can't offer you anything any more, Liza,' he said. 'Even if it weren't for...well, there's the war. I could be killed.'

"'I've lived through your death once already. God wouldn't make me live through it again, would he?'

"'I don't think God has much to do with this, Liza. I should never have married her. It's you I love; I always will.'

"'Don't talk about her, Daniel, please. I can't stand it.'

"I hadn't realised I was crying until he started to kiss away the tears. And I've never regretted what I did that night, despite all my mother's efforts to teach me her own high morals. He was so gentle, so afraid of hurting me, of awakening all those old fears. But he was all I wanted and if I couldn't have him, I had no one to blame but myself.

"So Daniel spent his few leaves with me, and neither of us ever mentioned the lady in America who thought he was being faithful to her. I suppose I should have been ashamed, spending those times with him, sleeping with a married man. I should have been scared of getting pregnant as well, but none of that seemed important. And it never happened, so I suppose I'm just one of those women to whom the good Lord chose to deny motherhood.

"Attitudes were changing a little, what with men coming home from the war, never knowing whether they were going to live to see the end of it. But it wasn't only that. Married or not, I thought of Daniel as mine and I knew I always would. Even if he went back to her when it was all over, he'd still be mine.

"Nina was as fond of him as ever and being more of a modern girl, with different values, she thought I was doing the right thing. Then he started telling her stories about America and how things were there, about all the opportunities that we didn't have in England then. And she began to get itchy feet. London had always been her world and I don't think she had ever been out of it, not even for a day trip to Southend. But it wasn't her world any more. I knew I was about to lose my little sister, and I couldn't blame her. I'd have done the same in her shoes.

"The day came when she asked me how I'd feel about her going to the United States to see for herself. The idea scared me; she was only seventeen.

"'But you don't know anyone in America,' I argued. 'You'll be all alone.'

"Daniel looked thoughtfully at his hands for a moment, then he glanced at Nina before he spoke. I had the feeling they'd already discussed this.

"'There is someone I could write to,' he said. 'Someone who'd take care of her and make her welcome. She's a very nice lady, really.'

"My eyes searched his. It was an idea that had never crossed my mind, that she might be a nice woman. He wouldn't have married a bitch, would he, no matter how much I chose to think of her as such?

"I gave him a little smile.

"'She must be,' I said.

"We arranged passage on a ship sailing to New York and Nina went off to stay with Daniel's wife. His wife! It hurts me even now to say those words, to think of her.

"But I had the best of him, that was my consolation, though I knew that one day the war would end and, if he survived it, he'd go back to her. But it was me he loved. And when he wanted peace from all the fighting and the dirt and the horror, it was me he came to.

CHAPTER TWENTY TWO

"When Nina sailed for America, I knew she wouldn't be back, that I'd never see her again. As I waved her off, it seemed that a part of my life was going with her and I suppose it was. Not long after she left, Daniel went back to the trenches and I didn't see him again until it was all over.

"I was all alone then, and it seemed all wrong somehow. When I was growing up, all of us in that one room, there was never an inch of space that wasn't already occupied. There was Billy as well then, the old man coming and going as it suited him, and babies being born. I used to think I'd give ten years of my life for a place to myself, but when I had my peace and quiet, it wasn't nearly as good as I'd expected.

"I missed Nina. She was the only one I'd had to tell things to. She and I used to natter for hours about things we'd never tell anyone else. And, although I'd never have admitted it at the time, I resented where she was living. Perversely, it seemed to me that, not satisfied with taking my man, this anonymous woman on the other side of the world had stolen my little sister as well. Such silly fancies you have sometimes, don't you? The poor woman didn't even know I existed, and there was I imagining she'd deliberately plotted to hurt me.

"But it was Daniel I missed most. I knew Nina was happy, but Daniel was living through hell in France and I had to face the fact that he might never come back.

"Once he was wounded and I knew as soon as it happened. I felt the searing pain in my shoulder, I heard him cry out. But I didn't jump to conclusions that time, like I had before. I waited for a letter and when it came it was full of concern in case I'd known and thought the worst. I've still got that letter; I've kept all Daniel's letters.

"We shared something special during those few, brief years. The strain of knowing how brief drew us closer together, like many young couples when they couldn't be certain there would be a tomorrow. But while other girls were rushing off to marry someone they hardly knew, that option was no longer open to me.

"I often wondered if my mother was looking down on us, if she knew that three of her daughters had sinned so badly. She'd have been devastated.

"But I did my best to get on with living. I worried about Daniel, I fretted about Nina. And I got on with things, with running the pub for Tom as well as doing a bit of work for the Countess and her friends.

"Mind you, there wasn't much call for new clothes during those years. There wasn't much about in the way of materials, either.

"I saw little of Rose and when I did see her, little Jimmy had grown so far out of his baby stage, I doubt that I'd have recognised him. He was a cute little boy, as little boys go, and he got more like his father every day. That must have rankled with Alfred.

"Rose never had any more children, so I don't know what went on between them.

"Tom was invalided home in January 1918, badly wounded in his thigh. He always walked with a limp afterwards and he complained of the constant ache in his leg. His only relief was to take long, slow walks.

"He was pleased as punch about the way I'd run things and he asked me if I'd carry on helping him. I had nothing else to do, so I agreed. He had our old room decorated and back upstairs I went. But it was much nicer than before. I had a bit saved up by then, so I managed to get myself some decent bits and pieces and I made into a real home, with proper wallpaper on the walls and white paintwork to brighten the place up. But I never touched Rose's money. That was for her whenever she needed it, and for Jimmy when he grew up.

"I'd never had a bank account before. You didn't in those days, not unless you were really well off. And there was I with all this money sitting in an account and it wasn't even mine. I used to worry sometimes about what would become of it if anything happened to me and I often thought of making a Will so she'd get it all back, but it was one of those things you think a lot about but never quite get round to actually doing. Not that it mattered anyway, as things turned out.

"I can't deny that I was thinking about Daniel when I did up that room, even though I knew in the back of my mind that he'd have to go back to her. But when he came back at the end of the war, I knew straight away that there was something different about him.

"I was in my room, still admiring my new decorations, even though they'd been done a while by then. I'd got mother's bobbins out and I was trying my hand at making some lace and wishing I'd got her to teach me when she was alive. That's the way it goes, though, isn't it? You always think you've got plenty of time for everything, then one day you realise your time's run out.

"He didn't knock, just opened the door and stood watching me. Tears sprang to my eyes when I saw him, when I realised he had really come home in one piece. I jumped to my feet and ran to him, but he didn't move, didn't even take a step toward me.

"I stopped a couple of feet in front of him. I saw at once how drawn and pale he looked.

There were lines and shadows around his eyes and all the laughter had gone out of them. You know, his eyes had always danced, even when he tried to be serious. Not any more.

"He didn't say a word, didn't even kiss me, just followed me into the room and sat down while I made him some tea. He took the cup and that's when I noticed how his hands were shaking. He couldn't hold the cup steady, and the hot liquid splashed onto his legs. He forced it to his lips and the china clattered against his teeth because he couldn't keep it still.

"'Let me help you,' I said and I reached forward to hold the cup for him.

"His eyes met mine and I was stunned to see the rage in them. I was frightened, too, because the man who sat beside me wasn't my Daniel. He had never been angry in his life.

"His fingers clenched around the cup, so tightly I was afraid it would break apart and stab the pieces into his hands. His lips pressed together and his jaw clenched, then he hurled the cup across the room. I ducked as it flew past my head and shattered, leaving a trail of tea across my newly covered wall.

"In that moment, I wanted nothing more than to get up and run and the only thing that stopped me was a sort of stupor. I couldn't accept that Daniel had done this, in spite of having seen it with my own eyes. I didn't run; instead I put my arms around him.

"'It's all over now,' I said gently.

"'Is it?' He answered angrily. "It might be over for you, but look at me! Look what they've sent back to you! I can't even hold a bloody cup!'

"He wrenched himself away from me and dropped his head into his hands.

"'I can't live like this, Liza.'

"He couldn't accept that he was ill, you see. Battle fatigue, shell shock, wasn't recognised as an illness then. What Daniel was suffering from, the War Office chose to call cowardice and many young men had been shot on that basis.

"'You won't have to,' I answered, but I was afraid to touch him, afraid he'd reject me again. 'You'll get over it, Daniel. You know I'm always right.'

"The last bit was meant to be a joke and he'd have taken it as such before. Now he just looked at me as though he didn't know who I was. I knew it would be a long time before I heard him laugh again.

"He walked about the place moodily for weeks after that, scarcely speaking, and though we shared the same bed, we shared nothing else. Like lots of the men who'd been fighting in the trenches, he couldn't bear the sound of any loud noise, jumped out of his skin at the sound of the door knocker sometimes.

"'I feel so useless, Liza,' he said to me. 'They should have lined me up against the wall and shot me like all the other cowards.'

"'That's not right and you know it,' I insisted angrily. 'That's what all the men feel, the ones who have had their nerves shot to bits. You'll be all right.'

"He looked at me as though I'd spoken a foreign language.

"'I can't go home, Liza,' he said, so softly I had to lean close to hear him. 'You know how I feel about the ocean. You don't know what it was like getting here in the first place, having to steel myself, tell myself it would be all right, every minute of the journey. I just can't do that now. I'll crack up and make a fool of myself, I know I will.

"'Then don't go,' I said eagerly. 'She'll understand, won't she? That you're ill?'

"'Would you?' He demanded, angry at himself. 'I haven't seen her for nearly four years! She'll expect me to come home now. How can I tell her I'm too scared to walk outside the door, never mind travel all that way?' He looked down at his hands, hands that still shook constantly. His mouth turned into a grim line, so bitter that I'd never have believed it could find a place to settle on his face. Then he said: 'if she has any pride, she won't want me back.'

"'Well, let's hope so!' I shouted angrily. 'Then you can stay here with me, where you belong!'

"I ran downstairs, afraid of saying something I'd regret. The idea that this woman, who I didn't need to meet in order to hate, might be too proud to care for my precious Daniel, made me want to murder her. But deep down, I knew he was wrong to even think such a thing. She probably felt the same way about him as I did; I could never imagine anyone not loving him.

"I walked for hours and by the time I went home, I resented him for forcing me to think about her. Perhaps I also resented him for not being the same man who went away, I don't know. I cursed everyone who'd had anything to do with the way things had turned out – the captain of the ship for allowing it to sink; my mother, poor old soul that she was; the Kaiser for starting the war; Edie for hiding Daniel's letter in the first place. But most of all, I cursed myself for not recognising what I had until it was too late.

"'I'm sorry, Liza,' he said, before I had even closed the door behind me.

I hugged him.

"'You've got no reason to apologise to me. But you're wrong, you know. She'll be so happy to have you home.'

"I still didn't know her name. I didn't want to know it and in all the letters I got from Nina, staying over there in her house, she never once mentioned her. She must have known it wasn't something I wanted to be reminded about.

"And I knew my share of shame about that, too. I had always prided myself on the way I could face up to things that others might hide from. Facts were facts, I used to say. But now I'd found something I couldn't face, that I couldn't bear to think about, and I was ashamed of that.

"Nina's letters were full of cheerful news about the way things were done in America and about the job she'd got, serving in a dress shop. She even had plans to set up her own shop one day. People were more equal there, she said. There were more opportunities for everyone. She loved the place and I was happy for her, though I knew she'd grow away from me and I'd lose her for good.

"I helped Daniel to compose the letter to his wife, telling her how ill he was and how he couldn't face going back until he was better. That was one of the hardest things I've ever had to do, but when I saw what he had written himself, how he'd underrated himself, I just couldn't bear the idea that she might read it.

"I should have anticipated the letters from her, I suppose. They came regularly, once a fortnight, and I began to dread the sound of the lid being shifted on the old tin bread box where Tom always put our post. The sight of her handwriting made me cringe and recoil into myself, made her seem real, where before she'd been nothing more than a phantom that had followed me out of my nightmares.

"Tom would look at me a bit askance whenever I saw him, especially when one of the letters had come. I expect he wondered what was going on. He wouldn't have presumed on our friendship enough to criticise or offer an opinion that wasn't asked for, but I knew he didn't approve. He didn't know Daniel was married and perhaps he wondered why we were living like man and wife without doing anything to make it legal.

"Of course, I knew that if she was writing to him, he must be replying, but he kept it to himself, never wrote while I was around. Still, I couldn't help wondering what sort of tone she wrote in, and my curiosity gradually grew into a nagging suspicion which filled me with horror. What would I do in her position? I asked myself. And I knew the answer without even considering it – if he couldn't come to me, I would go to him. The idea was only one step away from me being terrified, every time there was a knock at the door, in case I opened it to see her standing there. I knew I would never be able to tolerate seeing them together, but I let my fear fester and nag before I found the courage to put it into words.

"'She won't come here, Liza,' he assured me, looking up at me from the bed where he sat.

"I stood, leaning my back against the fireplace, carefully avoiding his eyes.

"'How can you be so sure? I would, if I was her.'

"He smiled indulgently, reminiscently, then slow shook his head and drew a deep, decisive breath.

"'What exactly are you asking me, Liza?' He said. 'I can't answer your question without telling you things about her you don't want to know. I could say she can't afford it, and that would be no lie, but you'd only tell me how you'd scrimp and save and go without food to get here. So, what I want to know is, do you really want an answer to your question, or not?

"I didn't really want to know, he was right about that, but at the same time I had to hear it, or I'd never have known any peace.

"'Well?' I replied after a moment. 'What makes you so sure she won't come here?'

"He gazed at me thoughtfully for a few minutes, as though ordering his thoughts to tell me something that was going to hurt. Then he sighed and began quietly, so that I had to strain to hear him.

"'Do you know where I met her, Liza? On a lifeboat, in the freezing ocean. She'd been travelling home from visiting her grandmother in England, a last meeting before the old lady died. She was sixteen years old and terrified but she was the one who was comforting the children, assuring the elderly that everything was going to be all right. And assuring them with so much conviction, so much confidence that none of us could doubt it. As I watched her, listened to her comforting others when she looked so vulnerable, looked as though she were the one in need of solace, I knew she was doing exactly what you would do in that situation, bury your own fears under everybody else's. That's why I kept in touch with her to begin with, because she reminded me of you.

"'She was the one who pulled me into the lifeboat, she was the one who saved my life. And she has the same dread of crossing the Atlantic as I have.'

"I couldn't think for a minute, couldn't begin to get my mind around what he had told me. It occurred to me that maybe he'd married her out of gratitude and the notion brought some much needed comfort, though I didn't want to think of her as a heroine, didn't want to have to admire her.

"'Is that why you married her?' I asked, hopefully. 'Because she saved your life?'

"'No.' He shook his head slowly. 'It was another two years before I finally gave up on you, when I decided to start looking forward instead of back. I thought I'd got over you and I still believed that until the night I arrived back in

England. I'd never have come here otherwise. When you rushed into my arms, three years dissolved away to nothing, as though they had never happened. I knew then that I'd made a terrible mistake; what I wasn't prepared to hear was that you'd made one, too.'

"He reached out and took my hand, but he made no move to draw close, almost as though he was afraid I might reject him.

"'She won't come, Liza,' he whispered. 'It would take her months to save the money and she'd be too frightened, anyway.'

"I nodded reluctantly. I wasn't quite convinced but I had to take his word for it, didn't I?

"During the months that followed, I did my best to help him back to his old self and it wasn't easy. Daniel had changed so much, I scarcely knew him. He was snappy, for one thing. He lost his temper at the slightest thing, yet before the war I wasn't even aware that he had a temper to lose. He'd shout at me sometimes, other times he just keep silent for hours on end. But it didn't matter. I knew he couldn't help himself, I knew he was ill, but what I mean is that none of his moods ever changed the way I felt.

"All that mattered was that he had come home, when there were so many men who never did.

"But the two who I might have hoped to get rid of managed to get away with not going in the first place. Your grandfather was one of them. He had an important job, so he said, that exempted him from enlisting. I only discovered that because Edie still kept in touch with Rose. I'd had no contact with either of them since the day I'd slammed Edie's front door behind me. The other one, of course, was Alfred.

"Strange as it may seem, it was Alfred who inadvertently got my Daniel back on the road to recovery.

"He came into the pub one night. Tom was out, as it was a weekday and quiet and he was still prone to taking himself off for long walks at night. I didn't mind; I'd managed by myself all that time, I could certainly manage now it was all over.

"I was washing glasses when Alfred came in. He'd already been drinking and he staggered over to the bar and demanded a beer.

"I served him his drink and started to turn back to what I'd been doing, when he grabbed my wrist. There was no one else in the bar, except Auntie Ann asleep in her usual corner.

"'Let go of me,' I said.

"'I suppose you think you're too good for me,' he slurred. 'Just like your whore of a sister.'

"I wasn't going to struggle to get my wrist free; much as I hated to admit it, he was stronger than me and I didn't want to give him the satisfaction of knowing it. So I just stood there, staring at him disdainfully.

"'D'ya know what I've just found out?' He demanded. 'After all this time she tells me she doesn't even own that house. She tells me she's got nothing except what she and her little bastard stand up in.' He leaned over the bar and peered at me, and his face wore the most hateful sneer I'd ever seen. 'She says she signed it all over to you. Is that right?'

"'That's right, Alfred,' I replied. 'She gave me everything before she married you. She knew you'd try and squander it all away, so she got rid of it.'

"'Well I hope for your sake you've still got it all,' he said. 'Because I'm going to the law. I'm going to sue you to get back what's mine.'

"I laughed; I couldn't help it. Just who the hell did he think he was? But my laughter only made him angrier and he twisted my arm and raise his hand to strike me.

"I didn't know that Daniel had come down and was standing in the back doorway at the side of the bar. Out of the corner of my eye, I saw a flash of shadow rush past me.

"The next thing I knew, he was behind Alfred and had his arm round the weasel's scrawny neck. I looked up at Daniel and saw fury in his eyes, but this time he was angry with someone other than himself.

"Daniel was a big man, as I've said, and the pressure of his arm on Alfred's throat was cutting off his air supply, making him choke. His face began to turn an alarming shade of bluish purple.

"'Let go, you snivelling little creep,' Daniel said menacingly. 'You lay one finger on her, it'll be the last thing you ever do.'

"Alfred let go of me quick enough then. He turned round and as he did so, Daniel punched him square in the jaw.

"'Come on,' he said. 'See if you can take on a man for a change.'

"I was smiling, because I saw that Daniel wasn't shaking any more. For the first time since he'd come home, he'd lost that haunted look. Up until then, he'd been afraid of his own shadow almost, and ashamed of himself most of the time. Alfred fled and I'd have been glad to see him go, except I knew he'd go straight home and take his temper out on Rose.

"'Are you all right, Liza?' Daniel asked, holding me against him. 'If he hurt you, I'm going after him.'

"I shook my head.

"'I'll live,' I said, then added with a chuckle: 'My hero.'

"He laughed then and what a wonderful sound that was. I'd begun to think I'd never hear him laugh like that again. But while I was happy for him, I knew it meant that I'd lost him.

"He lingered on in London for months after he could have gone back. I began to feel secure, in spite of the regular letters from New York, until the day he told me what one of them contained.

"I could tell from his expression, the regret in his eyes, that she'd written something more important than just chit-chat and local news.

"'It seems you know her better than I do, Liza,' he said.

"He was still holding the letter, staring at the neat lines of writing as though he could somehow change their message. I knew what he meant and there was no point in denying the reality of it.

"'She's coming,' I said quietly.

"He nodded.

"'It can't happen, Daniel. You know that, don't you? Leave me some dignity, please.'

"It was the end of 1919 before he finally set sail, having forestalled her journey with a hurried reply to her letter with a telegram. I'll never forget our last night together, even if I live for another hundred years.

"'I don't want to go, Liza,' he said softly. 'You know that, don't you?'

"We were lying in bed and he was playing with my hair as it lay across his chest.

"'You'll be all right,' I answered, deliberately misunderstanding. 'The journey'll be over before you know it. Stay in your cabin as much as you can with the blinds drawn. Then you can pretend there's no ocean outside.'

"I heard his laugh above my head.

"'That's not what I meant and you know it. I love you, Liza. I don't want to go back to her.'

"'You're not chained to her,' I suggested tentatively. 'You could leave her.'

"I suppose I was as contrary as most women. I knew, even as I said it, that it wasn't as simple as that. He turned his head and looked at me, trying to fathom, I think, whether I really meant what I said.

"'Could I?' He asked after a moment. 'Do you really think I could do that to her? Subject her to the shame, the scandal, and for what purpose? She'd never divorce me and even if she did, that'd mean dragging us all through a public trial. And what would a divorce do to her chances of marrying again?'

"Everything he said was true. I knew that, but I didn't care. The sensation of him slipping away from me was almost physical and no matter how tight I held on, he'd still keep slipping away, leaving my arms full of nothing. I was losing him, for good this time, and I was in no mood to be reasonable.

"'Is that all she's fit for, then?' I said spitefully. 'Being someone's wife?'

"'You don't mean that. She's not as tough as you and I couldn't do that to her. You know very well I couldn't.'

"'So what are you saying? That you love her?'

"He sat up and frowned at me, surprised, as though he thought I'd already know the answer to that one.

"'Of course I love her.' His words cut into me, more painful than any physical injury. 'I wouldn't have married her otherwise, would I? It's not her fault that I don't love her as much as I should. It's not her fault I'd rather have you.'

"I couldn't answer him; there was nothing to say. When someone married then, they married for life. I knew that as well as he did.

"He had to return to her; we both accepted that, and I even felt a little sorry for her that night. She must have loved him, mustn't she? It wasn't fair to blame her because I'd made a mess of things and sent him off to her in the first place. But I wondered if she'd ever guess, if she'd ever notice a distance in his manner that couldn't entirely be blamed on the war.

"'You do understand, don't you?' He asked. 'You can't always do what you want, can you? Sometimes you have to put others first.'

"'Stop it, Daniel,' I said bitterly. 'If I could put back the clock, don't you think I'd do it? I had my chance and I threw it away and wrecked both our lives in the process. Don't spoil tonight by throwing that back in my face, please.'

"'It wasn't your fault,' he insisted.

"'Whose fault was it then? You're in an impossible situation, I know that. And it was me that put you there, so don't go all noble on me and try to pretend otherwise.'

"He left the next day. I went to Southampton to see him off and all the way there we avoided talking about anything serious, just chatted and laughed, as though we were out on a day trip instead of parting company for good.

"That was the day he gave me the photograph, standing there on the quayside.

"'I got this for you, Liza,' he said as he handed it to me. 'Now you can tell everyone it was a conquering hero who loved you.' I tried to laugh, but I felt too miserable. 'Thank you for putting up with me and my tantrums all this time.'

"I gazed at him for a long time, wanting to argue, to tell him I'd do it all again, put up with anything rather than let him go. But what was the point? He already knew all that and putting it into words would only make us both feel worse.

"'Well, I just hope she appreciates it,' I answered, trying to make my voice sound light.

"He kissed me, pulled me close to him for a moment, then turned quickly away. My eyes followed him all the way up the gangplank and onto the deck.

"I stood on the quayside and waved until the ship was out of sight. There were tears pouring down my face and I didn't care who saw them. Of course, mine wasn't the only miserable face there. Hundreds of others had come to see off their loved ones, so many that I had to fight off competition to keep my place at the front of the crowd where I could see him leaning over the rail of the deck.

"I was pushed and jostled and felt like a punchbag, but it was worth every bruise and bump.

"I stood there for a long time after everyone else had gone, hoping to catch just one small glimpse on the horizon. I don't know what I thought, what I hoped for. Perhaps that the liner would re-appear, perhaps he'd make the captain turn back. I just couldn't seem to get my legs to walk away and I kept thinking, over and over, that's it. He's gone back to her and they'll settle down together and have babies and I'll never see him again.

"At last, I got out my handkerchief and dried my eyes. I realised I was still clutching his photograph and then I saw the words he'd written. Such simple words, nothing flowery or made up. Typical of Daniel. I put the picture away in my bag, then started to walk back to the railway station.

"There were none of these Inter City electrified trains in those days. The journey back to London took hours and all I had to do was think, think and remember all the cherished times we'd had together. You know how you sometimes can't stop reliving a special memory, or a scene in a film that really got to you? That's how it was for me, savouring every memory, reliving each embrace, each word that he spoke, all the long way home.

"A shock was waiting for me when I got there, something so completely unexpected, it almost succeeded in wiping Daniel out of my mind."

CHAPTER TWENTY-THREE

Auntie Bess exhaled a deep breath.

"Get us a glass of water, love," she said in a barely audible whisper.

When Stella returned, she was mopping at her eyes with her tissue. She wasn't alone; Stella, too, had an uncomfortable ache in her throat.

Stella returned to her seat, determined not to prompt her. She still didn't know what Bess was going to tell her about Rosina, and she wasn't at all sure that she wanted to.

The old lady gulped down half of the water before she went on.

"Despite the cold weather, I was hot and sticky and dog tired by the time I reached the Angel. All I wanted to do was go upstairs and sink down on my bed, but first I went into the bar to let Tom know I was back.

"'You've got a visitor,' he said, nodding to the corner where Auntie Ann would be found later in the evening. I turned round to look.

"Sitting at the table, a silly grin on his face, was my father. It took me a while to recognise him. His face was lined with deep grooves, his hair had turned almost completely grey and his eyes were clouded, in the early stages of growing cataracts.

"'What do you want?' I demanded.

"'Why, Bess,' he said, making no attempt to get up, 'is that really you? My, but you've grown into a fine young woman. It does me proud to see it.'

"'I don't know what you think you've got to be proud of,' I snapped. 'It's no thanks to you that I grew up at all.'

"I had been little more than a child when I saw him last, but now I just wished he'd disappear. I glanced over my shoulder at Tom and saw that he had averted his eyes, embarrassed by the exchange. I knew I should take the old man upstairs, out of Tom's way, but I didn't want him anywhere near my room. I felt he would contaminate it and not just because he was filthy dirty.

"His jacket was wrinkled and shiny and there was a line of dirt visible just below his greasy hairline. He wore a knotted scarf around his neck, a sort of bandanna that I suppose had once been red, though it was so dirty it was difficult to tell.

"'I'm your father, Elizabeth,' he said in what I suppose he thought was a stern voice.

"'Biologically, yes.'

"'Don't you give me any of your lip. I've been waiting here all day; I thought you'd be pleased to see me.' His voice softened and he got that wheedling look in his eyes that I'd almost forgotten about. 'I've had a rough time, Bess.'

"'Haven't we all.'

"'I've been kipping at the mission. You can't imagine what it's like, all those filthy men, home from the war and nowhere else to go. We'd have been better off if they'd stayed in Europe.'

"Wouldn't that have made you mad? That lazy old bugger, talking contemptuously about men who'd risked their lives for the likes of him. Men like Daniel, whose departure had left a raw place that was still too fresh.

"'You still haven't answered my question,' I said.

"'Come and sit down, love. Tell me what's been going on.' I didn't move. I preferred to stand, staring down at him. It gave me an edge of superiority. 'Like I said, I've been waiting for hours. Where have you been anyway?'

"'None of your business.'

"'Where's your mother? She should have finished with her doorsteps hours ago. What's she doing? I heard Rose got married but I thought Nina or Edie would have been here to make me welcome.' He nodded toward Tom and added: 'I wanted to go up and make myself a cuppa, but this old fool wouldn't give me the key.'

"'Thanks, Tom,' I said without taking my eyes off my father.

"Weariness overcame me and I let out a sigh and sank down in the chair facing him across the table. My eyes squinted against the smoke that lay heavily in the air from the cigarettes he had smoked while he waited. The ashtray was overflowing.

"'Nina's gone to America,' I said shortly. 'Mother went senile. I daresay you can give yourself a pat on the back for that.'

"'Senile?' He repeated stupidly. 'I don't understand. She can't have gone senile at her age. Why aren't you looking after her?'

"'Why didn't you? It might not have happened if you had. Anyway, she's dead now.'

"He didn't ask how she had died, only looked down at his feet, though whether I had managed to jolt his conscience I couldn't say. My eyes followed his and I saw that his soles were parting company with his shoes. He wore no socks and his feet were as dirty as the rest of him.'

"'What about Billy?' He asked. 'What's he up to?'

"Echoes of the past, I thought.

"'Billy's dead. Has been for years. I'm the only one here now. What did you think? That you could come back after all these years and find nothing changed?'

"He sat staring at his feet for a long time. I wanted to leave, to go upstairs with my memories and consign my father to history where he belonged. But that wouldn't have been very fair on Tom, would it?

"'Well,' he said finally, looking at me with what might have been a bright smile if he hadn't been so grimy. 'Let's go up then, shall we?' He half rose to his feet. 'Since you're all alone, I expect you'll be glad of the company.'

"I couldn't believe what I was hearing. I knew it was going to be torture, being alone now, but I wasn't quite that desperate.

"'You're not staying with me,' I answered. 'You can forget that idea straight away.'

"'It's my home too, Bess,' he said. 'If I want to stay in it, I bloody well will.'

"'No. It stopped being your home years ago, when mother made the separation official. I pay the rent and that's the way it's going to stay.' I got up and looked down at him, my hands leaning on the table. 'I don't know what gutter you crawled out of, but my best advice is that you crawl back in, because you're not welcome here.'

"'I've got nowhere else to go, Bess,' he pleaded. 'I'm going blind. Doctors say it won't be long before I lose what little sight I've got left. You wouldn't turn your old dad out in the street, would you?'

"I couldn't help laughing at his audacity.

"'So you're going blind, are you? So you thought you'd just breeze back here and someone would take you in and look after you?

Well, you were wrong. You can throw yourself in the Thames for all I care and good riddance.'

"I heard the door open, but I didn't take much notice until I heard a gasp.

"'George Shaw!' Cried Auntie Ann from behind me. 'I swear I'd just as soon see the Devil himself!'

"The look on her face shook me a little. She looked angry and frightened both at once, as though she had seen something that terrified her.

"'How dare you come back here!' She cried, her voice rising to a scream. 'After what you did to my sister, my poor Becky. You should be locked up, that's what! You shouldn't be allowed to roam the streets where decent people are!'

"She sounded on the brink of hysteria and her voice had begun to tremble by the time she'd finished her tirade.

"My father peered at her. His eyesight wasn't as bad as he'd made out, but I doubt he'd have recognised Ann in any case. She was thin and scraggy by then, her hair had gone white, and she was nearly as dirty as he was.

"'Who's there?' George said. 'I don't know you.'

"'It's Ann,' I told him. 'Mother's sister.'

"He sank back in his sear, his face showing his amazement.

"'Can't be. She wouldn't be seen dead in a pub.' He peered at her again as she drew closer. 'What happened to her?'

"I wasn't about to go into the details of Ann's decline for his benefit. Nobody really knew for certain what had happened to her and I sometimes wonder if she even knew herself.

"'Get out of here, father,' I said wearily. 'We don't want you. You'll get nothing from me.'

"'I'll go and see Rose,' he replied, getting shakily to his feet. 'She'll help me. Unlike you, Rose's got a heart.'

"I watched him go, watched Auntie Ann shuffle over to the bar for what turned out to be her last bottle of gin, then I went upstairs.

"At about nine o'clock that night, I woke up. Someone was gone; I could feel it, but I wasn't sure who and I couldn't do anything about it but lay and hope the old man had taken my advice and gone in the river, though it wasn't likely. I didn't care enough about him to feel anything when he died.

"When Tom tried to wake up Auntie Ann at closing time that night, he discovered that she was dead.

"Ann died of a heart attack and I felt certain it was the shock of seeing my father again that brought it on. I couldn't forget her face when she had called out his name.

"I had funeral arrangements to make and I had to see Rose, had to tell her about Ann and warn her about the ol' man. I didn't think he'd have much trouble worming his way into her house, then she'd have two lazy louts to wait on.

"It was the week before Christmas and on a table in the window, she had a small tree, laden with candles and sparkling bells. A silver-clad angel presided over the whole decoration and she'd placed little gifts among the branches.

"It had all been done for Jimmy. She'd never bothered before and the sight of it made me realise how alone I would be this year. Daniel would be spending the festivities with Nina, and with her.

"We could never afford Christmas while I was growing up, yet now I'd celebrated a few, I was going to miss it. It's funny how quickly these things become important.

"I shook myself out of these morbid reflections to concentrate on the purpose of my visit.

"'If he comes here, Rose,' I said, 'don't let him in. You know what he's like.'

"She gave me one of those languid smiles, then turned to watch Jimmy where he played on the floor.

"'You must have a better memory than mine, Bess,' she said. 'I don't think I can remember what he's like at all.'

"'Well, take my word for it, then. He's after a free meal and a free doss and someone to wait on him. Id have thought you had enough on your plate as it is, without him adding to it.'

"'But he's going blind, you said. How am I supposed to turn away my own father when he comes to me for help?'

"'I did.'

"'You always were tougher than me, Bess. Don't you think Jimmy's getting more like his father every day?'

"I looked at the little boy and had to agree. He was like James, the same dark hair, the same aristocratic features. Then my eyes moved up and I saw the photographs which lined the mantelpiece.

"'What does Alfred say about having James' picture all around the place?'

"She fingered the gold, oval locket around her neck, within which I knew resided yet another image of Viscount Hartford.

"'I take them all down before he comes home,' she replied.

"'Rose, it's not good for you, all this.' My arm swept the air, gesturing toward the photographs. 'It's not going to help you get over him, is it?'

"'I don't want to get over him. That's the difference between you and me. When you thought that Daniel was dead, you did everything you could to forget him. Now he's gone back to America, you'll concentrate all your efforts on doing it again. But I don't want to forget James. I want to remember him, to relive every minute we spent together. You'll never understand, will you?'

"She was right about that. I never would understand and I thought I had a little insight into the way things had gone sour in her marriage. I had no time for Alfred and I couldn't summon any sympathy for him, either. But it couldn't have been much fun for him, could it, having to share his home and his wife with a dead man?

"We were the only ones at Auntie Ann's funeral. Rose'd got a neighbour to look after Jimmy and we were standing by the open grave. It was right on a hill and that day you could see the city rooftops, the smoke coming from the chimneys. It was a cold day, but clear and dry. I couldn't help remembering, standing there, the time before when we had almost buried Ann. It makes me shudder to think about, but even so, it was funny, the way Edie threw her bonnet at the coffin.

"'It's a lovely spot,' Rose murmured. 'I'm glad she's got a nice spot.'

"'Oh, yes,' I answered flippantly. 'She'll be able to get up and have a sit in the sun in the summer, watch the sunset even.'

"I remember a time when she'd have laughed at that, given me that indulgent look and told me to behave. But now her expression showed not a trace of humour. She'd pulled her hair forward on her cheek and now the wind caught at it, revealing an ugly bruise beneath.

"'Why don't you leave him, Rose?' I asked her impatiently. 'No one'd blame you. For Jimmy's sake, if not for your own. It can't be good for him, seeing what his so-called father does to you.'

"'D'you want to kick him out of the house, Bess?' She asked. 'I must admit, I'd quite enjoy that myself.'

"'Then let's do it.'

"She shook her head.

"'Do you really think he'd let me go, just like that? He'd take Jimmy, just to get back at me. Have you never thought of that?'

"'But Jimmy's not his son.'

"'Try telling that to the law. Alfred's name is on the birth certificate and you know as well as I do that a father has more rights than a mother.'

"'I'm sorry, Rose. I didn't think of that.'

"'Why else do you think I stay? Anyway, father's there for now. We'll talk about it when he's gone.'

"'So you've taken him in, then?'

"'I told you I would.'

"'Well, if we're going to talk when he's gone, we never will, will we? How he's got a roof over his head, a cook and a skivvy, he'll never go.'

"She gave me a little half smile, then broke off a small spray of flowers from the wreath she had brought for Auntie Ann. She wandered away from the grave and I watched her for a while, until I realised she wasn't going to turn round and come back, that she was actually headed somewhere. I should have known where, I suppose, but I really had no idea he was buried in the same churchyard.

"I caught up with her near the front gates, where a massive mausoleum of solid, white marble presided over the corner of two pathways. It was like a little house, with a pitched roof and a front door, either side of which stood an angel with arms outstretched, ready to welcome the departed.

"The most recent name to be carved on the wall leapt out at us because of its newness. She bent down and placed the spray of flowers on the ground beneath his name.

"'He's in there, Bess,' she said quietly. 'Just a few feet away from me. I can see him lying there, asleep; I can almost reach out and touch him.'

"I tried, but I couldn't envision him like that. I saw him decayed, skeletal, all his beauty eaten away by the rats. I shuddered.

"'He's dead,' I told her. 'Let him go.'

"'When I remember him, I can make him come to life again.' She turned to me with a gentle smile. 'If anything were to happen to me, you would look after Jimmy, wouldn't you?'

"'Come on,' I answered impatiently. 'Let's get you away from this place.'

"I turned her predicament over in my mind, worrying and fretting about it all week. She wasn't well enough to be taking everything on her own shoulders and there was only one way to help her. Reluctantly, I made up my mind to go and see the old man, see if I could persuade him to leave, even if it meant having him to stay with me instead. I'd have made his life so miserable, he'd have been happy to go back to the mission.

"I could hear the screams before I even got up the front path, but it was raining heavily and I couldn't be sure where they were coming from until I got to the door.

"'Leave him alone!' Rose screamed. 'I don't care what you do to me, but leave him alone!'

"I still had a key to that house and this seemed like a good time to make use of it. I unlocked the front door and followed the noise into the dining room.

"The rain pounded against the window panes in sudden, violent gusts which seemed to coincide with the screams, making them louder and more terrifying.

"The table was set for dinner, there was a smell of roast meat in the air and on the table stood a joint of beef, the carving knife beside it.

"Alfred was standing over little Jimmy, a leather belt in his hand. The child's face was bleeding from an earlier blow and Rose had

Alfred around the waist, trying to pull him away from her son.

"I don't know how it happened. I remember glancing around for a weapon, something heavy I thought, to hit the bastard with, make him stop, but what I snatched up from the table was the knife.

"Then came her voice, hysterical, calling out: 'No, Bess! Give it to me!' I think I must have shut my eyes, because the next time I looked, Alfred O'Neill was lying flat on his back with the handle of that carving knife sticking out of his chest.

"I heard a rustling noise behind me, and I turned to see my father standing in the doorway, watching Rose as she struggled with the knife. I've never been sure what she was trying to do. Perhaps she thought if she pulled out the knife, Alfred would come back to life.

"'You'd better call the police, father,' I said quietly. 'Leave it, Rose. It's Jimmy that needs your help.'

"I pushed the old man out of the house, trying to make him do something useful for once in his life. I wasn't sure he was the right person to send; I suspected that he might not come back. As it turned out, it would have been better for all concerned if he hadn't.

"'Don't touch anything, Rose,' I said. 'Not until the police get here.'

"She seemed numb with shock, but it was Jimmy who concerned her, not herself, not me. She had scooped the child up in her arms and was rocking him back and forth, kissing him.

"'Is he dead, Bess?' She whispered.

"I nodded.

"'Take Jimmy upstairs,' I said. 'He shouldn't have to see this.'

"She did as I suggested, but she was back down again within minutes, her eyes moving around the room, looking at the body, at the blood soaked carpet. I think she wanted to start clearing up the mess; I know I did.

"Then the police arrived and after that things got confused.

"'Which one of you is Mrs. O'Neill?'

"'I am,' Rose said, stepping forward.

"'I'm arresting you for the murder of Alfred O'Neill.'

"I didn't hear the rest of what he said. I was too stunned by the unreality of the scene before me. Blood soaked the front of Rose's dress, her hands were crimson and the front of her hair was sticky with it.

"Behind the four policemen, stretching his neck to peer over their shoulders, stood my father. I thought I'd hated him before, but now I wanted to wrench the knife out of Alfred's corpse and stick it in him. There was a glow of excitement in his eyes. He wasn't worried, wasn't concerned about Rose, about Jimmy.

"'Father!' I yelled at him. 'What have you told them?'

"He didn't reply, only kept staring at the body as though he were watching a fascinating scene from a play.

"They were taking her out the front door when I came to my senses.

"'No!' I shouted after them. 'That's not right!'

"She turned and looked back at me, her eyes locked on mine, and I saw a warning in them.

"'Look after Jimmy, Bess,' she said.

"'You can't take her! She didn't kill him!'

"'What are you talking about, Bess,' my father said. 'Of course she killed him. I saw her with my own eyes.'"

Great Aunt Bess' story bore little resemblance to the accepted one, the version one can read in any publication which deals with famous murder trials. According to the official records, Rosina O'Neill killed her husband in a premeditated act, using the defence of her son as an excuse for the murder.

"So, she had good reason to kill him," Stella said. "She really was defending her son. And her husband wasn't the upstanding citizen he was purported to be." She breathed a sigh of relief. At least she knew now that her Great Aunt Rosina was not the heartless and cunning criminal she had read about. "I think I understand now, why you felt it so important to tell someone the truth."

Bess looked at her with those wise old eyes and offered her a self derisory smile.

"You understand nothing!" She declared harshly. "It wasn't Rose who killed Alfred. It was me."

CHAPTER TWENTY-FOUR

Stella's heart jumped and she stared at Bess stupidly, her fingers clutching the upholstered arms of her chair, digging into the floral covering as though she would fall out if she let go.

"You killed him?" She eventually managed an incredulous whisper.

Even as she said it, it seemed the most far-fetched idea. There she sat, withered and ancient, her voice cracking with age. She couldn't, not at any point in her life, have stabbed a man to death. That was the thought which kept recurring. It was a crazy notion, of course. Every killer born to man could one day grow old and infirm, especially since the abolition of capital punishment. But Stella still expected to see that little mischievous smile which would tell her the old lady was pulling her leg.

"Yes, love," she said at last, her grave expression confirming that she was in deadly earnest. "I killed him, I was the one who took up the carving knife from the table and stuck it in him.

"And Rose is dead and gone, while I sit here in a house paid for with her money and get telegrams from the Queen. Just look at all these cards." Her eyes swept the various surfaces which were covered with birthday greetings in every design and colour imaginable. "Most of them are from people I don't even know. Congratulations on living to such a great age. Me, who should have given up the ghost back in 1920."

"What happened? Why didn't you tell them?"

Her laughter emerged as a cackle, bitter and mocking and full of disgust.

"I'll tell you what happened," she replied. "When the police had gone, the old man wandered back indoors, looking very smug and pleased with himself. I'd always known he cared nothing for any of us, but I wouldn't have credited even him with bearing false witness against his own daughter.

"Can you imagine anything worse than your own father lying like that? He hadn't seen anything. He'd come in after it was all over instead of sticking up for her and his grandson, like he should have done.

"'Well,' he said, wringing his hands together like Uriah Heep. 'Who'd have thought it. A murder, right here in my own dining room. That nice constable said my evidence is of the utmost importance and I'm to keep myself available. "Utmost importance" – that's what he said.'

"I was sickened, so sickened I couldn't find words to express how much.

"'I'm taking Jimmy home with me for tonight,' I told him.

"'That's a good idea, love,' he replied, his eyes wandering greedily about the room. 'I'm not much of a one for kids under my feet.'

"I went upstairs and packed some of the boy's things, absolutely furious that he thought I was taking Jimmy for his benefit. There were many things I could have said to him, but I was too numb with shock to even think about them. I was shaking with rage and remorse and I knew if I stayed in that house a minute longer, I'd have found some other weapon with which to silence my father.

"There was a letter from Nina the next day. Tom brought it up with the morning newspaper. The headlines screamed at me.

FAMOUS MUSIC HALL STAR IN MURDER ENQUIRY
ROMANY PRINCESS CHARGED

"It showed a picture of Rose, all dressed up like she used to be for the stage, a picture of Alfred, and even one of Jimmy.

"I don't know how they got to hear about it so soon, but I always suspected my father. Nobody else could have given them the photographs.

"'Is it true?' Tom asked me.

"I nodded. I was trembling – it comes as a bit of a shock, seeing your own people blazoned across the front page.

"'She didn't do it, Tom. You know that, don't you? You know Rose as well as anyone.'

"'I didn't think it could be right, not when I think of her singing downstairs, such a lovely girl; everybody thought so. Mind you, I wouldn't have blamed her if she had done him in.'

"'You might not, Tom, but I don't suppose the law will see it like that.' I glanced at Jimmy, still curled up in my bed. 'Listen, Tom. Can you look after Jimmy for a couple of hours? I've got things to see to and I don't want him listening.'

"Tom agreed at once. He was a good man, Tom was, and I often wondered why nobody ever snapped him up.

"I went to see the Countess first. I regretted having to dump this on her just then, because she was busy getting things prepared for Belinda's wedding. That little girl had been swept off her feet, as she liked to say herself, by a cousin of hers from America. She thought it a huge joke because, being a cripple, she was never on her feet to begin with. I'd already made the dresses so that wasn't a problem, but I didn't want anything to blight her big day.

"I wanted to explain things to the countess before she got the wrong idea, but I was too late as it turned out. Like everybody else, she'd already seen the papers.

"'I could scarcely believe it,' she said. She guided me into my little sewing room and pushed me down into a chair. 'I've had so many telephone calls this morning from so-called friends, and there are two noble ladies currently occupying my drawing room. Belinda is beside herself.'

"'I'm so sorry. I didn't expect it to cause you any trouble.'

"'Now then, my dear,' she said. 'You mustn't worry about me. I don't care if half of London disagrees with me, you take as long as you want to help your sister.'

"I'd intended to tell her about Rose being innocent, but the words stuck in my throat. I might need her goodwill in the coming weeks. It was better not to say too much too soon.

"'That's just what I came to tell you,' I said. 'I have to leave here. It wouldn't be fair on you for me to stay. And I have Jimmy to look after.'

"'But that won't be forever, will it?'

"'I'm very much afraid that it might be.' I stood up and held out my hand, shook hers.

"This elegant lady had managed something that few people ever could – she had earned my respect and that deserved more than a simple 'goodbye'.

"'It's been a privilege and an honour to know you,' I added, 'Your Ladyship.'

"She put her arms around me and hugged me and I knew I had to leave, before my emotions got the better of me.

"From Regents Park, I went straight to the police station. I hadn't told Tom I might not be coming back, but there was no one else I could trust with Jimmy and I knew he'd take care of the boy, no matter how long it took.

"And I was sure I wouldn't be back, but Rose would. My steps faltered as I approached the police station, and I stopped outside, taking deep breaths to calm my nerves. I felt sure everyone was staring at me, that they all knew I had committed murder. I almost expected a mob to form about me, to drag me into the police station before I could get there myself.

"There was a damp mist in the air; it chilled my face and clung to my hair as I waited for courage to come and support me. It had to be done, I had to tell them what really happened and I knew very well what the consequences of my confession would be. I would be taken to Holloway Prison and kept there until the trial. Then I would be hanged by the neck until I was dead. I shuddered, pushed the visions out of my mind before they could make me turn back in terror, and walked steadily up the steps and into the building.

"That was my first jolt; the police wouldn't believe me.

"'You've got to listen to me,' I told the inspector in charge of the case. 'I killed Alfred. I'm the one who stabbed him, not Rose. She wouldn't hurt a fly.'

"'Now then, Miss,' he said with a silly grin on his face. 'Let's not be heroic. What you're doing is trying to pervert the course of justice and if you do it in court, you'll be charged with perjury.' He leaned across the table and patted my hand. He was getting on a bit and I suppose he thought he was being fatherly. That was funny, when you think about it, considering my old man's idea of fatherly. 'Go home, love,' he said. 'I know what you're up to, don't think I don't. You've got no husband and no one to look after you and you think it'd be better if you took the blame, rather than leave that little fella without his mama. But it's not right, is it? She killed him and she'll pay the price. There's nothing you can do about it. British justice will always win out in the end.

"'But she didn't kill him!'

"I could hear the desperation in my voice but I could do nothing to stop it. I had begun to realise that nobody was going to believe me, that I was going to keep on coming up against this wall of patronising conviction where I turned.

"'She says she did,' he answered kindly.

"I thought I must have misheard.

"'What?'

"'Your sister has made a full confession, admitting everything.' So now I knew and I was stunned. 'And you saw it happen. The prosecution will want you as a witness, so the sooner you put these silly notions out of your head, the better.'

"I left the police station even more worried than I'd been before. It hadn't occurred to me that I was a witness, that I'd seen what happened and they'd want me to testify against her. It was my chance, I told myself. When I got to say my piece at the trial, I'd tell them the truth then. But I reckoned without my father and without Rose herself.

"When I got home, I remembered Nina's letter, still unopened on the table where I had left it. It was an odd sort of letter, coming from her. It was like listening to someone who is trying to evade a certain subject – stilted and contrived. Of course, I knew what she was trying to avoid. Daniel was back home now and Nina was desperately trying to tell me what she'd been up to, while avoiding any mention of either of them. But that wasn't an easy thing to do; they were part of her life, of her every day activities.

"I sat down and started to compose a reply, but when I read it back, I found my letter just as evasive as hers. I didn't want her to know what had been happening. I crumpled my letter up and threw it away, deciding to put off writing for the time being. That was the beginning of the dwindling of our correspondence, until over the years, it finally came down to nothing more than exchanged Christmas cards.

"As soon as the police had finished at Rose's house, I packed my things and moved in. I thought it would be better for Jimmy to stay in his own environment. Not that I knew the first thing about children, but the poor little mite had had enough shocks for one so young and I didn't think that moving him to my room over the pub would do him much good.

"Father had been alone in the house for just three days and already it looked like a dosser's paradise. A layer of dust had settled over everything, bits of dried mud gathered on the carpets and the floorboards around the edge. There was a cigarette burn in the velvet seat of one of the armchairs and the air was thick with stale smoke from his tobacco. He hadn't even cleared the ash from the grate before he piled up more coal and it spilled out of the fireplace on to the floor.

"I glanced into the dining room, wondering if I'd ever be able to enter it again. The knife had gone; the police had taken that, but the joint was still on the table, dry and mouldering and the bloodstain had dried to a hard, brown mess on the rug.

"The stench of rotting meat turned my stomach. I sent Jimmy up to his room and turned to look at my father.

"'Right,' I said briskly. 'Get your things together. You're leaving.'

"'You can't chuck me out,' he protested. 'I've got to keep myself available. The police need me. Besides, this'll be my house soon.'

"'What d'ya mean, your house? Where did you come by an idea like that?'

"'Stands to reason, don't it? Alfred's dead and I don't see Rose coming back, do you? I'm her next of kin, ain't I?'

"I could feel the hatred in my eyes as I looked at him. I never met the man your mother married, but I hope you never had to know what it's like to feel that way about your own father.

"'Is that why you're doing this?' I demanded. 'Is that why you're lying to the police, trying to get rid of Rose? So you can have her house?'

"'I'm not lying! You don't know what I saw. Only I know that.'

"'I know you didn't see her kill him,' I spat. 'You couldn't have, could you? Because she didn't do it. I did!'

"He stared at me for a minute or two and then he laughed, really laughed, as though I'd said something hilariously funny.

"'You're a fool, Bess,' he spat. 'You'll never get them to let her off by lying. They'll never believe you. Now, if there's nothing else you want, I've got things to do. I want to get rid of some of these fancy female draperies she's got about the place.'

"It was no use arguing with him. I could see he didn't believe me, didn't want to believe me. I was going to enjoy turfing him out in the street with nothing more than he'd turned up in.

"'Rose signed this house over to me years ago,' I told him. 'It's my house and I want you out of it.'

"He stared at me with an expression of startled surprise, but it didn't take him long to put on that wheedling voice again.

"'I've got nowhere else to go, Bess.'

"'Go back to the mission. Who cares where you go? Just so long as it's not anywhere near me.'

"'I don't know what I've done to deserve such an ungrateful wretch as you for a daughter,' he muttered.

"'What do you imagine I've got to be grateful to you for? You don't give a damn about me, or Jimmy. And as for Rose, for what you're doing to her may God forgive you, because I know I never will.'

"'What d'ya mean?'

"'You're going to get her hanged! You never saw what happened and you know it! You're just trying to make yourself important.' I picked up his coat and threw it at him, finding my target as it hit him square in the face, making him stagger backwards. 'Now get out of my sight!'

***

"There were a few reporters hanging about the house for a week or so, but I soon made it clear they'd get nothing out of me. I tried at first, told them all she was innocent, that I was the one who had stabbed Alfred, but even they wouldn't believe me. They wanted all the juicy details about Rose, she was the famous one after all, otherwise they would not have been so interested. When I realised they were not going to print my version, I didn't have anything more to do with them.

"It must have been the worst time in my life, trying to look after Jimmy, eaten up with anxiety and desperately trying to get someone to hear my side of the story.

"I thought a lot about Daniel during those months. I needed him with me, to comfort me, to tell me it was going to be all right or even simply to hold me. But he wasn't there and he wasn't going to be there, and I'd sit for hours sometimes when Jimmy was sleeping with my eyes closed, just imagining he was doing all those things.

"I had a lot of visitors. neighbours wanting to black their noses, find out all the gory details, reporters still trying to get the inside story.

There was even a visit from Alfred's sister, raving about justice and how she'd kill Rose herself if she got off. I didn't bother much with any of them, just told them to push off.

"And I kept trying to tell the reporters what the inside story really was. But they didn't want to know any more than the police did.

"My last visitor proved to be more helpful."

CHAPTER TWENTY-FIVE

"I'd just got back from doing a bit of shopping when the doorbell rang and there stood the Earl. He didn't wait to be invited in, just took off his hat, stepped straight into the hall and made his way purposefully into the parlour.

"'I'll come straight to the point, Miss Shaw,' he said, seating himself beside the empty fireplace and looking up at me. He looked sad, somehow, and mystified and when he spoke there was a plea in his tone. 'I saw the pictures in the newspapers. I can manage simple arithmetic.'

"'Meaning?'

"'Meaning that the child is my grandson.'

"I leaned my head against the mantelpiece and gazed at the painted Chinese dragon on the fire screen, my mind busy. Rose and I had never discussed the subject, though I felt certain she wanted James' father kept in ignorance about Jimmy. But there was no point in lying to the man, was there? He'd guessed the truth and he was far from stupid.

"'I don't think it's my place to discuss it,' I finally replied turning to look at him.

"'I think it's going to be your place to do a lot of things from now on,' he answered kindly.

'It's no use lying to me, my dear. I can see the resemblance and then there's the name. I wish she had told me.'

"'What would have been the point of that? Would you have made him your heir? Given him James' title? That would've been rich, wouldn't it? Viscount Hartford, living in a terraced house in Dalston. Adopted father, professional layabout!'

"He got to his feet and came to stand beside me, putting his hand gently over mine.

"'Don't judge me too harshly, Miss Shaw. I only wanted the best for my son, like any father, and your sister would not have fitted into his world, any more than he fitted into hers.'

"I was torn between loyalty to Rose and what she would have wanted, and my own honest soul which knew he was only stating a fact.

"'I'm sorry,' I said at last. 'You're right, of course. They both knew it, too. But all Rose wanted was to do right by Jimmy. Bringing you into his life would not have accomplished that.'

"That was when Jimmy decided to come in from the back yard.

"'Sorry, Auntie,' he said when he saw the Earl. 'I didn't know you had a visitor.'

"He always had lovely manners for a little'n. Rose saw to that. Never could abide a rude child, she always said. The Earl smiled at him and squatted down to his level.

"'You must be James,' he said gently.

"'That's right, but they call me Jimmy. Who are you?'

"His grey eyes filled with tears and he swallowed hard before he replied in a husky voice:

"'Just a friend.'

"'Have you come to help my mother?' The child demanded.

"It was the first time he'd mentioned her since the night of the murder. I wasn't even sure until then that he knew what was going on and I was shaken a little.

I didn't want him to know what was happening, but there's not much that children don't notice.

"'If I can,' the Earl replied. 'I'll certainly do my best.'

"Jimmy didn't answer him, he just nodded silently and went back outside. It was almost as if he knew who the man was.

"'I can understand why she didn't want my help,' he said, turning back to me. 'But surely I can do something now, for the sake of James' memory. For the sake of that little boy out there. She is in need of a good counsel; will you at least allow me to provide it?'

"'Thank you,' I said and I meant it. The Earl's money and influence could mean the difference between life and death for Rose and I wasn't about to let her silly pride get in the way of that.

"It was a week after Alfred was killed before I got to see Rose. I'd spent all my time trying to get the police to listen to me and clearing up the mess in the house. I didn't want to leave Jimmy until he'd got used to me. He woke up nearly every night crying, not knowing what had upset him, but it wasn't difficult to guess.

"Tom looked after him while I went to the prison. He seemed to like Tom, said he'd played games with him and made him laugh. He badly needed to laugh.

"I felt the most overwhelming despair as those great doors closed behind me, as I heard the key turn in the lock and knew I couldn't simply leave whenever I wished. And if I felt that dread, what must she have been feeling, knowing she was innocent?

"She was dressed in some awful brown wool stuff, a full length, shapeless garment that made her figure disappear. An equally shapeless white cap hid her beautiful hair, and her complexion was as pale as chalk.

"I wasn't allowed to speak to her alone, of course. A pinched-faced wardress sat in one corner of the room, staring at the grey brick walls and listening to every word.

"'Rose!' I cried out as I rushed forward and gripped her hands.

"'No touching!' The wardress growled, and I quickly withdrew my hands.

"My voice dropped to a whisper.

"'What's going on?' I asked before I had even sat down to face her across the scarred, wooden table. 'What have you told them? They won't believe me.'

"'I've told them the truth, Bess,' she answered quietly. 'That he was attacking my son, so I picked up the knife and stabbed him with it.'

"'That isn't what happened!' I hissed.

"'Isn't it? Well, it'll do, won't it?'

"'Rose, you know you didn't kill him, don't you? You haven't convinced yourself you did, have you?'

"She smiled, a little secret smile, as though she had got what she wanted.

"'But I did, Bess,' she whispered. 'You're not going to take the blame for this one. You might have been the one who struck the blow, but I'm the one responsible. It would never have happened if it weren't for me.'

"'They're going to hang you, Rose,' I pleaded. 'D'you think I'm going to keep quiet and let that happen, when it was me all the time? What d'you take me for?'

"'And I suppose you think I'd let you hang instead,' she said. 'It was my fault. That's all that matters here. If I'd taken your advice years ago, if I'd gone away and pretended to be a widow instead of marrying Alfred, none of this would have happened.'

"I could see I wasn't going to convince her to change her story and would it have done any good if I had? I turned to the wardress.

"'Are you listening to this?' I demanded. 'I killed Alfred O'Neill! Are you going to report this conversation to the Governor?'

The little woman just stared at me disdainfully then continued her contemplation of the wall.

"'Who's paying for that fancy barrister?' Rose suddenly asked.

"'James' father,' I replied abruptly, prepared for an argument.

"'Thought so. He's not doing it for me, you know. He's doing it for James.' Suddenly she leaned forward and her eyes met mine. I saw more animation in them than I'd seen in years. 'This is the way it's going to be, Bess. Everything's as it should be. All you need do is take care of Jimmy and you can tell the Earl I don't want his help. I don't want some clever barrister getting me off, convincing them it was you instead.'

"'But it was me! I killed Alfred. I've told them and I'll tell them again. They'll have to believe me eventually.'

"She laughed, as though she were not sitting in a prison cell with a formidable wardress listening to every word.

"'No one will believe you, Bess. Why should they? They think you're trying to protect me for

Jimmy's sake.' She nodded toward the little woman in the corner. 'Even she thinks that. They've given you a motive for lying but they can't find any reason why I would.'

"She was right, too. Throughout the trial, she maintained that she had seen the knife on the table and it was all she could think to use that would stop her husband from hurting her son.

"The Central Criminal Court was still a comparatively new building then and the courtroom smelled of new wood and leather polish. I've never been able to stand the smell of those things since; they bring back a picture of that courtroom, an image so vivid it could have happened yesterday.

"'And is it not true, Mrs. O'Neill,' asked the prosecuting counsel, 'that the child you maintain you were protecting is not, in fact, your husband's son?'

"I've never known where they got that information from. It was such a closely kept secret, I thought I was the only one who knew. Mind you, there was a story in the papers afterward about two of the girls who were in the chorus when Rose was a star, all about what it was like working with her. It must have been one of them, I suppose, who put two and two together. But they never knew his name; either that or they were afraid to say. I'm glad about that. It would have broken Rose's heart to have his name blackened by it all.

"The question upset her; she didn't answer to begin with and the judge had to prompt her.

"'That's right,' she replied at last. 'He isn't.'

"'And is it not also true that your marriage to the deceased was your first and only marriage?'

"'Yes,' she agreed.

"Excited murmurs came from the gallery. Nowadays, the question wouldn't even be allowed, wouldn't be relevant. But it was all too relevant then.

"'Who is the father of your child, Mrs. O'Neill?'

"For the first time since it all began, she faltered.

Her counsel objected on the grounds of relevance, but I think the judge was more interested in the answer than the law would have allowed. He overruled him.

"'Answer the question please,' the judge ordered.

"'It's not important,' she said.

"'Come now, Mrs O'Neill. The court needs to know the true facts here. I put it to you that the deceased married you, believing you to be a maid and innocent of any carnal experience and believing for four years that the child was his own son. I further put it to you that when he learned the awful truth, that the child was the result of some former, clandestine affair, he quite naturally resented both you and the child. Isn't it true that the affair with the boy's father was still going on? That this man is quite possibly even now in this very courtroom?'

"He turned a full circle, letting his eyes sweep the packed gallery where James' father sat, his face impassive. Tears began to spill down Rose's cheeks, tears I hadn't seen her shed in four years.

"'That is not true!' She cried. 'He's dead. My son's father was killed in the war. He was given the Victoria Cross.'

"'Indeed,' said prosecuting counsel, raising a sceptical eyebrow. 'Then it cannot do any harm to tell the court his name.'

"'No,' she insisted. 'He died for the likes of you and I won't disgrace his name. There's no point.'

"I think I was the only one who noticed her glance up at the Earl and saw him answer with a grateful smile.

"Nowadays, such a noble gesture might have helped, might have raised her in the estimation of the jury, but not then. Living in sin with a man was not a crime, but in the eyes of society it was almost worse than murder. What an archaic phrase that sounds now – 'living in sin'. Things would have been so different for her today. Nothing seems to shock anybody any more.

"'Why did you kill your husband, Mrs O'Neill?'

"'Because he was hurting Jimmy. What's the point of all this any way. I killed him, I pleaded guilty. My father's told you what he saw, so why waste public money on this charade?'

"The judge banged his gavel and threatened to hold her in contempt. Not much of a threat when you were likely to hang anyway.

"'But we have the evidence of your sister, Mrs O'Neill. Your sister, who insists that it was she who stabbed your husband and for the same reason you yourself have given this court.'

"'Bess had nothing to do with it. I killed Alfred, and I'd do the same again if I had the chance.'

"She was still being defended by the Earl's barrister, whether she liked it or not, but there wasn't much he could do to save her, not when she said things like that, was there? The prosecution also had my father's lying testimony. It didn't make any difference to him which one of us did it, he'd have been just as important. But he'd been too busy lying in the first place and he couldn't change his story now or they wouldn't believe him at all. I found out later that he'd already made a deal with the newspapers for his story.

"'I heard a scream,' my father swore on oath, 'and I went into the dining room to see what was wrong. I saw my two daughters there and Alfred, who was, as far as I could see, meting out proper punishment to the boy like any father would. My daughter, Rosina, picked up the knife from the table and moved toward him with it. I cried out to her to stop, but she ignored me. I then saw her stab her husband in the chest with the knife. I could do nothing to stop her. It was all over very quickly.'

"There was whispering again in the gallery and I actually heard someone expressing sympathy for my father, having to stand up there in the Old Bailey courtroom and condemn his own daughter. I couldn't sort out my feelings, they were so confused between rage and sorrow and the awful sense of injustice.

"I thought a lot about James during the trial. I wondered if he was looking down on it all and blaming himself. If he'd left her alone, she might have grown old in peace. But that wouldn't have suited her, I don't suppose. The only time she was really happy was when she was with him.

"The prosecution presented Alfred as a hard working man, whose disabilities had prevented him from fighting for his country. They made the jury feel pity of him, that he'd married in good faith, only to find that his wife was carrying another man's child. It was all rubbish, but the jury didn't know that.

"And there was nothing I could do to convince them otherwise.

"The tension was almost tangible as I watched the jury file back to their seats. They hadn't been out for long, no more than an hour or so. Even while I prayed for just one dissenting voice among the twelve men, I knew the verdict was a foregone conclusion. They had already convicted her, whether she'd killed her husband or not. She was a music hall star and she'd had an illegitimate child, had actually lived with a man she wasn't married to, war hero or not. I've often wondered if it would have made them think differently, had they known who the man was. It might have. People were very class-conscious in those days.

"'Guilty,' the foreman of the jury announced clearly.

"That man's face has haunted my dreams ever since. I wonder about him sometimes, where he came from, that he had the power to decide my sister's fate. He was a little man with a moustache, about forty he was, with greying hair going bald on top.

"I'd never felt faint in my life before, but I really thought I was going to pass out then. My emotions battled within me, reached exploding point. I cried out:

"'No! I killed Alfred, not Rose. You can't do this!'

"'Any more disturbances and I shall have you removed from the court.'

"As it happens, I removed myself from the court. I couldn't bear to watch him put his black cap on his head and pronounce an undeserved death sentence. It should have been me he was condemning, not her.

"I was standing at the main door, my shoulders hunched up and my arms wrapped about myself to keep me from shivering from shock. I took deep gulps of summer air, anything to calm myself, but it didn't work. People waiting outside were watching me curiously. Most of them knew who I was, had read the papers and heard reports of how I'd insisted I was the guilty one. Not one of them believed me and I swelled with fury inside when I saw the sympathy in their eyes. Their compassion should have been for Rose, but all she got was hostility and condemnation.

"I felt too angry to cry. When you're telling the truth and nobody will believe you, it makes you so furious, you can't get your mind around anything else.

"When I felt a firm hand on my shoulder, I didn't even turn round to look; I assumed it was the Earl, though why I couldn't say. Then I heard a familiar voice, one I hadn't heard in a very long time.

"'Bess?'

"I spun around and found myself looking up at a round, freckled face, crowned with bright red hair.

"'Sam!' I cried, gripping his arms. 'What are you doing here?'

"'Thought you might need a shoulder to cry on,' he replied quietly. 'I'm sorry, Bess. There's not much I can say, I know. But fancy you trying to take the blame, telling all those lies to save her. We could have used your sort of courage during the war.'

"Another time, I suppose I'd have been flattered, but not then. I had got to a point where I couldn't feel anything, except anger.

"'They weren't lies, Sam,' I said.

"He stared mutely at me.

"'You can't mean...you mean you really did kill him?' He finally asked, and his eyes were so wide with incredulity, it was almost comical.

"'That's exactly what I mean. Please say you believe me. I'm so sick of nobody believing me.'

"He didn't answer, just took my arm and steered me along the street to a tea shop. We sat at a table in the corner with our tea and I had a sudden flash of deja vu. Hadn't I sat drinking tea at a corner table with him once before? And hadn't that meeting changed the course of my life? I put down my teacup; I couldn't drink it.

"'What can be done?' Sam asked after a moment.

"'Nothing. They've made their decision and there's nothing more we can do about it. I've told them I killed him; Rose's told them she did. In their place, I expect I'd believe her myself.' I sighed. 'There's no point to an appeal when she insists she's guilty.'

"'But why does she?'

"I gave a derisive laugh.

"'Because as far as she's concerned, she is guilty.' I explained. 'He was her husband, he was her problem. It wouldn't have happened if she hadn't married him. And I told her not to. So, she blames herself.'

"He looked sheepish for a minute, then he asked quietly:

"'So who was the boy's father?'

"Slowly, I shook my head.

"'That's her secret, Sam. She may have just forfeited her life to keep it; I can't tell you.'

"He watched me over the rim of his cup for a while, not saying anything more. There didn't seem to be much more to say. At last, he drained his cup and set it back in its saucer.

"'I thought Edie might be there,' he said at last.

"'No chance. They've completely disowned Rose. You're not still carrying a torch for her, I hope.'

"He shook his head.

"No. I just thought I'd see what she's like now. Maybe tell her about my pretty wife and my three lovely kids. But that's not why I came, though, Bess. Don't get me wrong.'

"'Why did you come?'

"'Just to offer a little moral support, I suppose. Your family always meant a lot to me. After Edie and I parted, it was the rest of you I missed, not her. I don't think I ever really loved her, not like I love my Daisy.'

"His words filled me with warmth. I smiled and I thought, at least I've done one thing right in my life. He was like a mythical knight out of a fairy tale that day, coming out of nowhere to rescue me from an almost suicidal depression, to bring a little spark of pleasure into all the gloom.

"I only saw Rose once after that, the day before she died, and she looked peaceful, almost serene, now it was all over. She still wore that awful brown smock, but her hair was flowing down her back, a sharp reminder that they would hack it all off before they put the rope around her neck. I let my imagination form a picture of her without it, then I blotted the image out with tremendous effort. It was too painful to contemplate, even for a second. She pulled a few strands of it from her crown and began to twirl it into a flat, round shape as she smiled at me.

"'There are some promises you must make for me, Bess,' she said briskly.

"'Anything I can do, Rose, you know I'll do it. How about telling them the truth?'

"She looked as though she didn't know what I was talking about.

"'It's too late for all that,' she said, still in a business-like tone. She handed me the strand of hair. 'Everyone likes to keep a lock of hair, don't they?' She said. 'Put it in James' locket for me, will you? I'd like that. I'm not afraid, you know. Death has never frightened me. We all go to a better place and this time tomorrow, I'll be part of it.' She paused and her eyes were wistful for a moment, as though she could see something which was invisible to me. 'I'll see Billy,' she said. 'And all those little brothers and sisters I never had the chance to know.

"'And James?'

"'She smiled, and it was the same, serene smile she'd had when he had first moved in with her and I'd been trying to persuade her to throw him out. I wondered if I could somehow swap places with her, like in A Tale of Two Cities. People always said we looked alike, though I could never see it myself. You have some really wild notions when something as bad as that happens. Panic thoughts.

"'Yes,' she replied. 'And there won't be any silly conventions to keep us apart, will there?'

"'I hope you're right,'

"She reached across the table and squeezed my hand, keeping a furtive eye on the wardress.

"'You will look after Jimmy for me, won't you?'

"'You know I will.'

"'But you must never tell him about me. You're his mother now, and that's what I want him to believe.'

"'Until he's old enough to know...'

"'No,' she said sharply. 'I never want him to know about me. It wouldn't do him any good to know his mother was hanged for murder, would it? And it wouldn't do him any good to know that his grandfather was an Earl, either. He'll forget about me soon enough; children are like that. And I want him to grow up believing you are his mother. I'll leave you to decide what you tell him about his father.'

"Panic twisted its ugly fingers about me then. This was really goodbye; this time tomorrow, I thought, she'll be just another rotting corpse beneath the earth.

"'Please, Rose,' I pleaded. 'It's not too late. It's you Jimmy needs, not me. Won't you please tell them the truth?'

"She only smiled and squeezed my hand one last time, before she went and stood in front of the door to the condemned cell behind her, waiting for the wardress to unlock it.

"I never laid eyes on her again."

CHAPTER TWENTY-SIX

"I've carried the guilt for nigh on seventy-five years," Bess said quietly. "And not a night has gone by that I haven't lain awake, asking myself if I tried hard enough, if there was some way I could have made them believe me.

"I wanted to tell someone when Jimmy died, but it didn't seem so important then. I never expected to outlive him. I never expected to outlive everyone I ever knew, come to that. You're the only one left. Jimmy and his wife only had one son and he was killed in the second war. In any case, I don't think today's generation would be ashamed of what their ancestors got up to, do you? The way they seem to take everything so casually, it seems to me they'd be quite chuffed to have a dark skeleton popping out of their closets."

"It must have been a terrible burden for you," Stella replied. "All that on top of what my grandmother did. I suppose you never saw Daniel again?"

"Well, dear, fate will play its hand, won't it?" She answered cryptically. "I don't know what became of my father. He must have died, mustn't he? But I never knew about it. I only hope it was the sort of slow and agonising death he deserved.

"You know, Rose always used to say that when she cried for someone who'd passed on, she was crying for herself, not for them. They had gone to a better place, she'd say. I know she believed that, and she seemed full of anticipation that last time I saw her, as though she were looking forward to an exciting journey. I've had to believe in that afterlife, too, or I'd never have been able to carry on. Well, let's hope she was right. I'll be finding out for myself soon enough."

Stella felt a little embarrassed at that. Of course, it was evident that at one hundred years old, she couldn't have more than a few years left at most, but it was still a sensitive subject to her, talking to someone about their own death.

"That morning," she went on, "the morning she died, I'd stopped the clock so I wouldn't have to know the precise moment. It did no good, but then I didn't expect it to. I didn't even go to bed the night before, just sat up all night, keeping my own private vigil. When dawn came, I was in the bedroom, watching Jimmy, afraid he might have inherited my own curse and know something was wrong.

"I didn't need a clock to tell me when she went. I felt it, that sudden empty wrench, and I knew she was dead.

"The very next day, there was my father's story in the newspapers, all about how he'd felt to have to testify against his daughter. I didn't bother reading it. I knew it would be complete bullshit.

"In the week that followed Rose's death, I was steeped in so much misery, it was the most I could do to get myself out of bed in the mornings. To tell you the truth, if it hadn't been for Jimmy and having to put his needs first, trying to keep things as normal as possible for him, I don't think I'd have survived at all. But I had to go out eventually, had to stock up the cupboards so we didn't both starve.

"I came home from doing a bit of shopping and found Tom waiting on the doorstep. I wasn't too surprised to see him. He'd kept himself in the background throughout the worst of it all, but he was always there, ready to lend a hand if I needed it. I was grateful for that, and I felt a bit guilty when I saw him, that I hadn't got around to thanking him properly.

"We went indoors and sat in the parlour.

"'You've been a good friend to me, Tom,' I said. 'I'll never be able to repay the way you've stood by me through all this.'

"He blushed and studied his restless fingers.

"'That's just it, Bess,' he said. 'I want to be more than just a friend.'

"I felt my mouth drop open. I was so surprised, so startled I couldn't speak.

"'We're both alone in the world,' he went on hurriedly. 'I know I'm a lot older than you, but we've always got along all right together, haven't we? I really admire you, Bess, the way you've coped with it all, your courage, your determination. You couldn't have done more.'

"I knew an answer was expected, but I was still dumbstruck. I had never even thought of Tom as a member of the opposite sex, really. He was just Tom.

"'Tom, I...' I began, but my voice dried up as no further words came to me. I took a deep breath and started again. 'Tom, I'm very flattered, but I don't think you've quite thought this through. I wouldn't make you a good wife. I wouldn't make anyone a good wife.'

"'I know you're not going to marry Daniel,' he said. 'I know now why he had to go back to America, who the letters were from.'

"I felt a tinge of disapproval in his tone that angered me.

"'Who told you?'

"'His wife,' he replied, making me stare at him with even more astonishment. 'I had a letter from her, thanking me for looking after her husband when he was so ill. I didn't write back, didn't disillusion her. After all, it's none of my business, is it? If that's what he wants to tell her, that it was me he'd been staying with, me who nursed him back to health, well it's the least I can do for you, Bess.'

"I couldn't think of a way to reject him, not a tactful one anyway. The thought of being married to Tom made me cringe and I got the idea that he thought he was doing me a favour, that no woman would want to remain a spinster, have people think nobody wanted her. And he knew I was no virgin. He probably thought no one else would have me, just like my mother would have done.

"'I'm sorry, Tom,' I said firmly. 'I'll never marry anyone.'

"'After Daniel, you mean?'

"'I love him. I always have and I always will and one day, who knows that he might be free. If that day ever comes, I'll be waiting. I appreciate your offer, I really do, but the answer has to be no.'

"When he'd gone I went straight out and put the house on the market. I'd been thinking about it for a while; it had always been part of my plan for the future if Rose didn't come back, and Tom had made me realise it was the only way to put the past behind me.

"I sold the house and moved here. It's a little further out but nobody knew us here and Jimmy and me could start afresh.

"Nina's letters got more and more formal, somehow, as though she'd lost the knack of writing her usual chit-chat. I wrote her that Rose was dead but I didn't go into details. I didn't think she needed to know and besides, I didn't want Daniel thinking I was hinting for him to come back.

"Life went on for Jimmy and me. I did as Rose asked, I never let him find out about her. But I couldn't pretend I was his mother. He was nearly four years old when Alfred was stabbed and he already knew an awful lot more than she gave him credit for. You know what children are like. You think you've kept things from them, then all of a sudden they come out with something to prove they've been having you on all the time. He didn't know what had happened to her, only that she'd disappeared from his life.

"I juggled with the truth a bit over the years. There had to come a time when he'd need his birth certificate for something or other, so there wasn't any point in pretending I was anything other than his aunt. I didn't mention the music hall; he might have put two and two together if I had. I just told him she died and left it at that. He had his photographs of her, he knew her name, and if he realised it was the same name as an infamous murderess, he never let on.

"He didn't ask about his father for a long time. There were so many kids then who'd lost their fathers in the war, I suppose he just assumed that his was one of them. And when he did finally ask, I told him about James. I didn't mention his title, of course, but the man I described to him was James and I found a photograph of him in uniform for the lad to keep.

"I gradually built up a dressmaking business from home, all exclusive stuff, thanks to the Countess. She let me use her name and she recommended me to all her friends to start me off. I kept myself busy, I tried not to think too much, tried not to brood on it all, and I don't think I did a bad job with Jimmy. He went to university, you know. Oxford. Rose would have been so proud. So would James.

"One day, when Jimmy was about twelve, I was hanging out the washing and I looked up to find Daniel standing beside me.

"'Hello, Liza,' he said. 'You don't know the trouble I've had trying to find you.'

"I know everybody says it, but he hadn't changed. He was still as good looking as ever, still had that playful smile of his.

"I didn't know what to say, so I said nothing. To tell you the truth, my heart was hammering so fast, I doubt if I could have spoken, even if I'd wanted to. I'd managed to shut him away all those years, in the dark recesses of my mind where I didn't have to wonder what he was doing, what time had done to him. But it was still there, that glow of warmth when I saw him, just as it had always been.

"'We went indoors and sat in the parlour and it was a long time before he said anything else. I was so confused and excited I didn't know which to be first.

"'I've heard all about it,' he said at last. 'I went to the Angel first, saw Tom. He told me all about Rose and what happened. I should have been here, Liza. I should have been here when you needed me.'

"'I didn't expect you to be.' I waited but he didn't say anything else, and I couldn't bear the suspense any longer. 'Why have you come back, Daniel?'

"'My father died,' he said, fiddling with his fingers. 'Now I've got his shops to run, as well as my own in New York. What with the financial crisis at home, I might have to close most of mine, so I expect I'll be coming back and forth quite a bit now.'

"I can't deny I was disappointed and I wasn't sure I wanted to see him at all, if I couldn't have him. He seemed to assume that I'd know his father had opened more shops, that he had a string of them himself. Perhaps he thought Nina had told me, or perhaps he'd forgotten how many years it had been. His reference to New York as 'home' raised a spark of resentment and I felt a moment of panic at the sudden idea that, if things were that bad in America, he might be planning to come back to England and bring his wife with him.

"'How's Nina?' I asked.

"'Fine. She's got herself a young man, nice sort of fella. I think she'll be getting married soon.'

"'I'm glad she's happy.'

"It was a strange sort of meeting. Daniel and I, we'd always known what to say to one another, but that day it was as though we were both treading carefully around each other's feelings. And I was too scared of getting hurt again to speak my mind.

"'You needn't think I've just turned up here expecting you to still be waiting, either,' he said defensively. 'I wanted to see you, to tell you I was here, in case you needed a friend. Better late than never, eh?'

"As soon as I heard the words, I knew I didn't want his friendship. Funny, isn't it? All those years before, when mother first put the idea of marriage into my head, I'd only been thinking of him as a friend. Now I couldn't tolerate the idea that I'd see him, touch him, and be nothing more than a surrogate sister.

"'Is that all?' I asked. 'Is that all you want from me, just to be my friend?'

"'I've nothing else to offer.'

"'Then get out.'

"He frowned at me. I think it was the first time in all the years he'd known me, that he hadn't accurately anticipated my reaction.

"'Sorry, Liza. I suppose I'm not doing you any favours, am I?'

"He started to get to his feet, but I caught his hand and held it firmly. It felt so good, so strong and warm in mine.

"'No, don't go.' I took a deep breath to give me courage. 'When I said goodbye to you, there at Southampton, when I watched you waving at me till I couldn't even see a dot on the horizon, I believed I'd never see you again. Now you've come back, and you expect me to say goodbye all over again. Well I can't do it. So if you don't want anything from me but friendship, just leave quietly and I'll try to pretend you were never here.

"He stared at me for a long time, then he folded his arms around me. I didn't know until then how very much I'd missed that.

"'Oh, Liza,' he said, his cheek against mine. 'What a mess I've made of things.'

"'We're not going into all that again, are we?'

"'I asked you to marry me once...'

"'Three times.'

"'What?'

"'You asked me to marry you three times.'

"'Did I? Well, I can't ask you again. I'll never be free to do that, not while she's alive.'

"'That never bothered us before, did it?' I said.

"So that's how it began. I suppose I was an early example of the other woman, though I could never think of myself as that. To me, she was the other woman, she was the fly in my ointment, because I knew him first. He was always my Daniel.

"It went on for more than thirty years. Every time he came over here, he'd stay with me and we'd be two youngsters in love all over again. I've often wondered whether he kept his father's business on because of me. I don't think it could have been making that much money, not enough to warrant him keeping paying out fares to come here. I like to think I was the reason.

"The neighbours all thought he was my brother, but Jimmy knew. Jimmy approved as well, he really loved Daniel, otherwise things might have been different.

"They were happy years for me, too, even when he was in America with her, because I knew he'd be coming back. I always had that to look forward to and my only real regret was that he died in her arms, not mine.

"But he came to me. I always knew I'd feel it when he went, but that day, I was setting the table, waiting for Jimmy and his wife to come for tea, and the radio was playing the Beatles 'I wanna Hold Your Hand'. I never hear that song without thinking of Daniel.

"His image was solid, but I knew it was only an image. He looked just like he had when I first met him, all those years ago when he'd come up to me in the park. He moved close to me and he said: 'Goodbye, Liza'. Then he vanished and I felt that familiar emptiness.

"That was in the sixties, so we were both getting on a bit, and it wasn't till then that I found out her name. She wrote to me. When I saw her handwriting on the envelope, it was like stepping back in time and I still felt myself shrinking inside at the sight of it. But it was a nice letter, telling me that Daniel had gone. She wasn't to know I didn't need to be told, was she? She'd known about me all those years, and she never once let on and there wasn't a hint of resentment, as though she'd been content to share him, if that's what it took to make him happy. So she must have loved him, mustn't she?

"It's funny how men always think they can pull the wool over women's eyes, but half the time they're not fooling anyone but themselves. She told me that Nina sent her love and she signed it 'Lucy Farringdon'. I'd have liked to wear that name myself; not Lucy, of course. Farringdon. Mrs. Farringdon, that's what I should have been, if it hadn't been for my own stupidity and Edith's need for vengeance."

"I'm glad he came back," Stella said softly.

She was still holding his picture in its silver frame, and she studied it now. Bess had made him come alive for her. Outside, the sky had grown dark and the moon cast its light through the open curtains. She got up and drew them closed, then turned on the lights.

"You're the only one left now," Bess said and as she spoke she slid the casket across the floor to Stella. "There are lots of things in there, pictures of James and Nina, as well as Edie. There's even one of Sam. And there are more posters, all Daniel's letters and Rose's gold locket. That's probably the only thing in there that has any monetary value, unless the posters are worth anything. You can throw out the lock of hair if you want."

"You don't want to be giving me all these things, Auntie," Stella protested. "You've kept them all these years. They're yours; I know how much they mean to you."

"That's why I want someone to have them," she replied. "Someone who knows the story and will appreciate them. They're only sentimental keepsakes, really, but I'd hate to think they might be thrown out with the rubbish when I go."

"You've got a long time yet," Stella argued feebly.

"Don't patronise me," she snapped. "I thought you and I had got to know one another a bit better than that. The only thing that scares me is I might get to the other side, only to discover that I've still got to share Daniel with his wife.

"My Will's in there as well. Like I said, you're the only one I've got to leave it all to. Just remember, everything in this house belongs to Rose."

Stella went and knelt beside the old woman, taking her hand. She didn't care about the house or the money, only that she'd found her too late. She felt tears burning her eyes.

"I wish we had met before," she said. "I'd so like to have known you better. Could I come and see you again?"

Bess smiled and shook her head slowly.

"I shan't be here, dear," she said. "In all the years I've lived with this so-called gift of knowing when someone's died, I've often wondered if I'd have any hint about my own end. Well now I know. I've said my piece, I've met you. Now I'm content."

THE END

Author's note

Thank you for reading The Romany Princess. I hope you enjoyed it and if you did, please consider my other books

<u>Historical Romance</u>:

The Scent of Roses

To Catch A Demon
The Wronged Wife
The Adulteress
A Man in Mourning
The Crusader's Widow

<u>The Holy Poison Series</u>:

The Judas Pledge
The Flawed Mistress
The Viscount's Birthright
Betrayal
The Heretics

<u>Mystery/Thrillers</u>

Mirielle
Old Fashioned Values

<u>Contemporary Romance:</u>

Fallen Stars

The first chapters of each of these books are available to read on my blog at:

http://historical-fiction-on-kindle.blogspot.co.uk

Made in United States
North Haven, CT
21 March 2025

67042315R00202